Praise for *Girl Und...*

"Your first must-read beach book of t...

—Oprah.com

"The riveting drama is sure to keep readers up into the night devouring each and every twist and harrowing scene."

—*RT Reviews*

"A romantic thriller full of raw and conflicting emotions . . . a roller coaster full of frustrating, exciting, heartwarming, and heart-wrenching moments that leave surprises at every turn."

—*Deseret News*

"Skillfully interspersing flashbacks with current events, debut novelist Kells has written an absorbing tale that will grip anyone who enjoys survival stories or psychological dramas."

—*Library Journal* (starred review)

"With its subzero temperatures that will make you reach for a blanket and a wounded but never-weakened heroine, Kells's assured debut is a winner."

—*Kirkus Reviews*

"Kells's visceral story is quite memorable and eminently readable."

—*Publishers Weekly*

"As a former competitive swimmer and the recipient of a medical degree, first-novelist Kells amply demonstrates her technical knowledge, lending realism to the story. . . . The story ably demonstrates that survival is not just physical, but also mental and emotional."

—*Booklist*

GIRL
UNDERWATER

CLAIRE KELLS

DUTTON
— est. 1852 —

DUTTON
—• est. 1852 •—

An imprint of Penguin Random House LLC
375 Hudson Street
New York, New York 10014

Previously published as a Dutton hardcover, 2015

First paperback printing, August 2016

THE LIBRARY OF CONGRESS HAS CATALOGUED THE HARDCOVER EDITION OF THIS BOOK AS FOLLOWS:

Kells, Claire.
    Girl underwater / Claire Kells.
        pages cm
    ISBN 9780525954934 (hardcover)   9780698186194 (eBook)   9781101983980 (paperback)
    I. Title.

    PS3611.E4443G58   2015
    813'.6—dc23
                        2014016965

Printed in the United States of America
10 9 8 7 6 5 4 3 2 1

Set in Walbaum MT Std
Book design by Alissa Rose Theodor

For Mom

've always loved the water. My earliest memory is opening my eyes in my neighbor's pool and seeing the world through this different state of being. It shocked no one when I begged for swim lessons at the age of three—far younger than my older, more adventuresome brothers. When my mother saw me flying off the high dive the summer before kindergarten, she was horrified but not surprised. She wanted to ban me from the pool for a week, but my dad had a different idea: put her on the swim team.

After the crash, my instincts changed. Even the smallest children know not to breathe underwater, but somehow, my mind railed against everything I'd ever known. I thought it was permanent.

I thought fear was forever.

The security line proceeds in its usual torturous fashion: in stops and starts, other people's luggage tumbling at my feet. After thirty minutes of halfhearted apologies, one of the TSA checkers waves me over.

He holds up my Massachusetts license and smirks. "You sure this is you?"

"Yep." I force a smile. That picture isn't my proudest moment: blond hair wild and windblown, eyes bloodshot, freckled skin paler than a baby's butt. It was February, the week before midterms. Never get your driver's license issued in February.

"You're a brunette now."

"Yep." Precious seconds tick by.

"Okay," he says, handing it over. "You pass."

I take my license and head for the closest lane. A family of six squeezes in right in front of me, juggling Uggs and Disney backpacks and a whole assembly of umbrellas. A toddler empties his pockets and fifty pennies scatter on the floor. I scoop them up while his parents chase down their other kids.

Five interminable minutes later, I'm through the X-ray machine, awaiting the verdict with my shoes off, arms at my sides. "Clear," the woman says, with the amount of enthusiasm one would expect from someone who's said it a thousand times today.

The crowds don't exactly part for me as I run for the gate, but I've gotten good at this. Some people run clumsily: handbags flying, suitcases bobbing behind them on carpeted floors. The business-class folks walk with a practiced, efficient grace. I'm somewhere in between: a little stressed but not crazed. Forget dinner, though. I hurry past the bars and fro-yo stands with a lurch in my stomach.

The thing is, I could have avoided all this; I could have been on time, relaxed, enjoying a decent dinner or at least some packaged sushi before my flight. Phil Markey offered me a ride to the airport after practice this morning, which came as a shock because senior guys don't often talk to sophomore girls—especially sophomore girls who don't exactly dominate in the pool. I didn't wonder about it too much, though. *A ride with the co-captain?* I said yes.

My excitement dimmed when Phil pulled up to my dorm with Colin Shea in the front seat. Colin Shea: serious and quiet and abundantly talented. Scarily talented. I'd avoided him since the first day of freshman year, and the thought of trying to explain why to Phil . . .

So I bailed. My excuse didn't even make sense—something about carsickness and country music. Phil didn't care, but Colin noticed. He always notices.

As if on cue, Colin steps out of line at Starbucks just as I'm rounding the corner. He's paying for a coffee—a venti, in fact. *Who buys coffee right before a red-eye?* Not just that, but a su-persized coffee. He doesn't even bother with cream and sugar. He thanks the exhausted barista, stuffs the tip jar while she isn't looking, and jogs up to the gate.

He's clearly the last one to board. Well, second to last. *Why did he wait so long to board?* I hope to God he wasn't waiting for me to show up. Phil knew we were all booked for the same flight to Boston, and Colin has a strange sense of responsibility about him. He probably thinks I'm late because of him. Which is true, but he will never know that.

I'll give it a minute and board right before they close the doors. Hopefully he's sitting way in the back somewhere. Some clever finagling scored me a seat in the emergency exit row, and I'm betting Colin just went for the cheapest option.

The gate agent responds to him the same way the barista did: stunned by his size and slick bald head, softened by his smile. She scans his boarding pass, hands it back to him, and even manages a sincere *"Have a nice flight."*

When the final boarding announcement sounds overhead, I make my move. The terminal feels more subdued now, almost quiet. Tomorrow, the day before Thanksgiving, the chaos will bloom all over again. A janitor empties huge recycling bins. Two Asian women scrub the countertops of a Panda Express. A bearded man in a tweed jacket sits in one of those massage chairs with his cell phone to his ear, rubbing his temples as the clock creeps toward midnight.

The gate agent offers me an empty customer-service grin, the kind that isn't meant to be returned. "Have a nice flight," she says. She's tired; I'm tired. I've averted disaster with Colin Shea and now I just want to *get there.*

As I round the corner, the cabin door gapes at me. A flight attendant mediates the transition from ramp to plane, where she greets me with a chipper "Welcome!" She doesn't seem perturbed that I've boarded precariously late, but the first-class passengers are. They wring out their hot towels and glare at me like I peed in the complimentary champagne.

I rush past those coveted rows and enter the cramped,

dingy quarters known as coach. The scene is familiar: tired parents and wailing babies, old men with canes, college kids sending a few last texts. Personal space doesn't mean zip in coach. People are leaning on each other, into each other, all over each other. Phil has one of the bulkhead seats. Lucky bastard. He winks because that's just kind of what he does, and I smile back.

"You made it," he says.

"Barely."

"Hell, isn't it?" He gestures vaguely to the chaos brewing behind him.

"A special kind," I say, trying hard to sell the joke.

He nods and goes back to *SportsCenter* streaming on his iPad. Not the best of interactions, but not the worst, either. At least he acknowledged me. I was worried he might never talk to me again after the whole carpool fiasco.

After a brief survey of unfamiliar faces, I drop my gaze and power forward. Up ahead, a generously sized man pours into the aisle. He catches me with an elbow, then a knee. No apology. It's fine. This is just how it goes on one of the busiest travel days of the year. Most people are wrestling with the overhead bins, but a few stare at me as I make my way down the center aisle. One brave-faced teenager actually swivels his head for a greedy look at my butt.

Ten . . . eleven . . . twelve . . . 12F. Window seat. It's not first class, but it's not 32B, either. I stop and look up. First order of business is to identify kids in the vicinity: Infants are bad, toddlers a nightmare. There are two of the latter sitting in the rows directly behind me. The little boy in 13E sports a baseball jersey, and 14F is swimming in a pint-size Indian kurta. All four parents flash me the same tentative grin, as if a positive attitude might just be the key to a seamless, whine-free flight. Another boy, maybe six or seven, sits in row 15, but he's all tuned in to his dad's electronics. This is a good sign. I just hope the younger boys skipped their naps today so they sleep through the flight.

The only other person in my row is a fortyish guy in an ill-fitting suit. He's on his cell phone, ordering some poor intern to finalize the paperwork before the holiday. The man looks like he hasn't cracked a smile since the eighties. I'm glad we're together, though. He doesn't seem like the chatty type.

I maneuver past his legs and settle into my coveted window seat. The shade is already up, revealing the nighttime extravagance of SFO and the Oakland skyline in the distance. Yellow lights pepper the hills to the east, disappearing in the hazy divide between sky and headlands. To the west, San Francisco sits in a steepening wall of fog.

"Excuse me."

The flight attendant leans into my row, pursing her lips with practiced professionalism. But my gaze doesn't linger on her for very long; it shifts to the six-foot-four, broad-shouldered kid next to her.

Colin.

I swallow hard. "Yeah?"

"This gentleman will be joining you in the emergency exit row."

The next seat over, Cheap Suit groans. Colin murmurs a thank-you to the flight attendant and shifts awkwardly into the dreaded middle seat. His legs are long and cumbersome, and he probably used them to barter for a seat in the roomier section. A wave of irritation surges through me. He definitely planned this—saw me walk down the aisle and take my seat, then concocted an excuse about his legs being too long for 32B or wherever he's supposed to be.

As Colin gets settled in, I make a point of rummaging through my bag. Laptop, e-reader, pens, a ripped swim cap. Some coins and other things I can't identify just by touch. I continue searching.

Laptop. Perfect. I put my earbuds in and power it up, but the battery's dead. *How did that happen?* I go for my phone instead. There's only one song stored on the hard drive, and it's a sampler from the phone company, but it will have to do.

So far, so good. Colin straightens his long legs and pulls his elbows in toward his body. For a tall person, he occupies amazingly little space. Most people his size park their elbows on the armrests the second they sit down, obliterating any sense of personal space. A good number of them proceed to nod off and snore or, worse, end up on my shoulder. At least Colin has some awareness of his surroundings. That or he's trying too hard.

He skims his massive hand over his bald head as he reaches for a dog-eared copy of *Great Expectations*. Although I'm doing my best to look elsewhere, I can't help but notice the handwritten plea to return the book if found, with Colin's name and Dorchester address scrawled on the inside cover. I resist the sudden, inexplicable urge to ask him about this: *You're from Dorchester?* When we met over a year ago, he told me he was from Boston. Which isn't exactly a lie, but Boston makes you think country clubs and old money; Dorchester means you probably learned to swim in a community pool behind a chain-link fence.

I suppose the details don't really matter. Best to act uninterested, to close my eyes and will the hours to pass. Because they will, and when we land, we'll go our separate ways.

The lights dim, the tires lurch, and the plane rumbles backward. The grump in the suit barks a final set of commands into his cell phone, while the gentleman in front of me is already snoring. It sounds like his throat is wrestling with his vocal cords, a real battle to the death. I blast the sample music. Slowly, peacefully, the sounds of air travel fade to a muffled drone.

I close my eyes. In six hours, I'll be there.

I'll be home.

●

A gray shore unfolds before me, cast under shadowy gray skies. The scene stretches on forever, sand and sky, two hulking ghosts in a lonesome embrace. The sea laps the shore, oblivious. It washes over my toes, my ankles, my knees. And then it recedes.

A wave is cresting in the distance—black, shapeless, inevitable. Although my mind processes the threat, my body refuses to respond. Muscles won't contract. Lungs refuse to inflate. Paralyzed, I stare at the wall of water as it swells before me, gathering strength before swallowing me whole—

The wave is not water but sound: human sounds. Crying, screaming. The distant echo of people's voices pitched with panic.

Gasping, I snap my eyes open and find that I'm not alone on some vast gray shore. I'm in my seat. Plastic tubes dangle from the ceiling. Serving trays rattle in place. The cabin pulses with light, though the sky beyond my window is a grim, starless black.

The man next to Colin has dropped something, and he's on all fours, crawling toward the front. The plane dips in that direction, pitching all of us forward, like an unbalanced seesaw. I blink a few times, focusing the images, praying they simply disappear—but the sound makes it real. *God, the sound* . . .

I cover my ears, only to feel the resistance of earbuds. The cord has no weight on the end of it, and in some distant corner of my mind, I consider the consequences of a lost cell phone. Then the plane goes into a dive, and my attention veers to the window.

The shade is still open, providing a pristine view of a great, mocking nothingness. We could be at the bottom of the sea or a million miles out in space—it's impossible to tell. I press my forehead to the glass, straining for a view of something. Anything. Lights, people, houses, cars. Or maybe a runway beckoning us to land.

But there is nothing out there. I've never seen darkness so absolute. We could be anywhere; we could be nowhere.

Oxygen masks bounce on seats like coiled springs. Someone's leopard-print luggage lands in the doorway between first class and coach. Lights are flickering. Alarms blaring. The whoosh of air threatens to burst my eardrums, even with my earbuds in. I pull them out to face the onslaught of what's happening.

It occurs to me then, finally, that we're going down. There are other people sharing this nightmare, two hundred of them, seeing the same horrors and experiencing the same despair and hearing the same staccato beat of air and engines. Our paths were supposed to diverge again in Boston, but they didn't. We're here. We're ending. Together.

I don't know these people. I don't love them or care about them or even know their names. Would it be easier if I did? Or would we cry even harder, holding on to the ones we love?

The plane jerks, and my neck snaps back against the seat. A sharp pain rockets through my chest, then fades. I feel a hand on my arm: warm, smooth, steady. And in that moment, everything goes quiet. Calm.

"Are you okay?" *Colin.*

His voice is smoother than I remember, and it takes me a moment to realize why: The uncertainty is gone. The shyness, too. The facade he uses to navigate our stilted interactions has been stripped away, replaced by a different, stronger, truer person.

In that moment, a single question floats to the front of my mind: *Why?*

Why is Colin Shea here with me now when he should have been sitting somewhere else? Why isn't he trying to save himself, as so many others are doing? Why isn't he calling his mom or dad or someone else he actually cares about?

Why does it suddenly feel like I've known him all my life?

My vision clears. I can see his eyes very clearly now: a pulsing, turbulent blue, the color of the sky just before dawn. Dark, but somehow comforting.

"I'm okay," I say.

He puts the armrest up and grasps my hand, and the panic tickling the back of my throat sinks back down. "I don't want to die." I say it more to myself than him, but he must hear me because he squeezes my hand even harder.

"You won't." He tightens our seat belts and hands me a pillow that he must have salvaged from the now-empty seat next to him.

"This isn't mine—"

"I know," Colin says. "Just try and support your neck."

The screams rise and fall with the dip of the plane; somewhere, a door slams against something else, and the drink cart tumbles down the aisle. Through all of this, Colin doesn't just keep his cool; he creates it. The hysteria surrounding us doesn't touch him.

He thinks we actually have a chance.

"Do you have a phone?" I start ransacking the seat-back pocket, tossing out magazines and life jacket instructions. My hands are shaking and everything looks blurred. "We should try to call someone—"

"We're not going to die." He positions the pillow under my neck and places a strong, steady hand in the groove between my shoulder blades. It's a small gesture, but significant in a world that feels like it's shrinking. He's so *warm*. So steady, too, like he was built for this. Built to be here, in this moment, for reasons I will never understand.

Together, we crouch down as much as our bodies and space will allow. Time stalls, then stands still. Oxygen masks skitter over my back like confused birds. Screams turn to sobs. The plane heaves up, down, sideways. I desperately want to look out the window, to get my bearings. To see one last thing—a star, a house, or maybe just the sky—before I die. Before everything ceases to be.

Instead, I stare at my shoes. A weathered pair of old Nikes, chlorine-bleached from all those hours on the pool deck. One of the laces is untied, but I can't tie them with my arms locked around my legs. So I just sit there, gazing at the faded Nike swoosh, watching my tears stain the industrial blue carpet. What an awful thing to see right before you die. Soda stains, dust, a dead spider. But I'm too afraid to look at anything else. I'm afraid to even move until Colin says my name and that awful terror recedes again.

We're only six inches apart, our faces so close I can taste the whisper of peppermint on his breath. He must've brushed his teeth after that coffee, which I know is a weird thing to think right now, but it streaks across my mind anyway, a grain of comfort in the chaos.

I'm glad he's here—someone familiar, if only in the loosest sense of the word. He must be thinking about his actual family: his parents, his siblings if he has any. The people who raised him, their alarms set for five o'clock on Wednesday morning, waiting for him to come home.

The question comes to my lips, unbidden. "Won't you miss your family?"

He looks at me for a long moment. A pained expression colors his face, then fades. "We're going to make it, Avery."

Something about the way he says my name makes me forget the hurtling luggage and blinking lights, even as the plane lurches forward, then dips with a violent shudder. A renewed chorus of screaming goes up. Something hits the ceiling, then drops, limply, onto the floor. I catch a glimpse of someone's head and close my eyes hard enough to hurt.

An announcement rolls over the speakers, as if it even means anything anymore: "This is your captain. Brace for impact."

This time the view out the window shows dark pines flitting past us like an accelerated movie reel. A lake glistens in the distance, reflecting the pale light of the moon. This isn't so bad, I think. To see something so magnificent, so natural, right before we die. I always loved the water: lakes, oceans, pools. I always felt at home there.

Then, I let it all go, finding Colin's gaze instead. It's only us now, our paths converging in a spiraling nowhere. As I try to process what it means to be with this familiar stranger, a strange serenity floats over me. It's as if all the thousands of horrible moments before this one have distilled themselves into something meaningful, something almost like fate. "You have the bluest eyes," I say.

A lone tear rolls down his cheek, the kind that comes without warning or expectation. I want to touch it. I want to make things right again.

Then, a roar. It sounds like the fingers of God scraping the belly of the plane, a gritty screech that makes my blood hum.

"Don't be afraid," he breathes.

And then we hit.

3

The date screams at me from the hospital white-board: WEDNESDAY, DECEMBER 10.

How did it get to be December tenth?

As I consider this, my nurse bustles in, tells me it's time for breakfast. She sets the tray on the table, and the stench of processed eggs fills the room. Unlike yesterday, or the days before that, there is no lunch menu this time.

No lunch menu because today I'm going home.

A pile of spare blankets sits in the corner. On the opposite wall, an electrical cord dangles from an unplugged flat-screen TV. I stare at the blank screen for hours on end, picturing the rabid faces of reporters and their sensationalist headlines. The same dated photos of those desolate mountains, recycled over and over again, like an overplayed commercial. I tried to watch different channels. Tried to read books or magazines. And even now, with the hulking thing disconnected, I hear the news and see their faces and wish it all away.

A lady with fire-red hair came by a few days ago to interview me. They brushed my hair and coated my face in makeup, covering the windburn as best they could. Someone handed me a bright red sweater to wear over my hospital gown; someone else helped me button it up.

Up until that point, everything felt almost normal, sitting in this room with my TV on and blue skies out the window and my parents perched on the foot of the bed. Nights were long and dreamless, the sleep of the sedated. Days had become a cycle of breakfast trays and lunch trays and naps. I'd been living in a haze—a warm, hollow, wonderful haze.

Then the lady with red hair started asking me questions.

What was it like when the plane was going down?

How did you make it to shore?

Were you afraid?

And, of course: *What* happened *out there?*

In the end, I threw the remote clean through the open window, which her hipster cameraman caught on tape. Two nurses ushered them out of the room. The haze, though, had cleared. After that, I dreamed in biting reds and oily blues. I saw pale, frozen faces, their mouths moving soundlessly, like dead fish. I saw belts with no buckles, and flames with no source, and a lake with no bottom. I saw three little boys, all dead in my arms. And I saw Colin saving someone else.

The doctors tell me this is to be expected. They say forgetting is the brain's best defense against the psychological devastation of traumatic events, and I'll be better off if I don't remember. Maybe the media doesn't think so, but they don't have the dreams. They don't wake up in the dead of night, gripping the sheets and wondering if tonight will be the night we freeze to death. The dreams make me wish I had died in the crash along with so many others. Then there would be no media, no lady with red hair, no questions. There would only be a bleak, logical narrative. A blitz of photos and sad stories. Instead, I'm an asterisk. A question mark. And for all those who celebrate my good fortune, there are others who must be asking, *Why her?*

My dad walks into the room as I'm wiggling my toes. It's become a habit, a daily check to make sure they still work.

"Sleep well?" He hands me a steaming cup of coffee. Black, a little weak. I usually take it with cream and sugar, but right now, all I want is warmth. The hot liquid courses through me, makes me feel human again.

"Not really."

"It'll get better." Spoken like a true physician. My dad isn't my doctor here, of course, but my being in a hospital blurs the lines between patient and daughter. He doesn't say anything to the staff, but he grumbles about my discharge planning to anyone who will listen. Except me. With me, it's a constant barrage of rehabilitation commands: *You should eat more. I want you out of that bed. Being in bed makes people feel even sicker than they are. Do five laps around the unit today. Six tomorrow.* And so on. No wonder why I'm so exhausted.

"Where's Mom?" I ask.

"Outside."

"Outside?"

He looks me in the eye as he says, "Avery, I think it's time—"

"No." Coffee sloshes over the cup and pricks my thighs. Dad steals it away from me, noting the little red marks on my skin with a practiced eye. When he decides it's no big deal, he crosses his arms and glares at me.

"This is your last chance to see those boys before we leave."

"I'll see them in Boston."

"Avery—"

"I don't want to see them." I turn toward the window, hating the tremor in my voice. "The doctors said they don't remember much anyway."

If I were one of the patients in his ER, he'd get up and

leave. My father doesn't argue with people. If you don't give a shit, he doesn't give a shit. But I'm his daughter, and so he stands there in silence, waiting me out.

"Fine," he says.

"Fine?"

"You don't want to deal with what happened, that's your choice. But you've got to give them *something*."

He walks out to the nurses' station and returns a minute later with his hands full. He's alone, thank God, but he has that doctorly, no-nonsense look in his eyes.

"What are you doing?"

"Giving you options." He lays out an assembly of items: his cell phone, a pen, several sheets of blank paper, three envelopes, car keys, and his iPad. He writes down an address and, beneath it, a phone number.

"That there is all the information you need to contact those boys."

"Dad—"

"I don't care how you do it. I really don't. But dammit, Avery, you are not going to leave here like nothing happened. You're stronger than that."

The truth is, I'm *not* strong. A stronger person would have answered the media's questions in details, and layers, and harsh truths; a stronger person would have found some way to cope. Instead, I told the world a story rooted in denial and self-preservation. *Survival.* What a magnificent lie.

He nudges the tray table in my direction. "I'll be back in an hour."

●

Right on time, my parents return with my discharge papers. Dad watches me crawl out of bed, a pathetic effort that

humiliates me to the core. Mom knows better than to say anything. The wheelchair disappeared days ago, never to be seen
again. I suspect he may have hurled it out the window while I
was asleep.

"You can walk, right?" he asks.

Not *Can you walk?* The expectation is clear. He hands me
a cardigan and watches me fumble with the sleeves. He doesn't
hurry me, but he doesn't help me, either.

When the ordeal of getting dressed is over, I tuck three
envelopes in my back pocket. Dad gestures to the door. My
mother does her best to set the pace, which is slow. Painfully,
therapeutically slow. An octogenarian on oxygen passes us in
the hallway.

Together, we make our way toward the elevators. I'm about
to push the button when my father starts walking toward the
stairwell. He just won't quit.

The stairs, as it turns out, are good therapy. My legs feel
stronger with each stride, as if my muscles are finally figuring
out how to work again. The cold had made everything so stiff:
bones, muscles, joints. My body was starting to shut down.

"Good," Dad says. "Looking stronger."

I refuse to acknowledge the veiled compliment as we approach the sliding doors. It's a long walk to the parking lot, but
we take our time. Dad allows breaks—just not very many. He
opens the door to the backseat and helps me inside.

"You know the address," I say.

It's a twelve-minute drive across town to Children's. Like
most hospitals built for pediatric patients, this one boasts a
bright and welcoming facade, with windows so sprawling they
shimmer with the reflecting sun. Parents and children and
babies and doctors flood the grounds, the kind of chaos that
breeds hope.

Dad pulls up to the main entrance; he must have decided I've walked enough for one day.

"We'll park and meet you inside," he says, leaving no room for an argument.

They drive off toward the lot. My first steps are almost mindless, a battle against nerves and impending doom. I shudder at the whooshing of the front doors, which sound different now that I've spent so many hours behind ones just like them.

The waiting room next to the ER pulses with the frenetic fear of the sick and injured. Babies wail. Parents wait with bated breath as the triage nurses call out names.

The letters in my back pocket rustle with each step, a constant reminder of what I'm about to do. It was never supposed to happen this way. I *promised* it would never happen this way. And yet it has, and it will.

What would Colin think of me now?

I make it to the main desk before the walls start to spin. A woman with an eighties haircut and purple glasses beams at me.

"Hello there, welcome to Children's. How may I help you?"

I *want* to say their names: *Tim. Liam. Aayu.* I can picture myself doing it; I can almost see their faces, their tiny hands, their little bodies swallowed by the duck-themed hospital gowns they put on kids.

"Ma'am?"

"I . . ."

As I stand there, fumbling with the contents of my back pocket, an alarm sounds. It is nothing like the steady patter of heart monitors. This is a shrill, desperate shriek, signaling impending doom.

"Code Blue, room 438. Code Blue, room 438."

This is your captain. Brace for impact.

And then it's not just the low drone of a standard announcement but a cruel, suffocating embrace. I'm so cold everywhere, a chill that starts in my feet and rises up, settling at the base of my spine. It feels almost feverish, like ice in my veins.

I turn toward the door, but I'm not fast enough. My legs give out, and the vibrant lights of the hospital turn to shadow. I decide to let it happen because this is who I am now. Damaged. Traumatized. Lost.

Sometimes I wonder if I really survived anything.

C old.

It hits me like demon's breath, angry and sharp. I wasn't sure what the actual dying part would be like, but this feels all wrong. Everything is too dark. Too noisy. And the cold isn't a dull passing-over from one place to the next; it bites.

I take a breath, my ribs splintering with the effort. Oxygen finds my lungs.

I'm not dead. *I'm not dead.*

Icy water is rushing in from somewhere, and it's already past my knees. My toes are numb, and my fingers are getting there. I try to move them, but my pinkie is broken and the others are damn near frozen solid.

Colin. His fingers are still intertwined with mine, his knuckles whiter than the tray table. I pry them open, but it takes some serious effort. He's got me in a viselike grip.

"Colin." I shake him hard. "Colin!"

His size made him an easier target for flying debris, but he seems to have avoided a mortal injury: no obvious head trauma, no penetrating wounds. His shirt, though, is spattered with a decent amount of blood. Selfishly, I hope it's someone else's because I want Colin to make it. He *needs* to make it.

"Colin, wake up—"

"Avery?" His eyes drift open. He's conscious; he's alive; he even remembers my name. I squeeze his hand again.

"You were right," I say, smiling in spite of it all.

He manages a weak grin. "Told you so."

The whooshing reaches a fever pitch, which spurs me on. I unbuckle Colin's seat belt and help him to his feet. The shift in gravity seems to rouse him. He grips the seat in front of him, straining for balance as the water swirls around our knees and the ceiling bends toward our heads. Our emergency exit row is horribly compressed, from seat to seat and ceiling to floor. A small fire has broken out nearby, consuming the unfortunate souls in the rows in front of us. The cabin looks like it's been put through a meat grinder.

We're barely into the aisle when a soft sob penetrates the chaos. It takes a second for my memory to catch up, to sort through everything that's happened, before recalling the little boys from earlier: the sleepy Indian boy, the toddler in baseball gear, the six-year-old playing on his dad's iPad. The younger two are crying as they cling to their mothers' lifeless bodies. The older boy peers over the seats, his dad's iPad still clutched in his hand. He meets my gaze with startling intensity, his eyes pleading with me to *do something*.

"Can you get the boys?" Colin's voice pierces the roar of rushing water.

The boys. How can I possibly just "get the boys"? They don't know me, let alone trust me. I will have to physically tear them away from their parents.

"Yes," I hear myself saying. "Yes, I'll get them."

Colin twists out of the row, grimacing as he puts weight on his left leg. "I'll check the back. See if anyone's alive back there."

I nod, too dazed to argue. As Colin heads for the rear, I dodge beams and wires and other debris in an effort to reach the boys. The younger ones tug on their mothers' shirts as I unbuckle their belts and scoop them up. The older boy comes with less resistance, but he refuses to abandon his shattered iPad. I gather them together in the emergency exit row, as far from the rushing water as possible. It's a losing battle. The rear of the plane is almost underwater, the aisle lights flickering into oblivion. We're going to sink—not like the *Titanic*, nose up, but like a giant car, dragged down flat and fast, weighed down by its undercarriage.

"Stay here a minute," I say to the oldest one.

His eyes widen, the iPad forgotten as it plunks into the water. "No, please!" He grabs my arm, his hand small but strong.

I don't have any experience with little kids. I'm the youngest of four, an afterthought in a family of boys. Babysitting was never my thing. Preschools terrify me; elementary schools give me nightmares. Just looking at this boy makes me feel adrift.

"I'm sorry, but . . ." I try to meet the boy's gaze. "I have to help him."

With a sigh, he lets his hand fall. "Okay," he whispers.

He watches me as I head toward the rear, bypassing a dozen decimated rows. The vast majority of passengers are dead. Some are unconscious. A doomed few are trapped, and they scream at me as I try to cut their seat belts or move a piece of debris. Their raw desperation roars in my ears. I can't bear to apologize; I just move on to the next person, hoping his or her luck was somehow better. Because really, the random placement of glass and metal and broken parts feels like nothing more than luck—good luck, bad luck, no luck at all. I know

I was lucky. Not because I managed to evade a hulking beam of steel, but because I was sitting next to Colin.

The younger boys are wailing by the time I make my way back to the emergency exit row. The littlest one climbs over the seat, trying to reach his mother. I pluck him out of harm's way and hold him close to my chest.

"Colin, we have to go—"

"Just a few more," he says, and dives into each row, yanking on seat belts and calling out to unconscious strangers. He pushes aside glass and debris and toys and magazines. Luggage and purses bob in the water like candy apples.

"Colin!" I scream until my throat is raw. The water swirls around my knees, rising at a fervent pace. With every passing minute, it gains on us.

At what feels like the last possible moment, Colin surfaces in the region of row 20. He's got a pregnant woman under his left arm, but she doesn't look conscious. As he lumbers up the aisle to reach us, I fight my way to the front, hoping to God there's a way out up there.

Suddenly, the splashing behind me stops. I turn around and see Colin studying the seats in what used to be the bulkhead, but the front wall has collapsed on top of them. The first row of coach is completely gone.

It hits me at the same time: *Phil.*

Together, we move aside as much debris as we can. The skeleton of the plane is exposed, wires sparking overhead. The bulkhead weighs more than a block of cement, but somehow, Colin gets it to move.

Phil is clearly dead. The left side of his skull has a sunken look, his hair matted with blood. His eyes, at least, are closed. Maybe he was asleep when it happened; maybe he died instantly. It's a small comfort, but better than the alternative.

"Jesus," Colin murmurs. For the first time, he looks shaken. He lets the bulkhead wall shift gently back into place, turning away at the last possible second as Phil's face disappears.

"I'm sorry," I say.

He nods, dazed. I want to say something else, something more substantive than a standard apology, but there is nothing to be done. Colin knows this as well as I do. And so we move on, toward the front. Toward salvation, if there is any.

The first-class cabin looks like a war zone. In some places, the ceiling has been compressed to almost floor level. Windows cracked, glass floating on the surface. The luxurious first-class seats are almost submerged, along with the passengers strapped into them. Blond hair floats up and around us like jellyfish tentacles. I cover the boys' eyes and push them past the bodies.

Overhead, a series of lights flicker, then die. A low rumble echoes beneath our feet. "Do you think there's a way out up there?" Colin points toward the cockpit.

I don't know. But if I've learned anything from the last twenty minutes with Colin Shea, it's that you have to sound like you *do* know. "This way." I point to the left. It's impossible to see much of anything in any direction, but up there, the windows look broken and the currents are calm. We're going to need both to swim out of here.

I hand one of the boys to Colin and hold on to the other two. It's much harder exploring the situation with my hands full, but Colin already has the pregnant woman to worry about, and he can only manage so much.

The water continues to rise. Chest, collarbone, neck. I hold the boys above the waterline so they can breathe. One of them cries again for his mom, and I try not to think of my own mother, asleep in her bed. Oblivious.

"Avery, hurry . . ." Colin calls out behind me.

Something in the paneling gives way as the water churns behind us. I kick hard against what remains, expanding a small opening just wide enough for us to swim through. Colin gives a nod, which I take to mean, *You lead. I follow.*

The boys, though, are more reluctant, their tiny bodies tensing in my arms. I try to convince them this is a game, something all the polar bears do. With some gentle coaching, they take a deep breath. *Please let it be enough.*

As soon as we're under, I kick harder than I ever have, a powerful dolphin kick followed by a frantic fluttering of my legs and ankles. The boys squirm in my arms. I push off the paneling and rocket upward, though there is no light to guide me, no real sense of up or down. Just instinct.

My lungs are bursting, chest aching. The water is ice, a cold fire that digs in and doesn't let go.

Breathe.

One final kick, and the surface gives way to a sprawling sky. Oxygen fills my lungs. The boys surface a split second later—one of them gasping for air, the other silent and still. I think on this for only a moment before focusing my attention on Colin, on the quiet, black waters where he should be.

"Come on, Colin," I whisper, willing him to hear me. The moon has passed behind the clouds, shrouding our surroundings in absolute darkness. The air is cold and raw, the shore cast in shadows. There are no lights peppering the distant horizon, no signs of civilization at all. We could be anywhere.

We could be nowhere.

As this thought bleeds through me, Colin finally surfaces. It takes a moment to decide he's real, to accept that we made it out of that plane. He waves at me, affirming the same thing, and we swim for land, side by side, holding on to other people's children. Only when the clouds part again and the moon filters through the haze do I see the trees up ahead, yawning over the lake like ghosts.

On the brink of total exhaustion, my foot hits something. Rocks, pebbles.

Shore.

Colin reaches dry land first, then runs back into the water to help me. He hoists the boys out of my arms, and one of them starts wailing. But the other boy, the one in the vibrant, torn kurta, doesn't so much as stir in Colin's arms.

"Breathe," Colin says, as he lays him down. "You gotta breathe." He gets down on his knees and gives the boy a gentle breath, careful not to damage his tiny lungs. I pump his chest with one hand as my father taught me—up and down, up and down—while Colin breathes for him. After two minutes, we switch. The older boy has stopped crying, but he watches us with naked horror.

Then, a shudder. A wet, feeble cough. I scoop him up, stroking his face as his mother would have done. The color returns to his cheeks.

"You're okay," I whisper. "You're okay." I rock him for a long time, telling myself that we saved him and three others and that should be enough. But the truth is, it's not enough. Not even close. As the wing sinks beneath the surface, releasing a slow gurgle as it disappears, I can't help but think about the two hundred souls we left behind.

Colin gives my shoulder a gentle shake. "Are you okay?"

"Yes," I say, dazed. "Are you?"

He nods, though I'm not entirely convinced this is the truth.

With the boys watching, Colin reaches into his pocket and pulls out a penlight. A surprisingly robust white beam scatters across the water, finally coming to rest on the face of the oldest boy, tall and thin with pale green eyes. He allows the tiniest of smiles.

"Is that a . . ."

Colin nods. "Penlight. Found it in a seat-back pocket."

"Wow."

Colin hands it to me, and I shine the light on each of the boys again, just to triple-check they're okay. Then I flash it on Colin, and the air leaves my lungs.

His leg is a bloody, mangled mess, the pant leg shredded below the knee. I lean over it, inhaling a whiff of blood and lake water. He tries to shrug it off, but this is no minor scrape. No wonder he was so dazed after impact. He's lost a lot of blood.

"Can I have a look?" I ask.

"It's fine. I can walk on it."

"If it makes you feel better, I have a little bit of training in, uh, this kind of stuff."

"Plane crash injuries?" His wince betrays the hint of a smirk.

"Sort of." I try to sound as nonthreatening as possible. "Just a quick look."

He reluctantly offers his leg, which looks like a ragged piece of meat under the light. It's a mess of blood, gristle, and muscle, probably the result of a stray piece of debris. At least the bones look intact—nothing broken, at least not from what I can see. And he didn't nick an artery: no spurts of blood, no high-velocity gushes. I've seen arterial wounds on Take Your Daughter to Work Day—which for me was Traumatize Your Daughter at Work Day. Now I'm starting to understand why my father made me watch all those gruesome trauma activations.

"I can't see how you can walk on this—"

"I can," he says. "I just did."

The look on his face ends the discussion. We round up the crowd, encouraging the boys to walk if they can. The pregnant woman, who looks even more pregnant on dry land, is still unconscious. Colin drapes her over his shoulder like he's carrying a heavy burlap sack. He tries hard not to limp, but it's a struggle. With blood oozing from the wound, he finally agrees to let me dress it. I use a scarf that washed up on shore and pray it holds.

The air, at least, is oddly still. The only signs of wind are the rustling of leaves and small waves lapping the shore. The temperature, too, is mild for November, although that can change. I don't know where we are, but I hope it's a small state park a few short miles from suburbia. I hope to God it isn't the Rockies.

"Here okay?" Colin stops and looks up. The brush is tangled and thick, overgrown with moss and spidery vines. The trees beyond it seem to stretch toward an infinite sky. If it rains—or, worse, snows—we might at least avoid the brunt of the storm.

We assemble a few fallen branches and leaves and huddle together. The bark of these towering pines is roughly calloused, but the naturalness of it makes me feel better for some reason. Like it's us against the world, and these trees are our allies.

"I thought it would be colder," I say.

He tosses a few pine needles, gauging the wind. "Strange for this time of year here."

"Where?"

He looks down at his fingernails, caked with grit. His silence says it all: He doesn't want to tell me.

"What time did we crash?"

"A little after one A.M., Pacific time."

"So we're in the Rockies somewhere."

His answer comes after some hesitation. "Most likely."

I wrap my arms around my torso and rub my shoulders hard enough to bruise the skin. It's going to get colder. Snowier. *Worse.*

Our clothes are soaked. No wind right now, but that could change. The boys may not survive a frigid night in an alpine wilderness. I start to suggest moving into the woods for shelter, but one glance in that direction makes me uneasy.

"We should build a fire," I say.

"A fire?" Colin looks skeptical. "With what?"

"Aspen." I clear my throat to summon some authority. "Rope, if we can find some. Shoelaces might work."

"Have you done this before?"

Yes, I'm embarrassed to admit. My father didn't take us camping for fun. He took us camping—and hiking, and climbing, and rafting—"to learn something."

I nod.

"Wow," he says.

"It's not easy," I rush on. "Not like they do it in the movies."

"It never is," he says teasingly.

"We need something sharp, though. A knife would be ideal."

"I'm guessing you didn't carry any contraband onto the flight?"

"Nope."

"I have something," the oldest boy says. He unfolds his fingers to reveal a sliver of his shattered iPad. "It's sharp."

I don't want to take it from him—*Hasn't he lost enough?*—but he forces the shard of plastic into my hands.

"This is perfect," I say, and he grins.

The forest is a haven for aspens, so finding a suitable spindle isn't a problem. The baseboard looks good, and thanks to dry weather, the kindling should work. No rope, but the boys are quick to surrender their shoelaces, and I use them to make a bow.

Colin and the boys look on, fascinated. *If this fails...*

I try not to think about the consequences of failure. This will work. It *has* to work.

When I did this with my father, my brothers and I had a knife. We had daylight. And if we failed, if the fire didn't start, we got a lecture and then tried again. If we failed again, then someone whipped out a match and that was that.

In this case, our knife is a piece of plastic, and it doesn't take kindly to molding wood. Even after multiple attempts to sharpen the drill, it barely fits into the baseboard. It's a cumbersome task, even with the bow, which makes it easier to spin the drill. I force it back and forth, back and forth, thinking, *Friction, friction, friction*, as if the thought itself will ignite a spark.

Sweat pours off my nose onto the wood, which makes matters worse. The younger boys are whimpering. The older boy's excitement has faded to a palpable anxiety.

"Here," Colin says, and puts his hands over mine. He doesn't take the bow away from me; he doesn't concede failure. He works *with* me, like a teammate on a relay, one relying on the other to win the race. If one gives up, or false starts, the whole effort is lost.

"Fire!" the boy in the baseball jersey squeals.

Fire. A delicate orange flame, fragile as a dream. I coax it to life with deep, desperate breaths, feeding the flame with the oxygen in my lungs.

It catches. Thrives. The possibility of seeing daylight becomes reality.

Daylight. Search planes. Hope.

"Nice work," Colin says, even though he generated the friction necessary to get the fire going. His arms are sheer muscle, strong and lean and perfectly coordinated. He worked that bow with the same talent he swims the butterfly.

"Thanks," I say. As the boys drift to sleep around the fire, the silence turns awkward. "You think they'll be okay for tonight?"

Colin nods. "They'll be okay."

"And her?" I glance at the pregnant woman, whose long brown hair has dried into tight curls. I don't look at her for very long.

He doesn't answer.

For a while, neither of us speaks. I have the sudden impulse to make conversation, *any* conversation. An hour ago, I was listening to sampler techno music to avoid unnecessary chatter with this guy. How things have changed.

"So," I say, "you were going home to Boston for the holiday?"

"Dorchester, actually. That's where I'm from."

It's the first time he's ever specified his hometown, which feels intensely personal for some reason. Or maybe he saw me staring at his book, and he knows his secret is out.

"Anyway, I didn't get there last year because the flight's so expensive, but this year . . ." He looks up. "I dunno. This year isn't last year, I guess."

His vagueness doesn't surprise me. Colin blew off a major meet two weeks ago, putting our entire season in jeopardy. I decide to let this go.

"I'm sorry that you have to miss Thanksgiving," I say.

He smiles softly. "You, too."

"Is it just you and your immediate family? Or do you have a big dinner?"

"*Big* dinner," he says. "Aunts, uncles, cousins. The black sheep kind of outnumber the other ones, but it's still a good time."

I can't help but smile. "Sounds fun."

"It is fun. I miss them."

"It must be hard going to school across the country."

He holds my gaze for a long moment. "I'm sure it is for everyone."

"Yeah." I think about my dad standing at baggage claim, waiting in a huge, tired throng of people. He works insane hours, but he's never missed an opportunity to pick me up at the airport. In a family as busy and dispersed as mine, the car ride home is often our only time to talk.

"How about you?" he asks. "Brookline, right?" The fact that he has to ask reinforces how little we've actually spoken despite spending so much time together.

"Born and raised," I say.

"It's nice there."

Nice meaning ritzy. And it is, in a lot of ways: old, stately homes, manicured lawns. A few blocks from the Harvard hospitals, a short train ride to downtown Boston. Aside from the hardened folk who park on the street overnight (which is strictly prohibited), Brookline doesn't have a whole lot of urban crime.

As for Dorchester, I've only been there for pit stops on our way back from the Cape. My impression is that it's a proud neighborhood with a lot of history. The bars are mostly Irish, dark, and crowded. People speak with thick accents, and they're damn proud of it. I know Colin would laugh if he heard my quick-and-dirty summation, but every Boston neighborhood has a certain reputation. Brookline has one, too—rich, snobby, and boring. Sure, part of this is true, but it's also homey, quiet, and beautiful. I love the regal homes, the windy paths and roads that lead, seemingly, to nowhere. Biking is hell, but walking has its charms.

"Dorchester's nice, too," I say.

He laughs. "So says the Brooklinian."

My cheeks flush. "I mean it."

"Dorchester's home," he says. "Good people. Strong community. I was sorry to leave it."

"I suppose I should have guessed from your accent."

"It's faded a bit since I moved cross-country. A few days at home'll change that."

He doesn't say what he must be thinking: *Not a hint of Boston in your voice.* Which is true. I spent the first two weeks of school beating it out of my vocal cords. Colin has no such self-image issues, which is strange, to say the least. He doesn't go to many parties; he resists the tide of popularity. I wonder why that is.

"You should sleep," he says. "We've got about five hours till dawn."

"I'm fine," I say, feeling my eyelids droop. "Not tired at all . . ."

He laughs, and it's so easy, so natural, it almost makes me forget where we are.

Almost.

When sleep finally finds me, what follows is a restless, fitful slumber. My dreams bring me back to the plane—to the screams and fires and an ocean of night—and when I wake, it feels as though a piece of me has slipped away.

5

I come to in the tattooed arms of a nurse named Burt. He lays me down in the pediatric ER's only open bed, its machines and gadgets all primed and ready to go. Burt is hooking up an EKG when my father takes him aside.

They share some words. Dad talks with his usual forceful brevity, while Burt nods along in gruff agreement. My mother stands on the periphery of their domain, wearing distress on her face like a second skin.

Another doctor comes into the room and joins the conversation. Meanwhile, I'm lying on a miniature hospital bed, staring at the ceiling while they decide what to do with me.

It's my father who ends the discussion and joins me at the bedside. His voice is one note past concerned but not quite grave. "How are you feeling?"

"Fine."

"Fine?"

"I had a moment."

"You syncopized."

I shrug. "A fancy word for 'a moment.'"

"Has this kind of thing happened before?" the other doctor asks. He wears sleek scrubs and Vibrams, which give him the appearance of going into battle—an unusual getup for a pediatrician, and all the more reason for me to run in the opposite direction.

"Many times," I say. "Giving blood. Getting shots. Standing too long in the sun." I glance at my mom and force a smile. "I get it from her."

"You collapsed, Avery," Mom says, sneaking a Kleenex back into her pocket. "It was awful."

"I'm okay." I grab her hand before she can reach for another tissue. "Really."

The militaristic doctor frowns, but Dad seems satisfied. He lets Burt do the EKG, and they run a few more tests. Pediatrics is starting to feel like death row before they finally let me go.

Burt insists on a wheelchair, and for once, Dad gives in. As Burt wheels me out, I try to remember those final moments at the reception desk. Did that woman even see the envelopes? Or were they forgotten as soon as my knees hit the floor?

"Dad . . ."

He puts his hand on my shoulder. "Don't worry about it."

"But—"

"I took care of it."

I'm not sure what he means, but I don't ask. It's time to go home.

My second discharge of the day occurs without further incident, until a nurse announces the bad news that they lost my clothes. My mother, always prepared for the worst, runs out to the car and returns with the small bag of belongings I left behind at the other hospital. The inventory isn't much: just a gray XXL long-sleeve shirt and black sweatpants, which I must have been wearing the day we were rescued. Both things used to belong to someone else, someone who's dead now. I don't want to take them with me. I don't want to see anything that reminds me of Colorado ever again.

We go out the back, bypassing the news trucks and obsessed reporters that must have followed me from the other hospital. The fans, though, are inescapable. When someone with an IV drip asks me for an autograph, I can't exactly say no. It's a small price to pay for survival.

●

Planes are out of the question, so we drive the 1,968 miles back to Brookline in a rented Chevy Impala. I tell my parents I'm not ready to confront the rest of sophomore year, or the swim team, or California until next semester. This is only part of the truth. The other part—a huge part—is that I'm not ready to face my boyfriend.

Lee called the hospital the day we were rescued, but I don't remember much about that day except the steady whir of the helicopter blades. He called the next day, too, and Mom answered and told him I was still too weak to talk to anyone. On the third day, he called four more times, polite as ever but refusing to take no for an answer.

At that point, he decided to fly to Denver. Lee had seen the headlines. He had as many questions as anyone—more, actually. He wanted to make sure I was okay, but he also wanted to know what had happened out there. The media hadn't reported many details thanks to my standoff.

He was on his way to the airport when I finally called him. His flight from San Francisco to Denver was already boarding. He had to go; his mind was made up.

I don't know if it was the psychiatric mumbo jumbo or the (faked) heaving sobs, but somehow I talked him out of it. Lee is a classic "tough guy"—he's thrown up more than once after a hard workout, he measures progress in terms of pain, and he can drink more beer than all the freshmen put together. But that day, with

me, maybe for the first time in his life, he just lost it. I could picture him wandering through the airport on his way to an empty
seat at an empty gate, searching for a corner of privacy. Or maybe
he didn't care. Maybe he cried right there in line, in front of
everyone, not really giving a shit because his girlfriend had almost died. Should have died. For days, he thought I *was* dead.

I needed to hear it, but it didn't go down easily. Lee's experience
was too much to process on top of my own. I needed days. Weeks,
maybe. I suggested he fly out to Boston for New Year's. Maybe by
then, I'd be in a better place to talk through everything.

He agreed to this only because he had to, although that
hasn't stopped him from calling. We talk three times a day
about stupid, meaningless things. Tracy Callahan broke her
foot attempting a backflip off the starting blocks. Tom Roche
partied a little too hard before the UCLA meet and threw up
on his second lap of the 100 breaststroke (he finished the race
with a personal record). McKellan screwed everyone over with
a ridiculously hard chem final, but Lee passed thanks to a generous curve (probably set by the water polo team, in Lee's
opinion). At first, our conversations felt awkward and stilted.
Over time, they've become easy, routine. I tell him about my
dad and the "acclimatization exercises" he imposes on me.
About the books I'm reading thanks to a generous outpouring
from elderly aunts. About the Christmas lights in Coolidge
Corner, which shimmer when it snows.

But there are certain things we never talk about: The media. Newspapers. Ski trips. Natural disasters.

Plane crashes.

He doesn't talk about Colin or Phil, not even in vague
terms. Like a seasoned pro, Lee steers the conversation away
from the past in general. We talk, instead, about the future:
My return to school. The team. The way it will feel to swim

again, surrounded by the familiar sights and sounds of Naudler Natatorium, bathed in the white wash of the overhead lights. We talk about the season: the races we want to swim, the goals we hope to achieve. We focus on what's to come.

It's easier that way.

●

As the holiday season makes its final push, the comforts of home start to ebb. Arrangements are made. Dinner preparations finalized. Family and friends swing by like it's the most natural, polite thing in the world to do so. I dodge them all.

The day before Christmas Eve, when Lee calls, I'm hiding in my room, my bare legs folded in front of me—Indian style, the way Tim always liked to sit. I can't remember sitting like this since elementary school, but lately, it feels comfortable.

"Hey," he says, in his slow Hawaiian drawl. People tell me Hawaiians don't have accents, but Lee does. I can hear it in the tempo of his sentences; the subtle blending of one word into the next, like a collective sigh. His first name, in the rare instances he uses it, sounds like poetry. *Kahale.*

"Hey." I crawl onto my stomach, propping myself up on my elbows. "How's life?"

"Great. Can't complain. Got my ass kicked in practice this morning." He proceeds to tell me about the mindless agony of swimming eight thousand yards at the crack of dawn. This is something I can relate to, something that feels safe.

Then he pauses, and the easy cadence of his words disappears. "Hey, uh . . ." He swallows a lump in his throat. "So—"

I cut him off. "What is it, Lee?"

"Did you get that e-mail from Coach?"

E-mail? My gaze drifts to the laptop on my desk and, beside it, a brand-new cell phone still in its box. They're like dams, bursting with information I have neither the desire nor strength to release. When Lee and I talk, it's on the landline preserved from my high school days. No Internet, no e-mail. Social media is a red zone.

"Um, no."

"Look, I just—I didn't want you to be surprised by it, is all."

"Surprised by what?"

He sits down on his bed, springs creaking over the line. "It's about Colin." He inhales, long and slow. I'm not breathing at all. "Maybe you should read it."

A flash of memory—blood, muscle, bone—flits across my mind. I blink hard, push it away. "What does it say?"

"Aves—"

"*What does it say?*"

The muffled chatter of the relatives infesting our house goes quiet. My shrieky voice has permeated the walls, poisoning the holiday air. A wayward sob escapes my throat.

"Aves . . ."

"I'll call you back," I say.

"Wait," he says; it sounds like a plea. "I'm coming out, okay? I booked my flight and everything." He takes a breath. "I miss you so much."

I know he does. I know because missing someone has become a part of me now.

Maybe all of me.

●

As the chatter downstairs resumes, the silence loses its fire. I lie on my bed and stare at the glow-in-the-dark stars that pepper the ceiling. In the daylight, they're a pale, putrid yellow, but when the sun goes down, they still twinkle. A two-dollar purchase that has withstood almost twenty years of dry winters and humid summers. How much does a commercial airliner cost? Two hundred million? And what about the part that broke? What's fair about *that*?

After hours of cycling these thoughts until my mind goes numb, I give up on sleep. The laptop sitting on my desk is an older model, my grade school "baby" that stayed behind when I moved to California. It wheezes as the opening screen comes on, like it's both excited and annoyed I've come to trouble it again.

The Internet is even slower than the processing system. The windows load in cumbersome sequence, and the hard drive is festering with viruses. When I got to college, my technical savvy multiplied by about a thousand; I bought what everyone else bought and installed when everyone else installed. I converted from IBM-ism to Apple worship. I ditched my BlackBerry and bought an iPhone. This was the price of fitting in, and I paid it willingly.

Finally, Internet Explorer flashes on-screen. I try to install Firefox and then Chrome, but both crash. It's thirty minutes before I'm even in my e-mail account.

801 new messages.

I archive five hundred of them in one fell swoop, careful to avoid anything from Coach Toll. It takes only a few seconds to find it, with its bleak subject heading and familiar list of recipients. It says, simply, *Update.*

My fingers tremble as they pass over the keys. I don't want to read it; I don't want to *know*. Anything. All those people. Crying. Screaming. Phil Markey's skull with its sunken look, blood draining from his left ear. Coach wouldn't mention those details in an e-mail, but *I* know them. I carry them with me. I'll carry them for the rest of my life.

I can't bear the thought of reading about Colin's fate. This is a fact of life, a simple acknowledgment of my physical and emotional limitations. For weeks, I wondered if time would change that, but it hasn't. Colin saved my life on that plane.

And for what? *Why?* So he could suffer in an intensive care unit for weeks afterward? I stopped asking the staff for updates after hearing the words "critical condition" for the twentieth time. I worried that one day, "critical" wouldn't suddenly be "stable," or "fair," or "good," as I'd hoped—but "gone." *Had that day finally come?*

I close the laptop and sit in darkness for a long time. In addition to the antique computer, my desk is cluttered with remnants of high school: handwritten notes, chewed-up pencils, a jar of change. A stack of envelopes crowds the far corner, as if banished there by some subtle force.

There are fifteen of them, all sealed. All addressed to Avery Delacorte, but with different return addresses. Newton. Watertown. Lexington. All Boston suburbs, all within easy driving distance. I open the one dated three weeks ago.

The spelling is horrendous, but someone has made the necessary corrections in a neat, tiny print. The writing itself evokes a strong sense of character that comes through in the straight lines and looping vowels. I know immediately who this letter is from.

> *Dear Avery,*
>
> *I got your ledder (letter). I love (loved) it. You shud (should) come to dinner at my house. Granddad liks (likes) you a lot.*
>
> *Love, Tim*

I read the others. Some are written in Tim's hand, but others provide colorful anecdotes of the boys' lives.

One letter. I sent *one* letter to each boy, none more than three pathetic lines long. There were no personal details—no details at all, really. Just condolences and apologies and a vague sense of regret. In the aftermath of so much trauma and sickness and loss, I figured they would never remember me. The doctors assured me they probably wouldn't.

In return, their grandparents and aunts and other relatives sent me pages upon pages of updates. Their words yearned for a connection I couldn't give them. If Colin were able, he would have confronted me by now. He would have demanded, *Why?*

With this thought, I open the laptop.

> *Dear Team,*
>
> *As you all know by now, our small community suffered a terrible loss when Flight 149 crashed over the Colorado Rockies. We lost an incredible person and a great swimmer in Phil Markey, who perished in the tragedy. He was a real asset to this team and will be sorely missed.*
>
> *Avery Delacorte is recuperating in Brookline. She informed me via her father that she will likely return to the team in January. We all look forward to her return.*
>
> *Colin Shea remains in critical condition. He has been transferred to Massachusetts General Hospital to be closer to family. Please keep him in your thoughts and prayers.*
>
> *Best,*
> *Coach Toll*

"Avery? You up there?"

Mom. My heart stalls, then ramps back up again. It's a full minute before I can even respond. "Coming," I murmur.

I close my laptop and make my way downstairs. I don't enjoy these dinners, with Mom overstuffing my plate and Dad asking intensely personal questions (*Does your face still burn? What's the pain like, on a scale from 0 to 10? Any issues with mobility in your fingertips? Tingling and/or numbness?* And so on . . .). Every time I sit down, he launches into a new History & Physical, just like the ones he made me take in high school when he'd drag me into work for an "educational experience."

For the first five minutes, we dine in silence. Everything tastes the same: like cardboard, sticking to the roof of my mouth while I swirl it around and gulp it down.

"I heard you on the phone, sweetie," my mom says.

"Yeah." I take a swig of chocolate milk. "Colin called."

The silence turns painful. Mom sips her purified water, the ice clinking the glass. Dad slices into his pork chop.

"I meant *Lee*. Lee called." I swallow hard, but the food isn't just tasteless anymore; it's nauseating. I feel like I'm going to pass out.

"Sweetie, are you okay?"

"Fine."

Dad puts his utensils down. "Any nausea? Light-headedness?"

"No." I force a glob of potatoes down my throat. "Where'd you get this from?"

My mom frowns. "Get what?"

"This pork chop."

"Oh. The butcher's. It's good, isn't it?"

I wince. So many unwelcome thoughts tumble around in my head. The word *butcher* makes me sick, as does the taste of meat, and yet I can't stop eating it. It's there; it's mine; I need to finish it.

Critical condition.

Closer to family.

Thoughts and prayers.

"Honey, if you don't like it—"

"No, it's fine." I try to smile, but she knows better. Her frown deepens.

"You don't look good." She glances at my dad, who studies me with his usual intensity. "Right? She looks pale to you, doesn't she? Maybe it's the pork—"

"I'm okay," I manage.

I stare at my food, arranged neatly in little piles. It's steaming hot, the way any decent dinner should be.

"Avery?" Mom kneels down beside me. She puts a gentle hand on my forearm, but it does nothing to quell the tremor in my hands. "Avery, it's okay."

I get up, knocking over the chair in my sprint for the bathroom. What follows is a violent, cleansing purge. After seeing the pork chop in reverse, I draw my gaze up to the mirror. The circles under my eyes are gone, and my cheekbones have lost their scary prominence. Even my hair is almost back to its natural hue, a soft, snowy blond.

Yes, it's true: The person staring back at me looks healthier. Robust, even. It's all such a magnificent ruse.

I return to the dining room to find my parents holding their breaths. Mom has that panicky look to her, but my dad manages to rein her in. "Are you okay?" he asks me.

Colin isn't going to make it.

I'm *not going to make it.*

Instead, I say, "Yep. Perfect."

She rises from her chair and reaches for my plate.

"Leave it," I say.

"Sweetie—"

"Please." Then, with desperation: "Leave it."

The nausea returns in full force, even worse than before. But it's not the food, and it's not my sensitive stomach.

It's me.

6

A red dawn skims the shadows on distant peaks. Heavy fog swirls around the mountaintops, the summits bald and raw. Even the lake looks monstrous in the daylight. This scene, as savage as it is beautiful, reveals a sobering truth: We're in the Rockies somewhere, probably hundreds of miles from civilization.

Colin takes a few limping strides toward the water's edge. All three boys trail behind him, imitating his every move. He picks up a burned piece of the fuselage, its edges charred black. He hands it to the older boy. It's about the size of a notebook, but there are other, larger scraps floating on the surface. Luggage, too. Things we need. Things that could be the difference between dying and surviving.

"I'll go in——" I say.

"No," he says, his expression hardening. "It's too cold."

"We have to try." I follow Colin's gaze to the boundless swath of the lake. "There could be food, medicines, supplies."

Colin stands in a contemplative silence, studying the horizon. Something orange, shapeless, and very far away catches my eye.

"Do you see that?" I ask, squinting into the pale sunshine.

He nods. "Could be an emergency kit."

"I hope it doesn't come to that." I keep my voice down so the boys don't hear the desperation in that statement.

"It's too far anyway." He shifts his focus to other, closer objects: A pink purse a couple hundred yards offshore, bobbing next to a giant, shredded suitcase, which appears to be leaking underwear. Beyond that, a plastic box. Boots.

I start peeling off my shoes. "I'm going in."

"Avery—"

"The sun's out. I'll air-dry."

"I'll go," he says. "You watch the boys."

"No."

"No?"

"You're hurt, Colin! Has that not occurred to you?"

"It's not that bad—"

"It *is* that bad. Last thing we need is you passing out in the middle of that lake."

Colin looks at the boys, at their eager, shivering faces. They don't say a word, but the prospect of losing the only man in the group has made them uneasy. "Ten minutes," he says. "Stop if you're cold or tired."

I don't tell him about the ache in my chest—probably a broken rib or two, based on my limited skills in diagnostics—but I've swum through pain before.

"I will." I fidget for a minute, unsure how to broach the next subject. "Uh, can you . . ."

He watches me fiddle with the hem of my shirt. These are the only dry clothes I have, and it seems silly to swim with them on. He swivels his head quickly enough to cause whiplash. "Yeah, definitely. Of course."

He grabs the boys' hands and turns them all 180 degrees so they're facing the trees. He didn't have to turn *everybody* around, but I'm sure he'd rather overdo it than underdo it.

The lake is huge: over a mile across, bordered by looming pines and rocky shores. I wade in—toes first, then ankles. *Too slow.* I need to just dive in, the way I do every day at practice, but something in me resists. It's a strange, aberrant feeling— an instinct gone bad. For the first time in my life, *I don't want to swim.*

Colin still has the boys turned around, facing the trees. I can't bear the thought of explaining why I've changed my mind, so I close my eyes and take a breath and plunge, fingers and hands and head first, under the surface.

The cold swells up my spine and settles at the base of my neck, flowing through me like a drug. The water tastes absolutely pristine, smooth as milk. It is nothing like the chlorinated pools I've been swimming in for years. Like nothing I've ever experienced, really.

The shuddering cold takes a moment to sink in, but when it does, my fingers and toes feel it first. Blood rushes to my core, but it's a battle just to breathe, to think. I can't seem to get enough air, and my muscles are feeling it. Everything starts to cramp up.

Keep going.

The fastest and most efficient way from here to there is freestyle, so I try to find my rhythm, keeping my torso high in the water. Hips roll from side to side; arms follow. Ankles flexible, legs beating to a steady, two-beat kick Coach told me went out of style in the seventies. Out here, it doesn't matter. I do what feels natural because muscle memory is all my mind can process right now.

I breathe side to side, then straight ahead, keeping my chin just above water to see where I'm going. In this case, I'm headed for a tangle of suitcases tied together with a bungee strap. The orange duffel bag is much farther off—a mile from shore, at least. *Too* far. So I settle for the suitcases and swim back to shore, kicking until my legs give out.

Colin watches me until I'm ten yards from shore, his face fraught with concern. "I'm okay," I say, reinforcing this with an overly enthusiastic wave.

As he turns back toward the trees, I stumble out of the water. With frozen fingers, I put my bloodied clothes back on. Hopefully these suitcases will yield a change of clothes, or at least something dry and warm.

"Okay, I'm decent," I say.

He turns around. One of the boys runs into my arms, which startles me a little.

"Fourteen minutes," Colin says with an exaggerated sigh. I know he's teasing me, but worry swims in his eyes.

"I'm fine," I say.

"Okay," he says, unconvinced. "Let's see what we've got." My recovery mission yielded three carry-on-size suitcases and a golf bag. One of the suitcases has standard female professional fare—push-up bras, blouses, dresses, and pantsuits. No coats. And, of course, she had to be a size zero. None of it does Colin any good, but the dresses and pantsuits could work for the boys, if we're creative. I opt for one of her larger, baggier sweaters. The thongs are hastily discarded before the boys can see them or Colin can comment on them.

Another suitcase must have belonged to an Oakland Raiders fan; every T-shirt, sweatshirt, and pair of sweatpants bears its logo. All medium size, which is bad news for Colin, but it will have to do. Overall, it's still a good find.

The golf bag appears to have lost its clubs somewhere along the way, but an assortment of useless crap fills the compartments—golf balls, tees, two golf gloves, and a pair of golf shoes. *Huge* golf shoes. They might even fit Colin.

He smirks as I dangle them in front of him. "You a golfer?"
I ask him.

"I guess I am now."

The smallest suitcase was clearly designed for a child, with
a kitten-themed canvas and pink wheels. I swallow a lump in
my throat. The clothes are even more indicative of its young
owner: pink stretchy pants, purple flip-flops, an unopened
package of headbands. The shirts are all tiny, but they'll work
for the boys. "I hope you like pink," I tell them. The oldest one,
who told me his name is Tim, reaches for a sweatshirt with a
horse on the front.

"I like horses," he explains.

"I like pink!" screams the boy in baseball gear. His name
is Liam, and he's four years old. He tells us this at least once an
hour.

The smallest boy isn't quite so selective. I think his name
is Aayu, but his voice is so quiet, it's hard to say for sure. He
struggles to meet my gaze, even when I hand him the only toy
in sight. The tiny smile on his face tells me he likes it.

"Pretty," he says, and hands it back to me.

Colin sighs as he sorts everything into little piles. "There
isn't much here for you," he says to me.

"Or you."

"I'll be fine," he says. "I'm bigger."

"That's terrible logic."

He smiles, but it feels strained. I wonder if he's thinking
the same thing: *Why are we even* looking *for clothes?* We were
on a commercial airliner, which means black boxes and media
attention and lawsuits. The NTSB probably started looking for
us the second we hit turbulence.

I hang everything on tree branches, while Colin does his

best to dry out his bulky winter coat for the boys to sleep in. We find a few other coats, too, but they're all saturated with either blood or lake water. It could take days for them to dry.

Colin tosses me a ski mask. The eyes and mouth are cut out, and I must look like a wilderness-based criminal when I slip it over my head. The two younger boys start to cry.

"I'm sorry!" I yank it off and pull them into a hug. They sniffle into my shirt. "It's not real, I promise."

I catch Colin watching me during this whole sad display, and he quickly averts his gaze. He must know by now I'm pretty much the worst caretaker ever. When the pregnant lady comes to, I can't wait to let her take over.

"You think it'll be enough for all of us?" I ask, gesturing to the clothes.

"I think so." He stands back to assess the display. "Let's walk the perimeter, see what else we can find."

We start at the water's edge and work our way south, returning to camp whenever our arms are full or one of the boys needs a breather. Colin makes at least a dozen trips lugging massive loads of fuselage—some larger than the hood of a car. The boys follow him everywhere. He refuses help, but I do my best to participate anyway, carrying as much weight as my weary arms will hold. Even with Colin's bad leg, he shows zero signs of exertion. The man is a machine, carrying loads that would pose a challenge to three or four men put together. I never doubted Colin's strength, but this is something else; this is adrenaline, and muscle, and the instinct to survive.

By midmorning, we've assembled enough scraps to build a small lean-to against the trees. Colin fortifies the walls while the boys and I sort through everything we found—which isn't much, aside from the fuselage. All told, we retrieved fourteen snack packs, featuring Doritos, peanuts, and Oreos. No vegetables. No protein. The meal trays must have gone down with the plane, along with the bottled water, first-aid kits, and everything else that might have improved our situation.

They'll come for us, I tell myself for the hundredth time. *They have to.*

Once the boys settle down, we all stop to admire Colin's handiwork. He's built us a fine shelter, with thick slabs of industrial-grade material and a durable roof. "Last piece is right there," he says, gesturing to a particularly forbidding piece of steel. "Can you give me a hand?"

He doesn't need my help, but a part of me swells with pride that he asked. "Sure."

While he concentrates on placing the slab in its proper place, I can't help but notice the rippling cords of muscle in his forearms and shoulders. His jaw is locked, his expression neutral. It's no wonder he dominates so completely in the pool. His competitive streak shines through even now, and his strength augments it.

He fastens the slabs with bungee cords and rigs the door so it won't blow open in the wind. "Where did you learn all this?" I ask him. "Civil engineering classes?"

"Nope. My dad's a roofer."

Another surprise, but he doesn't elaborate. The boys are watching us with googly eyes, and for the first time since we crashed, the prospect of bad weather doesn't feel like a death sentence. "It looks amazing," I say.

"You helped."

"Yeah, but you dragged half the plane across the shore!"

He shrugs, but his eyes tell me he appreciates the compliment. "Fuselage is lighter than it looks," he says, with the hint of a smile.

"It's a fort!" Liam cries. The boys pile in, and the make-shift door swings shut.

"I guess they approve," Colin says.

"I guess they do."

The moment lingers a little too long, at which point we disperse in a hurry. Colin goes over to check on the pregnant lady, while I join the boys inside.

"Look what I found!" Tim holds up what looks like an old Walkman. He's a cute kid: smart, funny, with the hint of a lisp he's constantly trying to correct by repeating certain words. His parents probably put him in speech lessons at the age of two. His parents who are gone now.

He manipulates the object in his small hands, the pieces of cracked plastic glistening in the morning sun.

"It's a golf GPS!" he says. "My dad has one." He gives it a hard shake. "Batteries are dead."

"Can I see it?" I ask.

He hands it over, and I know right away this pocket-size piece of technology has nothing to do with golf.

"See?" Tim says. "It's broken."

"Tim, I don't think this is a golf GPS."

He frowns. "Then what is it?"

"I think it's, uh, a transceiver." I leave out the part about *avalanche* transceiver. Best not to plant the idea of a deadly wave of snow in Tim's mind.

"Oh," he says, but I can see he's disappointed. The image of him clutching his father's shattered iPad sears through me.

"A transceiver is a fancy name for a radio."

"Oh!" His eyes brighten again. "Well, I'm going to fix it."

He digs through the next suitcase with unbridled enthu-siasm. *How many people travel with batteries?* And even if he does find some AAAs, the chances of their being dry and functional are close to zero. An avalanche transceiver is the kind of false hope we don't need; its only use is keeping Tim happy. *Forget about it. You won't need it anyway.*

Meanwhile, Liam and Aayu have discovered two My Little Ponies from the kitty-themed suitcase. "It's a horse," Liam announces.

"Horse," Aayu repeats. It sounds like *huss.*

The boys look nothing alike. Liam is freckly and blond, already flush with a mountain sunburn. Aayu is an ethnic mystery: lush mahogany skin, amber eyes, and curly raven hair. He held up three fingers when I asked him how old he was, but he seemed a little uncertain. He's small for his age, with a fragility that worries me.

I'm watching them play when Colin opens the door. "Can you come outside a minute?"

I tell the boys to stay put, but they're too invested in their new toys to acknowledge me. Three small children under control. I should savor this.

The makeshift door squeaks shut. Colin leads me toward the tree line, such that the fort is still within view but obscured by the low-hanging branches of nearby pines. His pace is strangely rushed.

Then I see her: the pregnant woman propped against a tree with her legs splayed out in the dirt. Her sweatpants are soaked from the waist down.

Colin stares at his mud-caked golf shoes as he says, "I think she's in labor."

Labor. The word lands in the air with a hollow thud.

"Are you sure? Has she come around at all?"

"No." He skims his head with his hand. "I was moving her into the sun, and she . . . I dunno. I think her water broke."

I kneel down next to her, this sad, tragic woman without a name. As her body contracts, her face registers no response.

"Can you get the penlight?"

"Penlight." He pats his pockets, comes up empty. "Yeah, sure. Hold on."

He returns a moment later with the penlight, its beam already waning. I shine it in both her eyes, searching for a response—an *equal* response. Her left pupil is fixed and dilated, which means the right doesn't matter. She won't survive this kind of injury.

I shake my head. Colin, in his quiet, stoic way, accepts it.

"How long does she have?" he asks.

"A few hours at most."

He kneels in the dirt, averting my gaze as he takes the woman's hand. I know he doesn't blame me, but blame is the only real currency we have out here. Blame the airline; blame the weather. Blame bad luck and circumstances.

I know this woman's situation is hopeless, but so was ours eight hours ago. We survived. We're still here, still fighting.

I place my hand on Colin's wrist, his body quivering with the unexpected touch. He looks up. "Can you get me some wet towels?"

"Why?"

"Because she's in labor, and that's what we need."

If he's surprised, he doesn't show it. He returns ten minutes later with two T-shirts, each freshly saturated with lake water. We have two water bottles on standby and a dry towel for when the baby is born.

"Now what?" he asks.

"Now we wait."

"How long?"

"Contractions are a couple minutes apart, so . . . I don't know. Soon?"

"Have you, uh . . ."

"Ever done this before?"

He waits for my answer.

"No," I admit.

"But you've seen it done?"

"A couple times."

He glances toward the lean-to, with its door hinged closed as a kind of curious-boys alarm system. The boys can get out, but the scraping metal will wake the whole forest.

"They can't see this," I say.

"I'll make sure they don't."

"Colin?"

He waits for me to draw in a breath, to say what must be said.

"If this doesn't . . . If I can't . . ."

He puts his hands on my shoulders—his massive, warm, life-saving hands. The gesture isn't meant to inspire confidence; it's intended to comfort. As if to say, *I know. I understand. We grieve together.*

Ten minutes later, the contractions stop.

●

I witnessed my first delivery in the backseat of a Dodge Ram; it wasn't my kid, thank God, but the girl was fifteen and so was I, and even now, I remember it as if the labor, and the pain, and the triumph of giving birth had happened to me. I remember the girl's gap-toothed smile at the end, her wails of agony in the beginning. I remember my father telling me to "catch" this brand-new human being as if a football were about to drop from her vagina.

More than any of that, though, I remember the moment when the whole process stalled, and the girl panicked, and Dad told her to breathe, just *breathe*, because her body knew what to do.

In her case, it did. The contractions went right along. The baby dropped into my waiting hands. A girl. A healthy, pink wailing baby girl.

Colin doesn't ask what's wrong, but he doesn't have to. The labor has stopped. The mother is brain-dead. The sheer insanity of this situation rolls through me.

"Colin—"

"Is she close?"

"Yes, but . . ." *I can't do a Cesarean in the woods!* I can't do anything because I'm not a doctor. I'm a doctor's *daughter*, with a high school degree and barely three semesters of college.

I rock back on my heels. For the first time since we crashed, my throat tightens and the urge to cry sweeps through me. Two more dead. *Two more who didn't have to die.*

Colin rubs my wrists with his thumbs, a rhythmic motion that slows my heart and settles my nerves. I try to think.

Think.

But there is no thinking in childbirth. There is just *doing*. I scramble back onto my knees and reach between her legs, and with wet, shaking hands, I try to *pull* the baby out. I don't know how this is supposed to work. Although my father has talked about using tools and hands and vacuums to facilitate the process, everything I'm doing right now feels grotesque and dangerous and hysterically stupid. My fingers slip.

Colin nudges me aside and attempts the same, although his efforts are somehow graceful, unhurried. I tell him to try repositioning her, which might give him a better angle. I don't tell him to try breaking the baby's collarbone. I couldn't stand it.

But Colin doesn't need my instructions—suddenly, wondrously, the baby slips into his hands and eases into the world.

A boy.

Our fourth little boy.

He doesn't cry as Colin places him gently in my arms, but I rock him anyway because he deserves that much. *I* need that much.

Colin doesn't say a word. He doesn't have to.

We grieve together.

●

Tim is the first to emerge from the lean-to. He finds me sitting at the water's edge, my palms splayed out over the surface. I dip them in the lake, and the water turns a rich, vibrant red. In spite of everything, my heart still beats; my blood still flows.

As only a six-year-old could, Tim wraps his arms around my neck and hugs me, hard, the kind of comfort that lingers for days.

"Tim?" I ask, after a while.

"Yeah?"

"Don't give up on me, okay?"

He digs his tiny hand into one of my red, wet ones.

"I won't," he says.

We watch a hawk skim over the lake, its wings spread wide as it slices through the sky.

"Avery?"

"Yeah, Tim?"

I wait for his reaction, but all he does is gaze at the sky. The sun swims in his eyes, makes them gleam. "Are we going to die?" he asks.

He probes my face with those piercing green eyes, squashing my first instinct to lie. I don't know what six-year-olds know about death. Do they understand it? Do *I* understand it?

All I know is what my own parents did: They told the truth. Especially my father. As soon as I was old enough to comprehend English, he told me what happened to people when they got really sick or badly injured: Their hearts stopped and they died.

"No." I say it fiercely, which surprises even me. "We're not going to die."

"Okay."

I don't have to wonder if he believes this.

He *knows* it.

●

Colin wanted to bury the bodies alone, so it falls to me to put on a good face for the boys. The little ones crawl out of the fort, both desperate for attention.

"I'm hungry," Liam says.

Aayu repeats: "Hungry."

I look past the lake, toward the trees on the eastern ridge of whatever valley we're sitting in. The sun has begun its slow descent toward the horizon. The fire flickers in the tease of wind.

"Try these." I dig into my pockets for the trio of candy canes Liam found in one of the suitcases. They're broken in a dozen places, which makes the choking danger a little less real. Even so, I do my best to crush the candy cane intended for Aayu. Tim helps me unwrap them.

With the younger boys sucking on the candy canes, I offer a bag of chips to Tim. He doesn't look thrilled, but he pries it open and munches on a soggy chip.

"What kind is it?" I ask.

He turns the bag over and reads the label, pronouncing each word with careful precision. "Sour cream"—he pauses—"and onion."

"Do you like it?"

He thinks about this for a second. "Sort of. Do you want some?"

I'm starving, especially since I missed dinner. "No, I'm good," I lie.

"We could look for berries," Tim says. "That's what we do when my dad takes me camping."

"Not all berries are safe to eat."

"I know." He swallows a big gob of chip. "But my dad has a guidebook."

"I wish we had one now."

"It's in my suitcase." He points in the direction of the lake. "Out there somewhere." The wind has picked up, sending a plume of ripples across the lake. Most of the debris is floating in the opposite direction from where we're sitting. Strangely, the orange bag hasn't moved—but it's still a long, long way off.

It won't come to that.

"Maybe it'll wash up later." I pat his arm, which feels awkward to me but has the desired effect. He sighs and resumes eating.

While the boys finish their snacks, I picture our lean-to on a map of the Colorado Rockies—a speck in the wilderness, as insignificant as a cottonwood tree. We're probably at least ten thousand feet up, which would explain the constant shortness of breath and the relentless ache in my hips and shoulders. It could take days for my body to adjust—maybe more, if we're thirteen or fourteen thousand feet above sea level. The boys seem okay now, but altitude sickness can take days to set in. It's a constant worry, with no easy fix. We don't have the resources to hike out of here on our own.

Then there's the climate: storms, snow, wind. Sunburn. Windburn. Dehydration. Exposure. Hypothermia. The sun looms over us like a giant eye in the sky, daring us to survive undetected. It feels like mockery. No matter how many coats and blankets and toothbrushes we find, we won't survive a blizzard in the Rockies. There are no ski lifts, no resorts bathing the landscape in a warm, welcoming light. This is the kind of wilderness no one comes to visit, the kind of lake no one ever swims in. We're the intruders, and we have nowhere to hide.

For now, the skies are a sunlit blue touched by wispy clouds overlaying the highest peaks. Completely benign, almost comforting.

"Don't worry," Tim says. He hands me a chip.

But I do.

The queasiness lasts for hours, making sleep impossible. Meaningless tasks like cleaning the bathroom and organizing my closet just make it worse. I doze off sometime after dawn. It's late afternoon when I wake up again.

"Avery!"

Mom again. She sounds peeved.

"What?" My voice barely carries, but that's intentional.

"It's Christmas Eve and I need eggnog for the dinner!"

Christmas Eve. For the first time in my nineteen years, I have completely forgotten a major holiday. I pull on a sweatshirt and hobble downstairs.

"Seriously?"

"Yes, I'm serious." She looks me over with obvious disapproval. "You're not wearing that to dinner, are you?"

"Maybe . . ."

"I hope that's a joke. Anyway, I need eggnog, *stat.*"

It never ceases to amaze me that my lawyer mother says things like *stat* and *critical* and *tachycardic*, while my doctor father avoids medical jargon at all costs. It helps, though. I know she's in crisis mode when she calls one of her codes.

"Mom, you know I'm not dying to go outside—"

"I need this, Avery. It's critical."

"How critical? Because reporters work three hundred sixty-five days a year. There could be one in the driveway right now."

"The only person in the driveway right now is your uncle Ted, who arrives two hours early to everything. Go tell him to take a walk and then get me my eggnog." She smoothes her apron and forces a smile. "Please, sweetie?"

I look her dead in the eyes. "Is this a Code Blue?"

"Yes," she says, with much gravitas.

"All right."

"Take my car. It's faster."

"I can just walk—"

"No. I need it stat. No time for dawdling."

"Whatever," I mumble. She doesn't understand how much I despise city driving. My high school friends used to call it a disorder.

But *stat* is *stat*, so I grab the keys and fire up her months-old Audi. It still has that new-car smell, the leather so stiff it hurts my butt. Even though the skies are overcast, I put on the sunglasses she left on the dashboard.

The closest grocery store is about a mile away. Turns out my mother isn't the only one who forgot something critical. The parking lot is jammed with anxious shoppers. Horns blaring. Carts scattered haphazardly across the concrete like the spoils of war. I want to go somewhere else, somewhere deserted, but there is no time for that. Our extended family knows to be at the house promptly at six. The clock on the dash reads 4:35.

I park two blocks away and walk with my head down, hood up. This is my first real venture into the public realm, and it feels monumental. Terrifying. Essentially the opposite of what I had hoped it would be.

I remind myself it's Christmas Eve. Family time. No one thinks about plane crashes or survivors or the news on such a happy holiday. Even reporters have boundaries.

The sunglasses are a little much, but my hood stays on as I enter the store. No one glances my way. People are too preoccupied by their tasks at hand. They just want to get their bonbons and cinnamon sticks and go.

There are a dozen other people swarming the milk aisle. This could be trouble. Eggnog is a hot commodity on Christmas Eve, unlike every other day of the year. I wade through the crowd and reach, painfully, for the last carton.

"Oh, that's mine," someone barks.

I glance over my shoulder. *Is she talking to me?*

The woman points to the quart of eggnog in my hand. "That's mine," she says again.

"Uh, it was on the shelf—"

She's starting to say something when her eyes go wide, her hands go to her mouth, and she squeals, "Oh dear God. You're that poor girl from the plane."

Her voice carries, echoing down the aisles as I weave through the crowd toward the exit. My mother will not be pleased if I come home empty-handed, but I can't stop at the checkout line. I just want to escape. Leave. Run.

For how long, though? Forever? Colin would tell me to make a stand.

Colin, who may never have another Christmas with his own family.

With this thought, I hurtle to a stop in the express checkout line. Hood up, head down. Eggnog on the conveyor belt, wallet in my hand. This will be easy. Fast.

Five minutes. Ten. Like airport security, now that I think about it. Someone's credit card gets declined. Someone else has to run back to the frozen foods section because he doesn't want asparagus; he wants artichokes. The mother in front of me tries to soothe her screaming baby, and I think about the baby whose mother died before she could hold him.

When it's my turn, I hand the cashier a five-dollar bill and hurry out. A raw wind hits me as the doors slide open, makes my eyes water. I put the sunglasses back on, no longer caring how ridiculous they look. *If someone else recognizes me...*

"Avery Delacorte?"

I stop walking. "Yes?"

A woman in a pinstripe suit thrusts a recorder in my face. My first thought is, *How did she get here so quickly?* A text? A phone call? Some anonymous tip line? I suppose it doesn't matter. She found me, and now she wants her story.

"I really need to get home." I start walking—fast, jagged, almost drunken strides. She gives chase in her four-inch heels.

"Avery, I had some questions for you regarding your account of what happened during your five days on that mountain. As you may be aware, Tim, the eldest boy, said you rescued him—"

"He's wrong."

"Wrong? He tells the story in great detail."

"He's six."

"Yes, but it just seems that he had a connection with you—"

"I don't want to talk about this."

"You don't *want* to talk about this, or you *can't* talk about this?"

She waits for me to answer, or at least turn around. Neither happens. I fumble with my keys as my mother's Audi finally comes into view. The eggnog slips from my grasp and splatters on the curb. Its thick, pungent liquid dribbles onto the street.

I pick up the remains of the carton. Any other year, I would have gone to some other store, if for no other reason than to refuse failure. Not this year. Maybe never again.

"Well?" she prods.

I shove the recorder aside, a meager act of rebellion that feels weak, and sad, and futile. She must hear the visceral ache in my voice. She must see the spilled eggnog and know, as everyone does, that I'm not the hero they want me to be.

"Two hundred and four people died that night," I say, seeing their faces, hearing their screams. "Shouldn't you be telling *their* stories?"

8

When Colin finally emerges from the trees, the boys forget their hunger for a minute. Spellbound by his long, lanky strides, they watch him cross the shore. When Colin sits down, Aayu holds out a hand covered in shards of candy cane.

"For you," he says.

"Thank you, Aayu," Colin says. "But that's for you. And so's this." He places a Hershey's Kiss in Aayu's hand. The kid's eyes go wide. Colin distributes two more to the other boys, their excitement palpable. I know we should probably talk about what happened, but I can't bring myself to ruin the moment.

"And one for you," he says. He places a silver Kiss in my palm. "I had them in my pocket. Forgot all about them."

"You walk around with Kisses in your pocket?"

The joke seems to startle him a bit. "Not sure I'm ready to answer that," he says, and smiles.

Liam makes the bold move of climbing into Colin's lap. Aayu's lower lip trembles, so Colin pulls him up there, too. Meanwhile, Tim presents the transceiver in all its hopeless glory.

"I cleaned out all the sludge to make room for new batteries," he says.

"Looks brand-new." Colin gives it a full inspection.

"Better than new, probably." He searches my face for a moment. "What is it?"

Tim's grin is triumphant. "A radio!"

"Hmm." Colin is still looking at me. "What kind of radio?"

"Very short range," I say. "For, uh, snow emergencies. For skiers."

"Ah," he says, grasping the unsayable word. *Avalanche*. He turns the transceiver over in his palm, his gaze hinging on the empty battery compartment. Yet another setback, although I try not to think about it this way.

"It's a great find." Colin hands it back to Tim, who glows with pride.

"I want to be an engineer someday." *Someday* sounds like *thumb-day*. He puts his tongue behind his front teeth and tries again.

"You can do anything, Tim," Colin says. "And you will."

●

The afternoon brings fatigue and fierce appetites. The boys doze on a patch of pine needles, while Colin fortifies the lean-to for the tenth time. The fire burns in fits and snaps, the smoke curling skyward. Still no wind.

"The weather's good," I say.

He peers up at the sky. "Pretty good."

"You don't sound convinced."

"Well, weather has a way of changing."

I keep my voice down just in case the boys are listening. "What are you saying?"

He steps back from the lean-to and sits beside me in front of the fire. As he talks, he focuses on the pair of bungee cords in his hands. "I checked the weather report before we left."

"For Boston?"

"For everywhere." Then, like he's embarrassed to admit this: "It's one of my hobbies."

"Well, that's . . . nice." It's the most personal thing he's shared since we crashed. Which is ironic, in a way, because weather is the talk of strangers.

"It's a little nerdy."

"I mean, sure. A little."

His smile loosens the tangle of nerves in my stomach. "Anyway, I'm guessing we're somewhere between Denver and Salt Lake City. The flight path is always more or less the same from San Fran to Boston."

"So . . . near Vail, maybe?"

"Maybe," he says.

"What did the report say?"

He looks up at the sky. "Snow later today."

"Snow?" The word creeps past my lips.

"A foot in Salt Lake." He pauses. "Probably more up here."

I crane my neck and search the skies for what feels like the thousandth time. The occasional plane cruising some twenty thousand feet above us doesn't reassure me at all; it just makes me feel smaller, like a tiny speck on a woodsy-green canvas. Even with the NTSB's technology and black boxes and GPS, searching the Rockies for survivors before a big storm hits puts other people at risk—especially if the powers that be assume no one made it out alive.

Colin abandons the cords and kneels in front of me. "They'll find us, Avery."

His eyes tell such grievous truths, which weigh on me more than anything—more than the altitude, or the weather, or the fact that three boys are depending on us. Because once someone decides we're dead, it's all for nothing. We won't make it out of here.

Liam wakes up and rubs his eyes. Dazed, he looks around and bursts into tears. Aayu quickly follows. So much for a peaceful nap time. Soon they'll be asking me for food, which I don't have. Or their mothers, who are dead. Or a warm bed, which they may never know again.

"Avery," Colin pleads.

I get up before he can say something that will make me feel worse. Because that's my problem with him—his lies are obviously lies, and his false reassurances make me feel child-like and fragile. His truths, on the other hand, are too raw for me to handle. The compromise leaves us in a silent stalemate, a comfort zone with a population of one.

The boys receive Colin with hugs, but they look to me for food. All I have to offer is salty peanuts and some waterlogged cookies. Liam wolfs them down, but Aayu takes his time in-specting every morsel he puts in his mouth. Tim eats with the cautious satisfaction of a picky eater. I can picture him at his kitchen table at home, eating Kraft mac 'n' cheese while his well-to-do parents dine on asparagus and lamb. But he doesn't complain. When I hand him a tiny packet of nuts, he thanks me politely.

Colin selects a bag of chips, then proceeds to offer all of its contents to the boys. I snatch it away from him. "Colin, you need to eat."

"I will when you do."

Tim has deposited two cookies on each of my knees. Both vanilla Oreos, which to me is an insult to standard Oreos everywhere, but they're still making my mouth water. Even so, it doesn't seem right. I can go a week without food if I have to. The boys can't.

"I'm not hungry."

Colin lifts an eyebrow.

"I had a huge dinner last night."

"In the airport?"

"Yeah."

"*While* you were sprinting to the gate, or before?"

The flush in my face settles somewhere along the span of my collarbone. "I can wait a while longer," I say. "Really."

"Eat those cookies, at least."

Liam's been ogling them with hungry eyes, but even he backs off at the sound of Colin's stern tone.

"Only if you have a chip."

"Deal."

I start with the cookie on my left knee. It's dry and crisp and delicious. Maybe I'm coming around on the vanilla Oreo thing.

Colin eats a soggy chip. The bag must have punctured in the water, and the contents look more like chip soup than a tasty snack.

He pops another one into his mouth. "Mmm. Delicious."

Aayu laughs. Liam holds out his hand. "Can I have one?"

Before long, Colin has given away the rest of his chip soup. He spins a fantasy for the boys—of feasts and cozy kitchens and McDonald's. Once he starts talking about Happy Meals, it's all over. The boys can't get enough. I don't know how he does this—how he gives these children hope without making empty promises. When he glances my way, I can't bring myself to participate. McDonald's seems impossible. A suburban dream.

I peek into the plastic bag. There are nine more snack packs, which should get us through dinner. Beyond that, I don't have a plan—because we weren't supposed to be here beyond that. I refuse to think about what nightfall will bring.

"Do you know any stories?" Tim asks. Colin shrugs, but

something tells me he's full of stories. His eyes are shining as he flicks his gaze over to me.

"I bet Avery has a whole stockpile of stories," he says.

"I don't really—"

"Tell us!" Liam exclaims. Tim watches me with wide summer-green eyes, flush with expectation. Well, he's about to be disappointed. I don't exactly come from a creative line.

"Maybe Colin knows a few . . ."

But they're all tugging on my shirt. Aayu looks at me with such intensity it seems as though he might cry if I don't come up with something soon.

"Um, okay," I stammer. Colin folds his hands and leans forward, like a kid at story hour. Liam and Aayu snuggle up next to him. Tim sits Indian style, as he probably does in his kindergarten classroom when his teacher gathers everyone up for nap time. Or maybe that's preschool. "Well, there was once a mermaid . . ."

"A mermaid?" Tim looks skeptical.

"Yes." I clear my throat. "A mermaid, and her name was Ariel."

Tim frowns. "I've heard this one before."

"Scratch that. Her name was Ophelia."

"Okay . . ." Still skeptical.

The story begins with Ophelia, the tentative mer-girl from Mermaidia who becomes a famous mermaid. I'm not sure where it all comes from, or how her simple tale morphs into something magical. Maybe it isn't magical at all. Maybe it's silly. But seeing the captive faces of Aayu and Liam and Tim is enough to justify all the nonsensical twists and gaping plot holes. They don't care. They don't even notice.

Of course, Ophelia isn't entirely fiction. She's largely

autobiographical—a shy girl (mermaid) born to a big family and high-stress, demanding parents. The youngest of four siblings, all boys except her. Two went on to professional baseball careers (Aqua-Ball, in this story); another works in Hollywood (Holly-Sea). But Ophelia was different. Ophelia lived in their shadows and tried to make their dreams her own, but it didn't work. She liked to swim and read books. She cowered on the edge of the sofa at parties. She didn't drink till college.

Colin doesn't know the real Ophelia—the Ophelia who moved to California (the Pacific Ocean) to escape the mountain of expectations back home (the Atlantic). But once she got there, she became someone else, someone she didn't recognize. Someone her brothers (except Edward, the youngest) would have liked and probably hit on if they weren't related. Someone her dad would have bragged about to his golfing buddies (golf is the same in Mermaidia). She wasn't sure how this transformation took place—just that it had. And now, removed from all those old expectations and faced with a set of entirely new ones, she realized that she kind of missed the older, less popular version of herself.

"So how does the story end?" Tim asks.

"I don't know." I look up to find Colin studying me with dark, discerning eyes. "To be continued."

His silence heightens the tension in a moment that lingers longer than it should. The boys don't notice, of course, but *I* do.

"Well," I say, slapping my knees to signal the end of story time. Liam jumps. Aayu is already dozing. Colin scoops him up and tucks him into a nest of blankets and coats. It's only midafternoon, but the poor kid looks like he could sleep for days. He's not the only one.

Liam settles in next to him, and soon he's asleep, too. With the younger boys sleeping, Colin and I are granted a rare moment of peace.

"I liked your story," he says. "I always had a thing for mermaids."

He acknowledges the joke with a smile, but I know what he really means. He hands me a waterlogged notebook, its pages dried to a near crisp.

"What's this?"

"For the sequel."

I flip through the first few pages. Blank, inviting. Tragic, too, when I think about whose thoughts and dreams were intended for it.

"Here." He places a pen in my palm—the tip chewed off, the ink green.

"I'm not a writer," I say.

"The boys won't care."

"What do you mean?"

"This is for them," he says, and I wonder what he means. Ophelia's story? Or the story I told to forty new faces on the first day of swim practice? I always believed people injected slight variations into their own biographies—until I met Colin. His has been constant.

"Someday, they'll want to know what happened out here," he says. "We need to give them that."

"I'm not sure I can do this." *The crash, those screams, that woman and her baby . . .*

"You can," he says. "I'll help you."

And so, with Colin's gentle encouragement, I start where our lives intersected on Flight 149. Rows 12, 13, 14, and 15. It aches to remember, but I can do it because Colin remembers, too. The fear. The skittering of pine and stars and nothingness.

The horror of leaving so many behind. This isn't my story. It's his, too. *Ours.*

I write until the fire burns out, whipped into submission by a howling wind.

Clouds are moving in.

9

Sometime later, I finally make it back to the house. Uncle Ted and a few other relatives have set up camp in the den. My parents corner me in the laundry room.

"What the hell happened?" Dad asks, adopting the same no-nonsense tone of voice he uses with his patients. "Your mother and I are concerned."

Concerned. I hate the ambiguity of that word, the way it echoes back to moody teachers and slave-driving swim coaches. *I'm concerned about Avery's ability to balance swimming and schoolwork. I'm concerned about Avery's adjustment to high school. I'm concerned about Avery's low self-esteem* . . .

"I don't have PTSD."

He swallows hard, momentarily thrown by this response. "No one said you did."

"You think that's what it is, though. I can tell."

He searches my face again. No one in this household tosses that word around lightly; my grandfather had what came to be known as PTSD, a product of his time spent in Vietnam. He put a bullet in his brain when my dad was five. "Avery," he finally says, "we'd like you to see someone. That's all."

"Who?"

He glances at my mom, who nods to confirm her approval. I wonder how many times they've rehearsed this conversation.

"We were thinking about Rachel Shriver."

"Who's that?"

"One of my colleagues at Mass General. She specializes in . . ." He takes a breath, skipping over that Unspeakable Word. "Issues like yours."

"What kind of issues?"

For the first time ever, he struggles to produce a response.

Mom rubs my arm. "Don't be defensive. We're just trying to do what's best for you."

"Rachel knows how to handle this," Dad adds.

"This *what*? You're not even telling me what you think is wrong." I pull my hood off, even though that makes the circles under my eyes more obvious.

"I made an appointment for you on Friday." His initial hesitation evaporates in the setting of renewed paternalistic conviction. "You will be there, whether you want to go or not."

"Dad——"

"This conversation is over."

"Lee's coming in on Friday! What am I supposed to do, make him sit in the waiting room with a bunch of schizo-phrenics?"

"Do not make light of this, Avery. I've seen what can happen to people like you."

"I'm not gonna shoot myself."

I've gone too far. His nostrils flare, but he doesn't say anything. The silence is even worse than the sting of an unwinnable argument. The silence tells me I've upset him, disrespected him, and, worst of all, disappointed him.

I brush by them and run upstairs. My muscles feel fluid

again, my toes and fingers working in finely tuned coordination. That leaves the damage that no one can see, the demons that no one can tame with operations or physical therapy. And I know, deep down, that Rachel Shriver can't quiet them, either.

In the end, I decide not to face any of it. I stay in my room for the whole night, while our curious relatives mill about the house and my parents make excuses for my absence. Only Edward, the youngest of my older brothers, dares to come upstairs. He knocks on my door just before midnight, soft and somehow comforting. He doesn't come in—just whispers a quiet "Merry Christmas," then descends the stairs in the telltale pattern of a natural athlete. The next morning, I find his gift outside my door: a new swimsuit, cap, and goggles, for the ones I lost on the plane. His card reads: *Some things never change. Love, Edward.*

All I can think is, *Yes, Edward, they do.*

●

The day after Christmas, Edward pounds on my door at dawn. "Time for a run!"

I'm awake, but that doesn't change my distaste for early mornings. "Go away," I mumble.

"Not going away!" He opens the door a crack and tosses a pair of dirty running shoes inside. They land on the hardwood floors with a heavy thump.

"That's not going to convince me!" I yell after him.

"Then Dad'll take you to the ER for the day. You can deal with all the hungover Santas."

Ten minutes later, I'm outside. The temperature is in the teens, with a biting wind that pricks my eyes. When we step off the porch, the dry chill takes me back to other things, other memories. Edward senses this and takes my hand, which he hasn't done since we were kids. "You'll be all warmed up in no time," he says. "Trust me."

I was never a runner. The rush of air against my face always made my eyes water—not that I was ever running fast enough to experience any great rush of anything. The rumble of cement under my feet made my bones ache, and every misstep turned into a stumble. Swimming suited me much better. In the water, I always felt at home.

But I have to admit, this isn't so bad. Edward has always run with the grace of a gazelle and the focus of a marine, but today, he falls into a gentle pace beside me. The air warms up a bit, or maybe that's just the blood in my veins. The sky is a pale robin-egg blue, the bluest it gets in December. Partially melted snow lines the sidewalks, shoveled aside to make way for a steady stream of pedestrians. For now, it's all ours. Brookline sleeps alongside its residents, awaiting the brunt of mall traffic later this afternoon.

Edward gives me plenty of time to find my stride, and much to my surprise, it finally happens as we cross into Allston. When Edward starts talking, I'm shocked to discover I can answer him without gasping for air.

"So," he says, the hint of a smirk on his face, "had enough of Mom and Dad yet?"

I smile at this, relieved by the question. Edward gets it; he grew up with them, too. "I'd say that's a true statement."

"They mean well, but they go about things the wrong way sometimes."

"Yeah."

"Most of the time."

"Especially Dad."

Edward nods, but he seems distracted by a memory. "I

didn't ask them about you. Figured it's your business if you want to talk about it."

We round the corner onto Commonwealth Ave and continue our charge toward the Charles River. The occasional early-morning riser—those of the nubile, female variety—steals a look at Edward, whose lean frame and natural stride have always turned ladies' heads. He's a professional athlete, after all.

"I'm quitting the team," he says. I trip on a curb, and he rights me with one swift motion without breaking stride. "Are you okay?"

"Yeah," I breathe, but it's hard to get the word out. *Edward's quitting?!* I thought I'd hear about my dad's conversion to naturopathy before Edward quit playing baseball. "Why . . . How . . ."

"I'm not enjoying it anymore."

"*Enjoying* it? You make like a billion dollars a year."

He smiles, but it's missing something. "Six-point-four million, actually. And you're right, no one plays pro sports for fun. At least, not strictly for fun. The money is king."

"You don't like the money?"

He laughs. "Money isn't everything."

"Dad would disagree."

"Believe me, I know."

"You told him?"

He nods. "Christmas morning, actually. Not the best timing, but it's hard to get his attention on a nonholiday."

A thousand thoughts flood my mind, none of them coherent. "Wow." I dodge the next curb, though I've lost all sense of direction at this point. "So what's the plan now?"

"I dunno. I've got a few things cooking."

"Wow."

"You keep saying that."

We come to a red light, and Edward slows to a full stop. For the first time since we left the house, we're standing face-to-face. His eyes are a bright, familiar green, full of boyish wonder. It's no surprise he's devoted most of his life to a game. "Why, Edward? Why now?"

He sighs, his breath fogging white as the wind whips around us. "Because I want to make a difference. Do something I love—and not just for me but for somebody else. Life's too short to pursue selfish interests."

"Baseball isn't selfish. You love it."

"I do love it. But something's been missing for a long time." The light turns green, but neither one of us moves. "Plus with my shoulder these last few years, always playing in pain . . . it's just not worth it anymore. I gave it a good go, and now I'm ready for other things."

"A good go? Edward, you're amazing. I see kids all over the place with your jersey on." Liam, for example. The image of his bloodstained jersey flutters to mind, then fades away.

He laughs. "Probably got 'em from the sales bin."

I roll my eyes, but he doesn't see it. We start up again, a slow return to our previous pace. A renewed blast of cold air greets us as we come upon the Charles River. It finds the water, too, churning the surface with a savage anger. I turn away from the river, focusing instead on the blacktop under my feet.

"Did my, um, experience have anything to do with this?"

He slows but doesn't stop. I've shaken his stride—a first. "To be honest, yes. It had a lot to do with it."

"How so?"

"I thought you were gone." His voice falters, but I can't tell if it's from fatigue or something else. "I thought . . ." He finds his stride again. "I know it's cliché, but I realized how short life is. How unpredictable it can be."

"So what are these things you've got cooking in LA?"

He shakes his head. "I'm moving back to Boston, actually."

"Really?"

"Yep."

"When?"

"Spring, if I can manage it. I have to sell the house, break up with the girlfriend—"

"You have a *girlfriend*? You never tell me anything anymore."

"Sorry, lame joke." His guilty grin makes me laugh. "No girlfriend. But I do have to sell the house."

It's been so long since any of us lived at home—or even in the vicinity of home. After high school, we all fled to the West Coast: Los Angeles, Seattle, San Francisco. As Edward says, it's easy to move away; it's harder to come back. Temporary situations become permanent. Relationships complicate things and change priorities. Career goals dictate the future. At school, most rising juniors spend the summer on campus, doing internships that put them in a good position for senior year and beyond. I've already had a dozen offers. Everyone wants to work with Avery Delacorte, Plane Crash Survivor.

It would be nice, though, to see Edward more. To talk to him when the world feels like it's closing in on me, as it so often does these days.

"So what about you?" he asks. "Any big plans on the radar?"

"Aside from going back to school?"

"*Are* you going back to school?"

I shrug. "I feel like I've worn out my welcome around here."

"Nah. Dad'll put you to work if you stick around."

"Great," I mutter.

"You know you secretly like it."

"Medicine? With Dad? It's like boot camp that never ends."

"Uh-huh."

We run in silence for a long time. My knees ache, but it's a purifying kind of pain. With each stride, it feels as though I'm banishing a period of permanent stasis. I never thought Boston would be the place for this to happen, especially in December. It's cold; it's miserable. Everything's gray. And yet, when we round the corner onto our street, I'm ready to run another mile.

Our house pulses with a cozy wintry light, inviting us in. We go in through the back, so as to spare my mother's hardwood floors. Edward kicks off his shoes and rubs his hands together to warm them. As he tosses my hat and gloves into the dryer, I can't help but think that for the first time in weeks, my house doesn't feel like a cave. It feels like a home.

"Thanks," I say. *Thank you for the present. For the run. For not asking questions. For being my brother.*

"No problem," he says.

Then he hugs the crap out of me, and I'm grateful for that, too.

always wanted a brother," Tim says to me. He wraps his fingers around a flat stone and tosses it into the lake. He's trying to skip it, but it lands with a heavy plunk.

"Here, try it this way," I say, curling his fingers around the edges of another stone. "Throw kind of sideways if you can."

He tries again, flinging his arm outward with the same result. "Like in your story," he says, plunking two more stones into the water. "The ones who played Aqua-Ball. Ophelia was lucky."

"Well, it's nice to have someone to look up to, but it doesn't have to be a big brother. It could be your . . ." My mind flashes to the man with the iPad, fair-skinned and green-eyed. In thirty years, Tim would look just like him. "It could be anyone."

"How about you?" he asks. "Who do you look up to?"

"You," I say.

He cuts off a throw midway through his arc. "Me?"

"The boys do, too. You're like a big brother to them."

Tim looks back at the lean-to, where Liam and Aayu are "helping" Colin sort the dried clothes. "I'm glad you're here," he says, and goes quiet.

We manage to toss a dozen more stones before clouds

eclipse the setting sun, casting the valley in shadow. Tim shivers but otherwise seems not to notice. He's still plunking pebbles in the water when snow starts to fall. Tiny flakes settle on his shoulders.

"Okay, Tim. Throw your last stone."

He doesn't protest, but he takes his time finding the perfect stone. When he finally settles on one, he hands it to me.

"I'll count the skips," he says.

"Are you sure you don't want to try again?"

"Yes." He curls my fingers around the stone. "I want to see you skip it all the way across."

I laugh, but his expression is achingly serious. The stone is, indeed, perfect for skipping: smooth, rounded edges, with two small grooves for my fingers. It fits snugly in my palm.

"Ready?" he asks.

I back up a few steps and angle my body sideways. *Power comes from the hips.* Edward's words come back to me in a rush, the memory so sharp it burns.

It's a good throw, maybe the best I've ever had, but the stone disappears at a decidedly human distance. I start to apologize to Tim, but his eyes gawk with wonder.

"Wow," he says. "You almost hit that cabin!"

"Cabin?" The word sounds almost foreign. "What cabin?"

"Over there."

He points at the tree line on the opposite shore of the lake, a haze of shadow and pine in the twilight. There are no obvious gaps in the woods, no prominent structures that my eye can see. Tim keeps pointing.

"Right there," he says.

"Where?"

"See that big tree?"

"They all look pretty big—"

"The biggest one."

I find it, but it takes me a second. Tim waits until I've identified it, then he shifts his finger two inches to the left. "See it? It's close to the big tree but back a little bit."

"Back where?"

"In the woods." He sighs, his impatience mounting.

Then I see it. A square, diminutive structure, with the haunted look of an abandoned outhouse. It blends in with the surrounding trees, as if consumed by them. In another hour, darkness will swallow it whole.

The *what-ifs* start next. *What if someone lives there, or at least knows about it? What if the Park Service keeps a radio in there? What if it has heat?*

The questions become more fantastical as they tumble over in my mind. A cabin—a tiny, deserted cabin. If someone lived there, he or she would have seen and heard the plane go down. We would have been rescued by now.

But food, or supplies, or a radio? Those things are still possible. Those things could save us.

"How far is it?" Tim asks.

"Too far to make it there now," I say, but I've already done the calculations: a mile and a half across the lake, at least six to hike there. The swim would kill me, but the hike will take all day. We don't have any gear for a backcountry trek, especially with three little kids . . .

Forget about it.

"Maybe tomorrow?" he asks.

"Maybe." I know what Colin will say: *Don't even think about swimming there.* This time, I won't argue with him.

When daylight breathes its last, we make our way back to the lean-to. Tim drags his feet, reluctant to let the cabin out of his sight. We both seem to sense that going inside means conceding hope for rescue, at least until tomorrow. I glance forlornly at the meager pile of ash on the shore. With snow on its way, we will have to go without a fire.

While Colin fortifies the walls for the final time, I gather up the clothes that have been drying onshore all day. Some of the heavier articles are still wet, but they will have to do. I round up the boys and tuck them into as many layers as they can stand: pants, shirts, hoodies, coats. As long as it's dry, it's fair game.

What's left goes to me and Colin. He's still pounding away at slabs of metal when the snow really starts coming down. "Colin," Liam sobs, pressing on the roof with his small but sturdy hands. "Colin's outside."

Colin must hear him because he comes in moments later, drenched in sweat. While he was gone, I found an array of trinkets to keep us hydrated: three mugs, four sippy cups, and a few punctured water bottles. I hand him a cup of lake water, which he downs in three swift gulps. I refill it twice before he stops to take a breath. He's working too hard. With his injuries, he should be lying down, keeping warm. Resting. Instead, he's out there moving metal and carrying debris, determined to provide for four other people. He doesn't seem to understand that he may need all that energy to fight an infection.

"You're overdoing it," I say.

"Nah." His eyes glisten in the waning light. "You'll know when I've overdone it."

"You mean when you collapse?"

He sips on his lake water. The contrast of the dainty little curlicues on the cup and his hulking frame makes him look awkwardly domesticated. "That won't happen."

"Colin, look at you. Your leg's a mess. You haven't slept. You've barely eaten." I try to keep my voice down for the sake of the boys, but Tim keeps tugging on his hat like he's trying to free his ears. "I'm worried about you," I admit, and it sounds strangely tender.

Colin stares into his cup, as if searching for the answer in its shallow depths. I exchange his cup for one of the mugs. He drinks it slowly this time, holding my gaze over the brim.

"Thanks," he says.

"You're welcome." I sigh.

He studies the new mug, this one proclaiming WORLD'S NUMBER 1 DAD in plump red letters. The irony isn't lost on either of us.

"So," he says, depositing the mug somewhere behind him as he sits down, "I thought you were going to Hawaii for Thanksgiving."

"Who told you that?"

He shrugs. "Lee."

"Lee told you? When?"

"About a month ago."

"You talk to Lee?"

He gives me a look that makes me regret asking the question. "We spend four hours a day together, Avery. Sometimes we exchange a few words."

"I'm sorry, I just—"

"Didn't think I talked to anyone?"

"That's not what I said." I shake my head, warding off some troublesome emotion. "Anyway, yes, I was supposed to go to Hawaii for break. I'm sorry I didn't."

I regret the comment as soon as it's out there, but Colin lets it go. He rubs the stubble on his jaw, a sandy blond that complements his olive skin. It makes him look rugged, a little wild. Nothing like the clean-shaven junior who keeps to himself at meets.

"Why don't you shave when everyone else does?" I ask. "You've been bald since summer."

"That's a weird question," he says, forcing a smile.

"Not for a swimmer."

Secrets. They share the space between us, louder than the wind hammering the trees.

"Lee's a good guy," he says. "I like him."

"Who's Lee?" Tim interrupts.

"A friend," I say, the half-truth just kind of slipping out. "We share a lot of the same interests."

"Swimming . . ." Colin lets the word dangle.

"Isn't that enough? Swimming takes up most of my time."

"True."

"It's hard to explain."

"Damn. 'Cause I've got a bus to catch in, like, two minutes . . ."

Tim looks confused. "He's being sarcastic, Tim." Still confused. "He's teasing."

"Oh." Tim ponders this for a moment. "So why aren't you laughing?"

Because I'm trying not to. Because it feels wrong. Because Colin isn't supposed to be funny; he's supposed to be the enemy. "My lips are frozen, I guess."

Tim smiles, but Colin seems . . . I don't know. Hurt? He reaches for his mug, even though the water is long gone.

"So," Colin says to me. "Ophelia has three older brothers in Mermaidia. That true for you, too?"

"Mmm-hmm. You?"

"Three little sisters."

"Wow. What was that like?"

"Brutal," he says, laughing. "Still is. Their favorite decorative item is a glittery sign that says, NO BOYS ALLOWED. Which means me, seeing as I'm their only brother."

So Colin has three younger siblings—maybe that explains why he's so good with kids. I look at the boys leaning all over him, and the picture starts to come together.

"What?" he asks.

"Nothing," I say, realizing too late my lips have thawed and I'm actually smiling. "So who taught you to swim?"

"Bug."

Tim giggles. "Bug?"

Colin nods, smiling at the memory. "Bug is a friend of mine from Southie. Huge guy, built like a linebacker. If you put me on a boat with a hundred people, I'd peg him as the first to drown." He laughs, remembering. "But Bug could swim. *Man,* could he swim. He'd put on a bit of weight and years by the time we met at the Dorchester pool, but he still had a beautiful stroke. My mom asked him to teach me, and he did."

"Wow," I say, trying to picture such a thing. Colin has never been one to say much about his upbringing, but the rumor mill still finds him. After blowing off the biggest meet of the season, gossip swirled, and grew, and curdled into something ugly. *Colin has legal problems. Colin's dad murdered someone. Colin's mom's in a psych ward.* It wasn't nice, or even fair, but by choosing himself over the team, Colin had turned everyone against him.

"Bug came to one of my meets last year," he says. "Big guy, Sox hat, sat in the top row?"

I shake my head. The only spectators worthy of my attention were my friends, whose presence I used to gauge my own popularity. Three or four of them would always come to home meets. Over time, they came to be known as "Avery Delacorte's entourage." To humor them, I would actually sign autographs as a joke. Colin must have watched this display and gagged.

"Well, he's coming again this year. To Nationals—if I qualify, that is."

"You'll qualify." Colin is as close to a sure thing as you can get; his freshman year, he qualified in six events. Seven his sophomore year. Earlier this fall, after missing two straight weeks of practice, he beat Beau Jennings, one of our co-captains and an Olympic medalist. Not a good moment for Beau—but even worse for Colin, as it turned out. The next week, Colin missed the meet, and his declining popularity bottomed out.

"I want you guys to teach me," Tim says.

"Anytime," Colin says, which makes Tim grin.

"All right," I say, pulling Tim's hat over his ears. "Time for bed."

"But I'm not tired."

"Colin will tell you a story, then."

"Well," Colin says, laughing as the boys clamor for space in his lap, "don't expect much after Mermaidia."

"Please!" they beg.

"Okay, okay," he teases.

As the boys settle in, he describes a Thanksgiving feast that sounds more like memory than fiction: an overcooked Turkey doused in gravy, enough stuffing to feed a herd of horses, cranberry sauce from the can and pies from the local grocery. He clearly doesn't come from a line of culinary geniuses, but the descriptions are vivid enough to make my mouth water. By the end, I can almost taste the lush sweetness of home-cooked apple pie. Or, rather, store-bought apple pie with Dixie Cup ice cream.

". . . And then everyone has a beer and dozes off in front of the TV. The end."

I'm the only one awake to enjoy the abrupt but fitting ending, and I show my approval with a polite golf clap. "A lovely complement to the mer-people," I say.

"I'm just glad he didn't ask me to sing him a lullaby."

"Maybe next time."

"Hopefully not. Trust me."

"Well, good," I say teasingly. "It's nice to know you're bad at something."

He looks at me like I'm speaking in tongues. "Avery, I'm bad at most things."

"Name a few."

"Gladly. Well, let's see. There's spelling—never quite got my mind around that one. Technically I'm dyslexic."

"Really?" It just slips out; I didn't expect this from a guy who maintains a 3.9 GPA. Not that he advertises this fact, but everyone in those brutal engineering classes knows who sets the curve. Another strike against Colin's popularity.

"My mom got me through it," he says. "Bought me all the classics and had me read to her growing up. I'm still an embarrassingly slow reader, but I actually enjoy it now."

"I didn't know that about you."

"Engineering majors don't have to read much. Anyway," he says with a smirk, "can I continue with the list?"

"Please do," I say, relieved that the easygoing mood has returned.

"Well, singing, as mentioned. Small talk. Hosting parties. Meeting new people in large group settings. Knowing when to shake hands or hug. I'm a hand shaker, but whenever I meet someone, it's a free-for-all. I hold out a hand, and then suddenly we're wrestling."

I laugh, having been in that exact situation many times before. In Boston, it's handshakes and Mr.-and-Mrs. In California, it's hugs and first names. I never thought I'd miss the stodginess of the old ways, but I do.

"Handshakes," I say. "Always the safer bet."

"Glad you agree."

"So . . . is that why you keep to yourself at parties?"

"I'm not as much of a loner as you'd like to believe. You just go to heroic lengths to avoid me." He doesn't say this with any spite, but it stings just the same.

"I don't avoid you."

He lets this go, but I deserve worse.

"Well, if you wanted to fit in more, you could do a few things differently," I say.

"Such as?"

"Like, I dunno, blowing off the Fall Qualifiers. You know you really screwed the team when you did that, right? Especially your relays. They were counting on you."

I wait for him to elaborate, but he doesn't.

"Do you have an explanation?"

"No." He looks at me as he says this, facing the challenge head-on. I don't dare ask him again, though it pains me to hear him lie. It hurts more than it probably should.

The wind screams at the paneled walls, and that's when it starts: the storm. Flakes of snow topsy-turvying above us, the tempo increasing with each gust of wind.

Frustrated, I move to the opposite side of the lean-to, a feeble attempt to create some distance between us. The younger boys stay nestled in Colin's lap, while Tim takes the space between me and Colin, providing a small but welcome barrier. His slight frame does little to diminish the tension brewing between us.

"You sleep first," I say, before Colin can utter a word.

He doesn't argue, but I know he won't sleep, either. As he pretends to doze, the snow sneaks through cracks in the roof, settling on our heads and shoulders. It reminds me of a finely tuned performance: nature's silent display of beauty, wonder, and merciless power.

"Avery," Colin says, his eyes closed as he whispers my name.

"Mmm-hmm?"

"Think of something nice."

I hate that he can read my mind, especially when I'm angry. "Like what?"

"I dunno." He shifts his weight, trying to get comfortable. "A good memory, maybe."

Nice encompasses so many good memories. Campus. Naudler Natatorium. Lee. Our first date. The night we danced under the fireworks. Our first polite kiss, our first real one. Seeing Hawaii for the first time in the company of a local. Sleeping on the beach under a moonlit sky.

My mind touches on these things but doesn't stay there. Instead, for reasons only my subconscious could possibly understand, it drifts to the first week of my freshman year.

Early September but it feels like fall, because in Northern California, every day feels like fall. Crystalline skies, a blazing orange sun. The outdoor pool glistens like polished aquamarine, beckoning me to dive in.

There must be a dozen—no, fifteen—lanes, and ten of them churn with the easy, practiced strokes of elite swimmers. Their mechanics are flawless: High elbows in freestyle, with a steady kick that propels the engine. The backstrokers keep their heads perfectly still, their shoulders subtly rotating as the arms follow. The breaststrokers cut through the water, a rhythmic, pristine glide that feels almost musical.

There is one swimmer, though, who stands out from the rest. A butterflyer. His dolphin kick is a powerful, undulating beat that starts in his quads and whips out in one fluid motion. He finally surfaces when it's *just* legal to do so, right at the fifteen-meter mark. His kick is that powerful, that efficient.

Once he takes a stroke, he has to battle surface tension and resistance.

But for this swimmer, these forces hardly seem at play. He doesn't cut through the water so much as ride it, his tremendous arms powered by a brutal kick. His body works in tandem, the kind of rhythm that eludes 99.9 percent of swimmers. It's the rhythm of someone who was born to swim.

"That's Colin Shea," says the girl next to me. Mandy, I think her name is. Or Marjorie. She's one of two other freshmen who *didn't* compete in Olympic trials last year. I like to think of the three of us as the clique of mediocrity.

"Oh. Who is he?" I ask, playing dumb.

"Who *is* he?"

Another girl chimes in. "He's the next Michael Phelps." Then, in a hushed tone, as if this is some kind of sacrilege: "He's *better* than Michael Phelps."

Someone blows a whistle, and minutes later, the whole team is on deck. The giddy chatter of my fellow freshmen dies down. Coach Toll delivers a stilted speech in which the core message seems to be, *These are our new freshmen. Be nice to them.* Then he drones on about practices, expectations, and teamwork. Oh, and have fun.

Fun?

The blitz of introductions is even worse. Names, faces, a roster of hometowns in states and countries I've never been. As the upperclassmen weave through the crowd, their small talk makes my head spin. They look intimidating, too. Pretty girls with copper complexions and perfect bodies. Guys who belong in *Sports Illustrated* or *GQ* or a hybrid of the two. A billion insecurities that had all but disappeared over the summer come rushing back.

"So, Avery," one of the seniors says to me. I can't remember her name. "What's your event?"

"Uh, distance."

"Distance?" She frowns. "I thought Coach said you were middle distance."

"Oh, right. Yeah, middle distance. The 200. I love the 200."

Her bronze face brightens again. I actually *hate* middle distance, but when Coach recruited me, he sold it as the perfect event for me. What he didn't say was that he already had a legion of talented distance swimmers, and that they were bigger and stronger than me, and that at five foot five and 125 pounds, I just wasn't *built* for the 1500. He also needed a middle-distance swimmer because his star 200 freestyler had graduated last year. His backup quit the team because of "academic difficulties."

The truth is, I would have swum the sidestroke if he'd asked me to. I wanted to be a part of this team. At the time, I wanted it more than anything.

"Anyway, I, uh . . . I need to use the restroom."

She laughs. "You asking for my permission?"

"Uh, no." I smile in such a way that hurts my face. "Sorry."

I make a mad dash to the locker room—to throw up? Cry? Flush myself down the toilet?—as the onus of what I've just done comes crashing down on me. A move across the country? To swim? With *these* people? I'm too small, for one thing. Those other girls could eat me for breakfast. In a Speedo, my modest chest looks flatter than an ironing board. My arms and legs are toned but thin. Too thin. And even though it's just after Labor Day, I don't have a tan. My dad enforces sunscreen use like martial law.

It's not that I'm uncomfortable with being an outsider; high school was not exactly a glowing chapter in my personal history. But college was supposed to be different. A chance to start over, maybe even be someone who mattered. Someone *cool*.

I retreat to one of the stalls near the showers. It's quiet here, at least. Hidden. I look down at my collarbone, at the purple suit straps sloping over my shoulders. A subdued purple but purple nonetheless, which is devastating because everyone else is wearing black. Of course they are. Everyone here is a professional athlete, and I show up all decked out in something from sophomore year of high school. The swimsuit's design is a loud, childish network of yellow stripes and green circles on a purple background. I used to think the flashes of green brought out the green in my eyes, but now I realize how stupid that sounds. No one at practice cares about my eyes. I should have worn black. Black is for blending in.

To make matters a hundred times worse, I start to cry. Big, fat, baby-doll tears, an emotional flood that won't stop until I'm somewhere safe, somewhere familiar. I want to go home, back to Brookline. Back to the swim club that nurtured me, back to the high school that made me feel safely invisible.

"Hello?"

It's a guy's voice: deep, husky, a little rough around the edges. As my mom would say, it has a "city flavor."

Oh God, I'm in the men's room.

"Um, yeah? I'll be right out. I'm so sorry—"

"Take your time. Just wanted to make sure you're okay."

He's not coming in. *Whew*. Maybe I'm in the right locker room after all. I open the door and perform a quick scan of my surroundings: no urinals. Just an endless row of private stalls, the shower drains clogged with hair. Yes, this is definitely the ladies' room.

I throw some cold water on my face and pat down my hair

to make it look like I ran off to fix some fly-aways. Not that this matters because we'll all be wearing silicone caps in ten minutes, but maybe he won't notice.

The mirror isn't friendly; my eyes are bloodshot, my cheeks puffy from all the crying. If I don't talk to anyone, I might be able to pass this off as an allergy to the sun. But the slightest provocation—a word, a memory, the sound of my name—will set me off again. And then everyone will see me for what I am: the mediocre swimmer from Brookline who thought she could change. Not just change but *contribute*. One glance at those forty faces, and I already know this team doesn't need me.

"You okay?" he calls out again.

I practice a few smiles in the mirror, take a deep breath, and head toward the exit. I'm barely out the door when someone—a very massive someone, *wow*—steps in front of me. He's at least six four, with broad, powerful shoulders. He has a warm, almost shy smile, though. It softens the electric blue of his eyes, the sharp angle of his jaw.

"Hey," he says.

"Uh, hey."

Colin Shea.

Of all people . . .

I recognize him from the roster, but his photo doesn't capture the athleticism of his frame, nor the grace with which he carries it. His face, too, looks different. He's the kind of person whose personality dictates how the world judges him: If he's an asshole, I might describe him as severe-looking, with the hardened eyes of a criminal. If he's nice, he's just ruggedly good-looking.

His voice already gave him away; the smile just confirmed it:

He's nice.

"Practice doesn't start for another twenty minutes," he says. "Wanna take a walk?"

He doesn't fully pronounce the *r* in *start*—a dead giveaway for a Boston native. My nerves meter goes from a ten to a seven, but I'm still worried about crying in public. That dam hasn't yet sealed itself off from disaster.

We head down a path that leads toward the university's golf course. Some older men are digging through the bushes, searching for wayward balls. A fake pond glistens under the morning sun.

He doesn't say anything until we've navigated the thick branches of a weeping willow, which protects us from flying balls and curious onlookers. He gestures to a wooden bench next to the trunk, and we both sit down.

"Sorry for the kind of isolated spot," he says. "I've been hit by too many golf balls to sit anywhere else."

"It's fine," I manage.

He holds out his hand. "I'm Colin."

"Avery," I say, giving it a firm shake. His strength seems to transfer through his fingers. It courses right through me, steeling my resolve.

"Great to meet you, Avery."

I smile—reluctant, shaky, but it's a start. The tears don't come. Something inside me seems to find its footing again, the ground steadying beneath my feet.

"You, too." I lean back a bit, watching the willow leaves as the wind takes them. "You're Colin Shea, right? You qualified for Nationals in six events last year."

"Should've been seven."

"Oh."

"Kidding."

I force one of those please-don't-think-I'm-a-loser smiles.

"I hope you didn't go memorizing the roster," he says. "Just do your own thing. Don't worry about anybody else."

"I didn't memorize everyone." Just him, because he's incredible—a future Olympian for sure. *Doesn't he know this?*

"Well, good. And forget all that stuff you read about me. It's hooey."

"Hooey?"

"My sisters tell me not to cuss."

"I see."

He extends his long legs as he puts his hands behind his head. His hair is a wild, sun-kissed blond, though it probably gets a shade darker in the winter. He runs a hand through it, mussing the ends as it curls around his ears.

"Anyway," he says. "I want to apologize for eavesdropping, but I heard you talking to Kara."

"Kara?"

"Scary tan. Red cap. Asked you about your event?"

"Yeah," I say softly. "Right. Sorry, I forgot her name."

"It's okay. I just call her Scary Tan."

I see him smiling, and for the first time all afternoon, my heart finds its rhythm.

"Anyway, I know you hate middle distance."

"What?" The defensiveness in my tone surprises even me. "I never said that."

"Yeah, but you do. I can see it."

"How? You just met me."

"Well, you swam all the distance events in high school. Open water, too." He studies his hands to avoid looking directly at me. "Sorry. I admit I did a little research. In any case, you're a distance swimmer."

I can't decide if I should be peeved or flattered that Colin

Shea *researched* me. "I'm done with distance. Coach is right—I'm not built for it."

"You're built just fine for it. Don't let Coach talk you out of what drew you to swimming in the first place."

"But it's better for the team."

"It's better for the team if you love what you do."

"Not always."

He shrugs. I can't believe I'm arguing with Colin Shea. *What a disaster.*

"What do you like about the longer distances?" he asks.

"As I said—"

"I'm just asking."

"It's stupid," I mumble.

"Try me."

"Well," I say, finding my voice again, "people always ask how I can stare at a black line for hours on end. But for me, swimming those kinds of distances was never about staring at a black line on the bottom of the pool. It's about shutting everything else out and existing in your own head, your own thoughts, until the world is ready to have you again."

He says nothing, but he doesn't have to. I know he gets it. *He understands me.*

"Is that dumb?" I finally ask.

"No," he says. The intensity with which he looks at me makes my nerves hum. "It means you're a distance swimmer. It's in your blood, your heart, your soul. Don't ever lose that."

"What are you suggesting I do?"

"Talk to Coach."

"On the first day? I can't."

"You have to."

I set my sights on the next golfer, a pudgy retiree. "You don't understand."

"I *do* understand." He pauses, like he's building up to something. "Don't take this the wrong way, but when I saw the list of incoming freshmen, I kind of picked you out of a crowd. No one here's from Boston." He stares at the dirt for a beat before continuing. "Anyway, I struggled in my first few weeks here. Practices were tough. The culture was kind of a shock. I grew up swimming in a community pool in a working-class neighborhood. We didn't have 'equipment.' I barely had a suit. Sorry to say I borrowed my cousin's, which is nasty, but money was tight in my house. Here, cash flows like a goddamn river." He shakes his head. "Gosh-darn river, I mean."

I've never seen someone so angry with himself for unleashing a *goddamn*. " 'Goddamn' isn't that bad a word," I say.

He looks up, fighting a smile. "Yes, it is. It counts in my sisters' book, in any case."

"The Book of Cusses?"

"That's right." He takes a breath, and for the first time, he looks a little uncertain. "The truth is, I just wanted you to feel welcome here. And part of that is swimming your event."

"Well, I appreciate that. But I'm on a team now."

He nods, but I can tell he's holding something back.

"Look, you're the best swimmer on the team," I say. "It's different for you."

"How's that?"

"Because everything you do contributes to the team. You win all your events; you swim on multiple relays. I just want to be a part of things here."

"On whose terms, though? Coach's?" He doesn't balk at the question. "Or yours?"

I don't know how this happened, this uneasy tension that

makes me feel as though I've disappointed him. Everyone else has set expectations for me in terms of times and splits and races. His expectations are personal. It doesn't make sense. In a span of five minutes, Colin Shea has somehow identified himself as the enemy.

"We should get back," I say.

"Sure." He hangs his head. "Look, if I said anything that made you uncomfortable—"

"You didn't."

The tension breaks with the approach of footsteps and a hearty "Yo!"

I whirl around, expecting to see the whole team staring at us, but it's only one person: Kahale Cooper, one of the freshman recruits. He flashes a wide, easy grin, so unlike Colin's brooding seriousness.

"Hey," he says to me. "You're a frosh, right?"

"Yeah." I glance over at Colin, but he's already on his feet. He shakes Kahale's hand and heads toward the golf course without another word.

"That Colin Shea?" he asks.

"Uh, yeah. I think so," I say, watching him go. "Why?"

"Great swimmer. Serious as all get-out, though."

"Yeah, but he's . . ."

He raises an eyebrow, hanging on the words I haven't said.

"Never mind." *Nice.* I was going to say nice, and I'm not entirely sure why I didn't.

"I'm Kahale, by the way. Lee to mainlanders."

"Mainlanders?"

"I'm from Hawaii."

"Oh."

He grins, as effortless as before. I've never met someone so comfortable with total strangers. "Has anyone ever told you your hair looks like fairy dust? I'm serious." His tone is teasing, but he also seems genuinely captivated by my hair. "Does it have magical powers?"

"I think it's the chlorine."

He laughs. "Nah. It's not that sparkly green color yet."

I resist the urge to glance up the hill, to see if Colin has changed his mind. *About what?* He didn't seem the type to waffle on things. He wanted me to talk to Coach; essentially, he wanted me to *be myself.* Well, that would be easy if I had the natural abilities of Colin Shea. Instead, I'm Avery Delacorte, borderline in all respects.

"So," Lee asks, "what's your event?"

This time, I don't hesitate. I *want* to be on the team. I *want* to contribute.

I want it more than anything.

"Middle distance," I say, and so the fiction begins.

11

Friday.

The day before New Year's Eve; the day of Lee's nonnegotiable arrival. I started the morning by blowing off my appointment with Rachel Shriver. My parents will never understand the fundamental truth that *she can't help me.* Waste of time and money.

Lee's plane landed at 4:05 P.M. He rejected my offer to pick him up, insisting he could handle a cab. I'm not fooled, as the real reason for this kindness has nothing to do with Lee's industriousness and everything to do with my new fear of airports. He was just too nice to say so.

I've never been a nail biter, but my thumbnails are withered down to nubs by the time a grungy yellow cab rounds the corner. It stops at the house next door, and a muscular guy in jeans, sandals, and a light jacket steps out. On anyone else, this fair-weather ensemble might be annoying, but Lee always dresses for summer. The sight of him in those faded blue jeans reminds me that while some things change, others don't.

"Lee!"

He drops his luggage, slipping on slush as he turns toward me. His breathless grin warms my fragile, confused heart.

I thought about this moment for weeks. Anticipated it.

Dreaded it. Longed for it. But when it happens, it feels like my old life clicking in place with the new, the before finally finding a thread of attachment to after. When he kisses me, I taste ChapStick on his lips and the echo of cinnamon on his tongue. His lips are cool from the New England chill, but soft and familiar. He isn't tentative or nervous. He just kisses me as he always has, as if nothing has changed.

When he breaks away, his cheeks are flushed. His hair is long and windblown, his face in dire need of a shave. He looks happy. "God, it's so good to see you," he says.

The sight of him on my lawn sends a calmness through me, making other thoughts seem far away. "You have no idea," I say, releasing a breath I must have been holding for hours. "I'm the next house over, though."

He carries his suitcase—the roller is broken—and follows me into the house. Both my parents are working late, which means an hour to ourselves. I lead him up the stairs and take him directly to the guest bedroom. If he's disappointed, he doesn't show it.

"Damn," he says. "Nice house. Seems old. I mean, historic old. Nice old." He fidgets with his suitcase. "Is it?"

"Early 1800s." I knock on the walls, which respond with a hollow echo. "Be careful, though. It's haunted."

His eyes go wide. "Are you serious?"

"No," I say, laughing. "Although my brothers liked to say so when I was growing up. Murders, rapes, even a few hangings . . ."

"Where are these brothers of yours? I kind of want to kick their asses."

He gives an easy smile as he sits on the bed, which groans with his weight. The same thought must flit across both our minds—*It'll be impossible to hook up in here*—as we blush in

unison. This is the second time in a minute for Lee, which is
unusual, to say the least. Even when his Speedo came off during a race last year, he emerged from the pool like nothing had
happened. After a brief discussion with the officials about
equipment malfunctions, he dove back in to retrieve it. Naked.
A collegiate skinny-dipper with an audience.

"Is the bed okay?" I ask, which does nothing to help the
blushing.

"Great."

"Cool."

He grasps my hand and pulls me down onto the bed, which
brings a new wave of butterflies—but good butterflies. Normal,
the way things should be after a long separation. Our reunion
is no longer an obstacle to overcome or a milestone to be
reached. It happened. We're good. In the wake of five grueling
weeks, I'd forgotten what it's like to be in the company of
someone so low-maintenance.

"So." I look down at our hands, linked together. It sends a
flutter through me, mingling with a memory that doesn't belong anywhere near here, like a mismatched current. "Excited
to meet my parents?"

"Hell yeah. I think I'm gonna like your dad."

"Really? No one likes my dad."

"Your mom must like him a little bit." He brushes a strand
of hair from my face, twirls it in his fingers. Still captivated by
my hair—maybe even more so, now that it's blond again.

"So how's the team? How's school? I'm so out of the loop."

"The team's good. Coach took the, uh . . ." He clears his
throat as he scrambles for different words. Lee knows the rules
now. "Coach took some time off at the end of last semester."

"Oh."

"The team is kind of like family to him, so, you know, he

took it hard. But he'll be back in January." Lee clears his throat, tries to sound casual. "So . . . are *you* coming back in January?"

There is no hesitation in my voice when I say, "Definitely."

"Really?" He jumps off the bed and does a fist pump that would make Edward proud. "That's awesome, Aves! I knew you were kind of on the fence . . ."

"I want to come back. My life is in California now." *My life.* My life should have ended at the bottom of that lake, but I don't tell Lee that.

He sits back down on the bed, his voice quiet. "I . . . prayed for you. I know, it sounds nuts—I was raised by atheists, for Chrissakes." He laughs nervously, like he's trying hard to keep it together. "When Coach burst out of his office during practice and told us you'd survived, I cried in the pool." He gives me a sheepish look. "I know, crying in the pool is for pansies, but I did it."

I reach for his hand. "I'm sorry, Lee."

"No, I'm sorry. And I know you don't like to talk about this, and I get that, I really do, but it's just been weighing on me."

"I know." I pull him close, wanting to reassure him even though words are just words, and they don't change what happened.

"Anyway, you hungry?" He settles easily into his usual good mood. "'Cause I'm starving."

I don't dare admit that my stomach has been in knots all day. "Sure, I could eat."

"I'm so relieved you said that."

"Well, I'm no stranger to your eight-thousand-calorie diet."

He grasps my hand and twirls me off the bed. "I need my strength to seduce you," he says, then laughs when he sees my eyes roll.

"I don't think it'll take eight thousand calories to seduce me."

"Five thousand?"

"Maybe."

"Okay, well, before that happens, I need to wash the plane off me."

"Good idea." I hand him a stack of towels before he can propose any other seduction activities. Emotional intimacy is one thing, physical intimacy quite another. I know the subject will come up, but I'm not ready to broach it now.

As Lee digs into his suitcase for a change of clothes, I can imagine Rachel Shriver's two-hundred-fifty-dollar words of wisdom: *Give it time.*

Such a fallacy.

●

Lee lets me pick the restaurant, so I choose Anna's Taqueria in Brookline: quick, crowded, and very loud. Lee gives me hell because this isn't California, and any burrito consumed outside that state is substandard, but I like Anna's. And, most important, it's quick, crowded, and very loud, which means we'll blend in. If a reporter *does* stumble in, Lee will beat him down—or at least throw him out.

Lee knocks on my bedroom door. "You in there, babe? I'm ready for this shitty East Coast burrito you promised me."

My turnaround time is usually fast. As a swimmer, I've developed a routine: alarm, snooze, pee, brush teeth, put suit on, walk to pool. I don't shower or even brush my hair. Don't check my e-mail. I just get up and go, barely conscious as I stumble across campus while most people are still sleeping off a hangover or pushing through the worst hour of an all-nighter.

But tonight, I can't seem to mobilize. I've been in my room for over an hour, fussing over my hair and clothes and accessories. Anna's Taqueria is not a fancy place. Plastic chairs,

Formica tables, paper cups. The ordering is done assembly-line style. Two sweaty guys behind a glass divider spoon out beans and meats and guacamole. Sometimes cheese. Lots of salsa. If you don't know what you want, they tell you to get out of line so someone who *does* know can eat. Their entire business model is based on efficiency, although the food's pretty good, too.

The point is, I could show up in sweats and fit right in. But because tonight is about Lee instead of me, and because I'm so desperately fixated on what it means to be *normal*, and because I haven't really left the house except for the occasional snowy run with Edward, I want this to be perfect. I want it to mean something.

And so I find myself standing in front of the mirror, appraising a pair of skinny jeans and a top that really has no business being worn before April. It's a bright, satiny white, which is not a color I often wear. Admittedly, the white brightens me up—my pale, freckled face; my spectral green eyes. Even my hair looks a little blonder than usual, which may just be the dye fading. I went back to my natural color as soon as I was able to shower on my own.

"I'm hungry!" Lee wails. He leans against the door so it squeaks in the frame. I locked it earlier, but if he knew this, he'd probably be hurt.

"Coming!"

It takes me a solid minute to find a matching pair of earrings: small silver hoops embedded with three turquoise stones. This is why I stopped wearing anything other than cheap studs. Not only did the pool eat them all, but searching for jewelry adds precious minutes to my morning routine.

I stab the hoops in my ears, put on a jacket, and throw open the door. Lee's jaw drops as his eyes wash over me like a warm rain. A mischievous smile curls at his lips. I brush by him before my blushing collarbone can give me away.

"Should I change?" he calls after me. "I thought you said this place was casual—"

"It's casual. Let's go."

I hand him my dad's down coat, which matches my own except for size. It's hideous but warm, packed with goose feathers from hood to heel, although on Lee, it barely grazes his calves. He's a good bit taller than my dad, but shorter than Colin.

Colin. His name keeps popping into my head in ways that threaten to ruin the whole night. After Coach's last e-mail, I shut my laptop down for good and exchanged my smartphone for a cheapie off eBay. Unfortunately, I haven't found a way to shut down my own thoughts.

"Is this place far?" Lee asks.

"Not too far."

"Like, are we gonna freeze before we get there?"

"Not if you zip up that coat."

After fumbling with the zipper, Lee loops his arm through mine. His first step is a near disaster on a sheet of ice, thanks in large part to a pair of Edward's old Nikes. They have to be at least a decade old. "Nice shoes," I say.

"You're sure Edward doesn't have athlete's foot, right? 'Cause I see enough of that in the locker room . . ."

"I'm positive," I say, smirking. "Edward is very hygienic."

"I can't believe you hid my sandals."

"Well, I don't want you to get frostbite." My fingers start to tingle, but my mind wills it away. "You'll thank me later."

"I'm sure I will." He grins. "So. Excited for this shitty burrito?"

"Are you gonna give me a hard time about it later if it's bad?"

"You bet." He gives me a nudge, which sends him careening sideways on the ice. I can't help but laugh a little bit.

I slow my stride until he's found his footing. He stares at his feet, waiting for them to betray him again. "You're really not a cold-weather person, are you?" I ask.

"Who would voluntarily live in a cold climate? I'm serious. Answer me that."

"It grows on you."

"Well, I'm glad it doesn't have to. I'm sticking with Cali."

He exhales through gritted teeth as he proceeds to walk with his head down, eyes on the ground. He keeps his arm looped around mine, but it's more for support than affection. I like it, though. Lee has always been the strong, confident, gregarious one. Even when we're alone, I sometimes struggle to be heard. But here, on the streets of my hometown, those battles don't exist. I'm in my element. The size and spectacle of California is three thousand miles away, along with all the insecurities that go along with it.

"You sure this place is walkable?" Lee asks.

"Just up the block." I point toward the quaint, haphazard intersection known as Coolidge Corner. Few of the streets in or near Boston are aligned or even planned out, and the intersection of Harvard and Beacon is no exception. Little side streets branch off the main thoroughfares in every direction, confusing tourists and frustrating shopkeepers. But the locals navigate them with ease, like it's some great secret we're all in on.

"Weren't we just on this street?" Lee asks, dazed.

"No."

"It looks familiar . . ."

"Anna's is right up that way." I point across the street and up the hill, toward a little storefront with yellow paneling and a cozy interior. Despite the chill, the night feels electric, swollen with anticipation. Then again, tomorrow *is* New Year's Eve, and people always get excited about the illusion of a fresh start.

Lee has found his balance in Edward's Nikes. As we cross the intersection, the din of conversation and the scent of Mexican food waft down the street. I hike up the hood of my coat and practically strangle myself with the neck strap. Better to be unfashionable than to be recognized. Last thing I need right now is a repeat of the eggnog incident.

"Aves, is that really necessary?" Lee tugs on the strap. "You look like an arctic bag lady."

"It's cold."

"True," he muses. He pulls his hat over his ears.

As we walk, I keep my head down, my gaze trained on the shoveled sidewalks. People in Uggs and heavy boots swarm around us, fading from my field of vision as they pass and disperse. The smell of carnitas and hot sauce makes my eyes water.

"Okay," Lee announces. "We're here."

I look up to see Anna's familiar yellow veneer. The line reaches almost to the door, and most of the tables are taken. Lee doesn't seem concerned.

He holds the door open for me. "Ladies first."

"Thank you," I say, and squeeze past. The line moves quickly, and we order like pros—me because I've been here a hundred times, and Lee because he's frequented a thousand taquerias in his lifetime. He knows the routine.

"Two burritos, huh?" I say, as he orders our drinks. "That gonna be enough?"

"It's a start."

I start to pay, but Lee hurls his credit card onto the counter.

"Whole weekend's on me." He points to the corner before I can argue or even thank him. "I see our table."

While he heads in that direction with our food, I fill two cups with lemonade and grab five packets of salt, which would clog a horse's arteries, but Lee loves his salt. The tables are not just full but overflowing. Some people are standing. It's a wonder he managed to jump on one so fast—

No.

No no no.

The lemonades in my hands hit the floor as Colin Shea rises from his chair. His gaze never leaves mine, the kind of connection that smolders, then burns, as the possibility of each other becomes reality.

"Aves?" Lee has scrounged up some napkins. "Aves, we've got a situation here . . ."

"Sorry," I mumble to the soaked teenager on my left. He starts to say something nasty, but Lee tames him with a stern look.

"Aves?"

I stumble backward, into the crowd and toward the door. An elderly gentleman catches me before I trip over his granddaughter's purse. There are shouts and taunts and then, horribly, the flash of someone's iPhone. Pictures. Video.

Hey, it's that girl from the plane crash!

I run hard—a dangerous, panicked sprint through the streets of Brookline. Twice, I slip on the ice. The third time, Lee catches me.

He looks on the verge of tears. "What the hell are you doing?"

"Him." I can't bring myself to say Colin's name. "You just . . . Why didn't you tell me?"

"Why are you so angry? Shea isn't some rando off the

street." He takes a breath, and his tone softens. "You of all people should understand that."

"Fine. You're right. Go have dinner with him."

"What's your problem?"

"*My* problem?" I bark out a laugh. "Oh, I've got problems you can't even imagine, Lee. Go ask Colin if you really want to know."

"You're acting crazy."

"Maybe because I *am* crazy." The words lurch from my throat in a soundless sob. Lee watches this humiliating display for a moment, but only for a moment, because he's good like that. He wraps his arms around me until I can breathe again.

Lee walks me home. He doesn't leave me to talk to Colin; he doesn't even go back for the burritos. We walk side by side in a tight, desperate embrace. I hate that I need him like this. I hate that he knows that *normal* is just a dream.

When we get back to the house, we order takeout and talk about the safest, most mindless things: Zach Kincaid's crush on Marjorie Kline. Alice Lien's disqualification from the homecoming meet because she tried to rig the starting blocks. The padding in various individuals' swimsuits, guys and girls. These stories help me look forward to the future, but more than that, they help me forget the past.

Later that night, we rendezvous on the guest room's embroidered bedspread, but it's a lost cause because the mattress creaks so badly—at least, that's what I tell myself. In the end, I go back to my room, and he stays in his. He sleeps soundly, as he always does, his soft snores percolating through the walls.

Meanwhile, I dream . . . and dream . . .

And dream.

Colin.

Some time later, I awaken to a velvet sky, thin clouds

teasing the Boston skyline. Icicles hanging from my window glimmer in the faint morning light. Last year, I would have described it as magical. Now, the word that comes to mind is *haunted*.

My parents are two doors down; Lee is a dozen feet away, separated by a thin wall my dad built during a costly (and pointless) renovation. Two of my brothers have gone back to their lives in Seattle and LA, but Edward is asleep in the basement, which has been his room for as long as I can remember. His yellow Lab peers up at me from the foot of my bed, his eyes somehow lost, like he's failed as a guard dog for reasons his brain can't quite process.

I have never felt so alone.

12

wake up with a start, sensing an absence that wasn't there before.

"Colin?" My mouth is like cotton. The air that finds its way into my lungs is cold, *so cold*. If only my father had taught us how to build indoor fires.

Without the penlight, the lean-to is steeped in darkness. I fumble around for it, careful to avoid the boys' tiny bodies. Their soft sighs and restless legs confirm their presence. At least they're all accounted for.

"Looking for this?"

Colin turns on the light, a feeble glow that nonetheless makes me feel better. He places the penlight in my hands, his calloused palm brushing mine.

"Have you been awake this whole time?" I ask.

"No," he says. "I slept while you were awake."

"Liar."

He peels off his coat and hands it to me. "You're shivering."

"I'm fine."

"Please—"

"*No*, Colin." I put the coat back in his lap.

We sit across from each other such that our legs are side by side, but not quite touching. Two inches is the most distance we can manage in these tight quarters.

"Tim saw a cabin," I say.

He searches my face for clarification, but the word itself holds so much promise. *Cabin.* Food, shelter, supplies. It needs no further explanation.

"Why didn't you tell me earlier?"

"He saw it right before dark. There was nothing we could have done anyway."

"We have a light."

"A *pen*light." I wait until he looks up. "Colin, don't even think about it. It's too far."

"How far?"

"Across the lake."

"Directly across?"

I nod.

"So a day's hike, or an hour's swim."

"Less than an hour for you."

"Not in these conditions," he says. "In any case, you're the distance swimmer."

So he remembers. I stuff my hands in my lap.

"It's too cold," I say, which is a fine, acceptable excuse. Except Colin doesn't believe it. He sensed my hesitation on the shore this afternoon; he senses it now.

"I think I should try," he says.

"Colin, *no.*" It feels like an affront.

"I know you could make it, but you've already gone in the water twice. It's my turn."

"What if you drown? What if you get there and can't make it back?"

"I'll make it back."

"You don't have to go. We could just wait for more suitcases to wash up onshore. It's happened a few times already—"

"I have to go."

He puts his coat at my feet, yet another offering that makes me feel weak and incapable. I know that later, when sleep takes hold of me again, he'll drape it over my shoulders. There is nothing I can do or say to change his mind about swimming for that cabin. About anything, really. He will do anything for those boys.

When I wake at dawn, the coat sits on my shoulders, and Colin is gone.

●

He scrawled a message on a two of hearts:

I have to try.

I rip the playing card off the paneling and stuff it in my pocket. My first instinct is rage; the second is terror. His conviction straddles the line between risk and insanity.

The fuselage dips and groans with every gust. The morning sky has gone a deep, angry gray, leaden with snow. Aayu navigates a restless sleep, while Liam dozes, oblivious to the storm raging inches from his body.

Tim watches me with sleepless eyes. "Tim, over here," I say, trying to keep my voice down so the others won't wake up. "Come on."

He crawls over, hands and feet padding a swath of towels we rescued from someone's shopping bag. I pull him into my side and adjust the makeshift ski mask on his head so his ears are covered.

"Where's Colin?" he asks.

"I don't know," I lie. *Out there.*

"His stick is gone."

Colin told the boys the stick was like a sword, but Tim suspects its real purpose: fending off unwelcome creatures. Bears, wolves, mountain lions. I hope to never see or hear one. When we were sitting by the fire, I always faced the lake.

"I'm going to go out and see." I check Tim's coat to make sure every button is fastened. "Stay here and be brave, okay?"

"No," he cries, tugging on my shirt. His eyes are wet, his ski mask damp with snot.

"I won't go far. You'll be able to see me the whole time."

His fingers grip the hem of my coat as I shuffle outside. At the door, I turn and take his hands, trying to warm them, even though his color is good. I do it because my mom used to do it for me, and it always made me feel better.

Tim's sobs turn to sniffles, and the tension in his little body slowly drains away. I blow on his hands a few more times to warm them.

"You're so brave, Tim," I tell him. "Braver than me, that's for sure."

The wind prickles the skin on the back of my neck. Tim pulls my hat down, careful to avoid tugging on my hair. "Don't go far," he says. "Please."

"I won't."

My first step outside is a savage one. A blitz of arctic air drives straight to the core, like falling through ice. Snow lashes my skin. The lake is barely visible in the distance, the forest an alien dimension with a thousand entrances and no exit.

"Colin!" I call out, screaming from the depths of my lungs to generate volume. The wind drowns out my voice, reducing it to a dry wheeze.

I stumble toward the lake, slipping on snow-covered rocks and ice. Any hope of seeing Colin's red shirt in the distance vanishes with the onslaught of blowing snow.

A small voice calls to me from the lean-to. "I heard something!" Tim half shouts, half whispers.

He points toward the trees behind him and, beyond that, a gaping void of shadows. I don't see anything. Just trees and blowing snow. "Where?"

"Over there!" He points again, same direction. A shudder rolls through me, but I don't know why. The only thing there is wilderness.

Or is there?

When the wind eases for a moment, I put my fingers to my lips and try to whistle. A sharp pain rattles my rib cage, but it doesn't compare to the thought of losing Colin. *Nothing* compares to losing Colin. I should never have told him about the cabin.

Then, in the distance: a second whistle. At first it sounds like an echo, but this one goes on longer, like it originated from someone with twice my lung capacity. The strange thing is, Tim was pointing in the other direction.

I scramble toward the woods, remembering too late that Tim is watching. He pushes open the scrap of fuselage and crawls out, but he has the good sense to close it behind him.

"Go back inside, Tim! You'll freeze!"

He pauses, probably a knee-jerk reaction to a command from an adult. I turn back toward the trees. Snow hits me from every direction—above me, around me, even from below. The wind kicks it up, whips it into a frenzy. When I turn back around, Tim is gone.

"Tim!" I stumble back toward the lean-to, squinting into the haze. "Tim—"

He barrels into me, all elbows and knees and soft sobs. I scoop him up and hug him, even though he's tall for a six-year-old and his legs dangle almost to my shins. I wonder if he feels the desperation in my arms, the relief in my voice.

"Tim, you can't be out here."

"I want to help."

His nose is red and his lips a worrisome plum, but otherwise, his skin is covered with scarves, hats, gloves—anything I could find. Good. At least I did something right.

"I know you do. But I can't . . . We can't . . ."

The determined look in his eyes turns sympathetic. "We can do it," he says. "I heard the whistle."

"You did?"

"Out there." He gestures vaguely toward the trees.

"I thought you said you heard something from over there," I say, pointing south, using the lean-to as a landmark. He's looking north.

"I did . . ." He furrows his brow. "I thought I did."

I whistle again. Tim counts to five. A second whistle carries through the stillness, and Tim claps his hands. "See? It's coming from over there!"

Over there doesn't make me feel any better. The only thing in that direction is woods, an endless sprawl of woods.

We're only a few yards from the lean-to, but the blowing snow makes it feel like miles. I keep glancing at the door, waiting for Aayu or Liam to poke their heads out. If they do, I'll have to herd them inside and hope Colin finds his way back. I can't be out here with three little kids.

"Whistle again," Tim says.

So I do. Every inhale hurts more than the last—a raw, splitting pain that grips my chest and shocks the bones all the way up in my shoulders. *Tough it out, Avery.*

Every time I whistle, the answering whistle is a little louder. A little closer.

And then, suddenly, it stops.

My eyes well with freezing tears. Snow gathers in the

wetness under my nose, melting with each breath. My ribs ache like I've been kicked.

Tim's desperate screams for Colin have faded to a whisper. I have to get him back inside, but my feet refuse to move. I have to find him. I *need* to find him.

"There!" Tim whirls around, tugging on my arm. "The noise I heard before." He points dead ahead. The brush rustles underfoot, a deliberate shifting of branches and sticks.

The shadow is all wrong. Steady, constant, in a way that shadows shouldn't be. It hovers in the frail light of dawn, as if suspended there.

"Tim," I say, surprised by the eerie calm in my voice. "Get back inside."

"But I want—"

"Now, Tim."

His innate response to adult authority wins out, but not before he reaches into his pocket and hands me his favorite toy: the avalanche transceiver. It feels heavier than before. *Batteries?*

"Maybe this'll work," he says.

"Tim, it's broken—"

"Just *try*." He dashes back inside.

Clarity washes over me, through me. I bend over to retrieve the razor-sharp scrap of fuselage Colin had been using to cut bungee cords. The metal looked dull in the waning sunlight, but out here in this world of white, it shines. I tap it against a rock: tentative at first, then louder. Faster. I start talking. It's the same story I told hours earlier, the one about Ophelia and the mer-people and Holly-Sea. But the cadence is all wrong. Chillingly low. Steady. Controlled. This isn't a story for children.

It's for bears.

13

New Year's Eve in Brookline dawns cold and raw. Lee wanted to see Boston, especially Fenway, but he changes his mind when we step outside. So we stay in, watching movies until the skies pink again, with dusk on the horizon.

When we've had our fill of mindless entertainment, Lee prepares me for a grand announcement of our evening plans. He leaps off the bed and spreads his arms wide. In one hand is his phone, a text message blinking on the screen.

"Gruder's having a party," he declares.

My heart sinks. Gruder is one of the co-captains, although he looks more like a rugby player than a swimmer. Barrel-chested, thick arms, hair everywhere. Whenever he shaves his body for big meets, he breaks out in a swath of red skin and pimples, which probably intimidates his opponents more than the Tarzan-like whoop he releases before every race. But Gruder is also cool. Getting invited to a Gruder party means you've made it, at least on the social scale.

"I'm confused. Why isn't he in California?"

Lee shrugs. "Sounds like he came here for break," he says. "His half brother lives in Southie. Do you know where that is?"

Southie is right next to Dorchester. "Yeah."

"Is it far?"

"Not too far."

He bumps my arm. "What's wrong?"

"Nothing." I try to sell it with a smile. "I'm just surprised we were invited, you know . . . being underage and all."

"Never stopped Gruder before."

"Yeah, but this isn't college."

"You think the Boston cops are gonna spend their New Year's Eve busting kids at house parties?"

"Maybe." He's right, though. New Year's Eve is mayhem in the city. My dad took me in for the New Year's shift during my senior year of high school, an experience not soon forgotten. The ER was a war zone, with doctors and nurses on one side and all the drunks on the other. The patients were either belligerent or near death, soaked in urine and vomit and other fluids better left unidentified. I realized this was my dad's way of telling me to drink responsibly in college, and while I did my fair share of shots at parties, the message stuck. I was often the DD, and never more than tipsy if I wasn't the DD.

"Look, if you don't want to go—"

"I want to go."

●

The party takes us to a two-story walk-up in a sorry stretch of South Boston. A pub occupies the corner, but the landscape is otherwise desolate: vacant lots on one side of the house, an abandoned row house on the other. Stray cats dash across the street, irked by the steady stream of cabs disrupting the peace. Bone-splitting music blares from the walk-up's open windows. A defiled snowman rots on the front lawn. Overall, it's a miserable place, with an air of badness. Or maybe it's just my mood. Ever since the incident at Anna's, I've been on edge.

We pull up just after ten, the requisite time for arrival without seeming overeager or unfashionably late. As Lee helps me out of the cab, the last of my cranberry-vodka sloshes over the brim of my cup. The cabbie glares. Lee smiles apologetically as he tosses him another five.

"Take it easy, little lady," he says to me.

Edward has always had two rules about drinking: (1) Don't drink alone, and (2) Don't drink when you're in a bad mood. I don't want to admit I've broken one of those rules—if there ever was a time to be happy, this is it. I'm going to a party in the city, hosted by a senior, with my hot boyfriend. And I have to admit, though Lee is very attractive at baseline (i.e., first thing in the morning, hair unwashed, eyes bloodshot from lack of sleep), he takes it to another level when he goes out. His thick brown hair is a little wet, a little wild. His jeans hang loose on his hips, accentuating his washboard abs and long, lean legs. Even those ratty Nikes are starting to suit him. And he smells good, too—like Christmas spice, colored by the fresh scent of his usual aftershave. I bury my hand in his, savoring the feel of him.

"You look amazing, Aves." His voice barely rises above the din of the music, but I love that, because it means the compliment is just for me. There is no one around to hear it, no one to question or cheapen it.

I smile up at him, the familiar buzz of vodka coursing through my veins. He kisses my temple, warming the skin there.

"Aloha!" Gruder pulls Lee into a man-hug and claps him over the back with enough force to shake a lung loose. "So pumped you could make it, man."

"Yeah. Hey, thanks for the invite."

"Absolutely, buddy. Happy to have ya." As Gruder's glazed

eyes drift to me, he shamelessly scans my breasts, hips, and bare legs. The dress Lee picked for me—a siren-red halter-top scandal—accentuates all three. "Avery. Damn. You look fantastic." Then, in a voice reserved for common courtesies: "Horrible what happened to you guys—"

"Nice place." I step into the house, brushing close enough to feel his chest hair poking above his collar. "Did you grow up here?"

"Nope. My dad's originally from Boston, but he moved out west and met my mom after he and his first wife split." He opens the door wide and lets us in. The house inhales as we enter, taking stock of each guest. It's the kind of house that closes in on you, makes you feel oversized in narrow halls and cramped rooms. The stairs twist upward, the musky darkness punctuated by occasional slants of pink, blue, and white lights. The house pulses with it—the lights, the people, the noise. Music coalesces into a chaotic drone of blending sounds and thumping floors. I take a swig of cran and squeeze my eyes shut, stealing a moment of calm.

"Wow," Lee breathes. "You really went all out, man."

"So," I say, butting in, "did you invite Colin?"

Lee's face pales. Gruder allows a bit of a smirk.

"What, the plane crash hero? Nope. Didn't invite him."

"Why not?"

"Well, for one thing, Lee hates him." Gruder punches Lee in the chest. "He just doesn't like to talk about it."

"You *hate* him?"

Lee starts to explain, but Gruder cuts him off. "You didn't hear about this? Shea took his place on one of the relays. I mean, Coach didn't have much of a choice—Shea swam the faster split—but still. Sucks to get bumped the day before Qualifiers."

I turn to Lee. "You were supposed to swim at Fall Quali-fiers?"

"Yeah, but . . ." He stares at the floor, which makes him seem smaller somehow, vulnerable. "It doesn't matter anymore."

"He's right, it doesn't," Gruder says. "Shea said, *Fuck it*, and never showed up to the meet. The whole relay had to scratch because the B-relay had already swum."

The pieces start to fall into place. "And everyone on the A-relay . . ."

"Lost the chance to qualify for Nationals. Yeah." Gruder clapped a hand on Lee's back. "I'm sorry, buddy. Look, if it makes you feel any better, I hear the guy's out for good."

"It doesn't," Lee says, and shrugs him off. "I wouldn't wish that on anyone."

"Yeah, yeah. That's not what you said a couple months ago."

"I'm over it." Lee struggles to meet my gaze. If he has an explanation for the meet-up at Anna's Taqueria, he doesn't of-fer one.

Gruder's foul breath fans my face as he leans in close. "In any case, no, I didn't invite him. Why? Did he, ya know, get a little *primal* out in those woods—"

"Shut up, Gruder," I snap, which stuns Lee more than it does me, but Gruder laughs it off. With a bizarre sense of pride, he leads us through the house's claustrophobic layout. The kitchen light is broken, and pieces of the shattered bulb litter the tiled floors. Every so often, the sound of crunching glass pokes through the constant thrum of rap music. A waifish blonde who decided to go barefoot leaves a trail of blood in her wake.

Most of the crowd, including the blonde, is gathered around the two kegs by the window. One is for keg stands and the other for socializing. Three girls in skimpy dresses surround the second one, whispering and giggling as Lee walks past. I give them a little smile—okay, maybe a slightly bitchy smile—and they look down at the fizz swirling in their cups. They start giggling again as we leave the room.

We meet about a hundred other people before we encounter Gruder's older brother, also called Gruder by his friends, which just confuses everyone. They could be twins with their curly chest hair and thick, squat skulls. Old Gruder is clearly no athlete, though. He has a portly belly and chubby arms. His hairline is receding at an Olympic pace.

He nods at my diminished bottle of cran. "Need a refill?"

"Yeah—"

"Nah, I think she's good," Lee says. He squeezes my hand but doesn't look my way.

"I'll take a refill," I say to Old Gruder. I release Lee's hand but don't dare meet his gaze. Doesn't matter; his stare burns a hole in my skull as Old Gruder pours me a healthy cup of booze.

"Aves, I'm just saying—"

"I know. Take it easy."

"It's only eleven, okay? Let's try and make it till midnight."

I start for the kitchen, but he grasps my wrist. "Do you have your phone on you?"

"Um . . ." I dig into the area where my pockets should be. No pockets. No coat, either. Must have taken it off earlier . . .

Lee frowns. "Where's your coat?"

"Dunno."

"I think it's in the kitchen. Keep your phone on you, okay? In case we get separated."

"We're in a house, Lee." My voice sounds thick and goopy, the words a bit slurred. I tell myself to try harder next time; it's no fun to look drunk.

"Just do it, okay? Please? For me."

"Okay." He watches me as I follow Old Gruder toward the kitchen. Despite the broken radiators in every room, the house is a sauna. Sweat drips down the backs of my bare legs. My hair is damp, the ends curling up like they do on humid afternoons. Even my muscles feel slow and languid, like I'm wading through sand.

Old Gruder takes me by the hand—*Whoa there*—and guides me through the crowd. The kegs are in their assigned positions. A large drunken idiot tries to get his balance while another holds the hose up to his mouth. It all strikes me as a little silly.

"What's funny?" Old Gruder asks as he thrusts a red cup in my face. His cheeks are flushed and plump, like a younger, swarthier Santa Claus.

I didn't even realize I was laughing. "The keg stands."

"You wanna do one?"

"Oh. No. I don't think . . ."

"*Come onnnn.*"

And then I'm up there. In a dress. Someone attempts to keep it from flying over my hips, but it's not like my dignity is a priority right now. The spray of beer finds my face, going pretty much everywhere except my mouth. By the time I'm back on my feet, my dress is ruined and my hair has lost its luster. Old Gruder doesn't seem to mind. He twirls the damp curls in his fingers and licks the split ends.

"Hey," I say, no longer caring if I'm slurring my words or not. "Wanna go to Dorchester?"

He smiles, but it's more like a creepy smirk. "Dorchester? Why the hell would you want to go there?"

"Because I know someone there."

"Uh-oh. Not a little boy toy on the side, I hope." He winks like he hopes it's exactly that.

"No," I snap, surprised by the forcefulness of it.

Old Gruder doesn't seem to notice. He plows on, his pupils gleaming. "Hey, I don't judge. We can go if you want."

Thoughts flutter through me—heard, reacted to, forgotten. Old Gruder keeps talking, oblivious to my inner turmoil. "So"—he leers—"you wanna go?"

"Go where?"

"Dorchester."

"Oh." I smooth the folds of my beer-spattered dress. My silver necklace has somehow tumbled into my cleavage, and Old Gruder fishes it out. I'm admiring Lee's taste in jewelry— he gave me this necklace for my nineteenth birthday—when Old Gruder grabs my hand and whisks me out of the room. Earsplitting music rolls through the speakers positioned throughout the house, even the bathroom. I almost trip over someone's coat before realizing it's mine. At least, it looks like mine. I hike it over my shoulders and follow Old Gruder outside. The music wafting around us cuts out, and the slow, melodious wail of "Auld Lang Syne" fills the night.

"Happy New Year," Old Gruder whispers, but his attempt at romance sounds like a wheeze. He takes a swig of his beer and tries to lay a wet one on my lips.

I turn just in time. Lee. *Where the hell is Lee?* Memories of kissing his freshly shaven chin and squeezing his hand feel like vestiges of some other life, even though it was only hours ago that those things happened. I'm still trying to process this when Old Gruder yanks open a car door and shoves me inside.

"Hey!" I kick the door open as he climbs in the driver's side. He grabs my elbow and pulls me back in, yanking me hard enough to cause pain. I snap back and catch him in the jaw, but it's a glancing blow. The booze is everywhere now, like sludge in my blood. Old Gruder doesn't seem the least bit affected by it. Did he even drink? Did he *plan* this? I try to kick open the door again, but he's locked it using the kid-safety thing. It won't open. I'm trapped. *Trapped.*

The flashback hits me hard and fast. It sneaks in through my fingertips and shoots up my spine, findings its target right behind my eyes. My vision changes. Old Gruder is no longer an ugly twentysomething with a square jaw and beady eyes. He's huge. Red eyes, snarling breath. The interior of the car recedes into a savage, snow-blown landscape. A child screams.

Or is it me, trapped in a terrifying nowhere?

14

The earthly stink of blood and sweat announces the presence of a fifteen-foot behemoth. A grizzly lunges out of the brush, shaking snow off its shoulders as it slashes the air. It glares at me, roaring so violently it sounds like a scream.

I know a thing or two about bears—thanks, again, to my dad. He taught me and my brothers how to make fires with shoelaces and how to catch fish with sticks, but he also made sure we knew how to survive an encounter with carnivores. First, always be talking—let the bear know you're there. Next, back away slowly; hope he takes the hint and leaves you alone. If he doesn't, find something to bang. Bears hate noise as much as people do. If these techniques fail, stand your ground. Don't. Ever. Run.

This bear has no intention of backing off. Paws the size of car doors, with claws to match. His snout glistens in the slants of morning light. He sees me, stares at me, and bares his teeth.

I bang and yell and throw pebbles at the trees. The little boys are surely awake by now, and I can only pray that Tim is strong enough to hold them back.

"Go away!" I scream. "Leave us alone!"

The bear lurches onto its front paws, ready to charge.

Don't. Ever. Run.

Its eyes are rheumy and white; mine are bloodshot and a very human green. I wonder if this bear has ever seen one of us before. I wonder if he's *eaten* one of us before.

I take a slow step forward. This isn't exactly a charge, but it's close. I scream and yell and try, frantically, to turn on the transceiver. The on-off switch does nothing. The batteries must be dead. Then, impossibly—it starts to beep. A low, sonorous sound, but enough to disturb the silence. I start waving it around, a flash of color and noise.

The bear roars.

"This is our territory." I take another step. "Leave!" A dozen feet separate us, a distance a bear could probably cover in less than a second. Certainly close enough for it to reach out and pulverize my skull with a single swipe.

It paws the snow, its fury mingling with confusion. I won't run. I won't let those boys lose someone else. Not like this.

Maybe it knows this. Maybe it senses desperation, or resolve, or the budding maternal instinct that every species shares. Whatever the reason, it casts me one final glance, turns on its heels, and disappears into the trees.

When time starts up again, it looks like this: Tim sprinting out of the fort, trailed by Liam and Aayu. Their arms around my hips, their faces in my coat. My legs collapsing under me. The snow swirling all around us, feathering our heads and shoulders like fairy dust.

And through it all, one hammering thought:

Colin.

15

olin.

    The memory of him—or maybe just the loss of him—pulls me back to reality. Old Gruder is driving like a maniac, his eyes wild with lust and abandon. My dress is hiked up to the hem of my underwear, way past where it should be.

As my vision clears, I turn my head to take in the sight of Gruder's brother. I hate him. I hate the booze, the keg stand, the goddamn kidnapping—but worst of all, I hate the way he brought me back to that place. To the lake, the bear, the terror.

Riding this wave of uninhibited rage, I yank on the steering wheel and pull hard to the right. Old Gruder yells like a little girl. He scrambles for the wheel as the headlights swerve into the darkness, the sights and sounds of South Boston rushing past. One of the windows sinks down of its own accord, and January's first breath hits me like a splash of cold water. I inhale, savoring the taste of freedom.

The tires skid on black ice, round and round and round, until the car simply spins itself out. It comes to rest on faded yellow lines, one of the tires jammed in a pothole. The exhaust pipe coughs once, as if to confirm the fun is over. Old Gruder peels his hands off the wheel, pitches forward, and vomits a chunky mixture of beer and Chinese food. I give the car door a healthy shove. It opens easily now, as if the outside world is finally ready to have me.

A light snow has begun to fall, melting in the folds of my hands. I walk toward a row of subdued houses, some illuminated by the eerie glow of televisions, others completely dark. A diner sits on the corner, languishing in yellow streetlights, its *E* burned out so it reads DINER—HOT ATS 24/7. A few old men are inside, gripping white mugs.

The peel of tires on a potholed road echoes somewhere behind me, then vanishes into the night. That, too, is already starting to feel like a memory. The keg, the almost kiss, the slam of a car door that shook my eardrums. Old Gruder's jowly face recedes into my subconscious like a wisp of smoke.

The door jingles as I enter. A solid-bodied waitress barks a greeting and points at one of the booths along the window. The menu quickly follows.

"Whatcha want?" She pours me a cup of coffee as she asks me this.

"Um . . ." The words are blurred, but the crackling of the fryer makes the menu irrelevant. I want eggs. Maybe some pancakes.

"Well?"

"Two eggs, over medium . . ." I say from memory; diner waitresses hate when you read the menu. Not knowing what you want makes you look like an amateur. "And a short stack of pancakes."

She stomps off, her stark black uniform contrasting with the diner's warm interior. The red booths have that lived-in, lovingly used feel, like a grandparent's living room. The floors are recently swept, and the silverware sparkles. The air of cleanliness and efficiency conveys a proud establishment, owned by someone who cares.

The coffee is a dream: hot and fresh, brewed by the diner gods. As I'm wrestling with both sleeves to get them over my wrists, it occurs to me why it's such a struggle to get the thing off: I'm wearing my dad's coat.

This realization comes to me in slow motion, like trying to put together a simple puzzle. I'm staring at the buttons when the waitress comes by again.

"This yours?" She holds up a cell phone.

"No."

"You sure? 'Cause I found it right under your table." *Un-dah. You-ah.* Her accent reminds me of every gritty mob movie ever set in this town. In a subtle yet more immediate way, it reminds me of Colin.

She puts the cell phone on the place setting across from me and continues her coffee rounds. The home screen display looks familiar—a picture of me, actually. Suntanned and smiling but caught unawares; the kind of photo that means something to someone.

I scroll through the list of contacts. Teammates, Coach, Gruder . . . there are about a hundred missed calls in the last hour alone. Odd.

I sip my coffee. The old-school clock on the wall ticks past one o'clock.

Oh no.

It's *Lee's* phone. I fumble through the missed calls—all sent from *my* phone. Of course. He must have my coat and, therefore, my phone. And wallet. And everything else.

Not good.

My fingers slide down a menu of hundreds of names. Girls with strange descriptors (Rita Gap Teeth, Marie Tongue Ring, Elise Religious . . .). Guys who go by their initials. Then the difficult-to-categorize: Coach Evil, Doober . . .

Shea.

Selecting the number opens up a text message. It all seems very benign—a blank screen, nothing else, with no anxious waiting period or awkward silences. Much less personal than a phone call, but more casual than an e-mail. Plus I'm drunk, so everything feels like a good idea right now. I ignore the forty-eight missed calls and type in a message.

Are you awake?

I hit send. No hesitation—not even a blip of nerves. It comes naturally, like something I've done a hundred times before.

The waitress returns bearing a steaming plate of food, which she practically hurls onto the tabletop. At first, I think she's angry with me, but no, this is just her style. The clatter of plates is this place's elevator music.

"Thanks."

She grunts in response and turns back toward the kitchen. I look down at the phone. The light is blinking with a new message.

Is this Avery?

I sent three little words from Lee's phone—*How could Colin possibly know it was me?* Maybe guys don't ask each other if they're awake on New Year's. Or maybe they do. I don't know.

I'm at the diner on

I actually have no idea where I am. I flip open a spare menu perched between the saltshakers. The Wheelhouse. I delete the previous message and type in its place:

I'm at the Wheelhouse.

Send.

Ten seconds pass.

Are you okay?

I ignore the purple bruises marring my forearm and push the thought away. I'm so tired of people asking me that question: *Are you okay? Are you sure?*

I send a reply: *I'm fine.*

Nothing for a while. Then:

Okay.

The phone rings two more times—both from "Aves"—before I can type in a reply. I dismiss both of them and stare at the blinking cursor.

Come?

Send.

A shorter pause.

Be there in ten.

I close my eyes, processing what I've just done. Colin is coming. In ten minutes. Because I asked him to.

I could undo it. I could call him and tell him never to text me, talk to me, or interact with me in any way ever again. And he would honor those requests because he respects the choices I've made, no matter how selfish or ill-informed.

I pound out a second message, this one to "Aves"/Lee:

I'm fine. Crashing at a friend's house.

Two more missed calls. The little blue light on the display blinks with a new message:

PICK UP THE PHONE.

Another missed call. I'm tempted to turn it off, but Lee's next call will probably be to the Boston PD. I hit the callback number and wait for his diatribe. After a single ring, he picks up—but it isn't rage I hear on the other line. It's fear.

"Aves!" He exhales like he's been holding his breath for hours. "Where the hell are you?"

"At a friend's house."

"Which friend?"

"Uh . . ."

He cuts me off. "Someone saw you leave with Gruder's creepy-ass brother. Are you sure you're okay? I got a real bad read on him—"

"Yeah. I ditched him. Don't worry about it."

I hear Gruder's muffled voice, then Lee telling him to shut up. His voice is quieter when he comes back on the line, as if all his bluster has suddenly left him. "You can't just say that to me, Aves." His next breath catches in his throat. "You can't."

"Lee, I'm sorry. I'm okay. I swear to you."

I hear him sit down, and the rest is easy to visualize: one hand rubbing his neck, the other gripping the phone like a lifeline. Before the crash, our relationship was so breezy—the good times were great and the bad times were nonexistent. Our biggest fights were about which cafeteria to go to for lunch, or which party to hit up first on a Saturday night. We're both products of charmed childhoods. Two-parent families. Stable incomes. No real tragedies except the death of the family pet.

But things are different now. The process of putting things back together when the pieces don't fit anymore is becoming a reality not just for me but also for him. For us. He talks to me like I'm encased in glass. He holds my hand as if it might, at any moment, disintegrate. When he looks at me, he seems to be searching for my very soul.

"Lee?"

He sighs, letting the distant sound of music float through the silence. "I need to know you're okay. That's all I'm asking."

"I am. I promise."

"Put your friend on the line."

"My friend?" My voice is a squeak.

"The one you're staying with. Put her on."

The front door's jingling bell alerts me to the entry of a new customer. It all feels so preordained, in a way. The timing of a question, the jingling of a bell. The seat assignment on an airplane. The failure of an engine that had worked a thousand times before, only to give out while we were flying over some of the most savage terrain in the United States. These are all things that brought me here, to this moment, like a scripted play. These are the moments that make the world turn on its axis. This is why I'm here. Alive.

Colin.

He found me.

16

brush the snow off their bodies and herd the boys back
inside.

"Where is Colin?" Liam asks. Aayu starts to cry.

Tim says nothing, but his somber mood mirrors my own.
When he thinks I'm not looking, he glances at the door, willing it to open.

We settle down in a tight huddle, maximizing body heat.
A cold wind slinks through the cracks in the fuselage, mocking me for every millimeter of skin that isn't covered. At least
the boys are bundled up. Liam and Aayu finally doze off, but
Tim continues to sniffle as he picks at the threads of his ski
mask. I told him to take it off for a while because it was so wet,
and now he holds it in his lap like a consolation prize.

"I'll find him, Tim." I take his hand and squeeze it. His
gloves are red and blue, emblazoned with the Patriots' mascot.
I can barely feel his fingers through the plump material.

"He stopped whistling."

"He must've had a reason."

He yanks on one of the threads until it comes loose. "What
if there are more bears?"

"Well, they live here. How would you feel if a bear broke
into your house and slept on the floor?"

"I'd be mad."

"Me, too. But what if the bear explained to you that he was lost, and he needed a place to stay for a while?"

"Bears can't talk."

"That's right, they can't." Tim's logic makes me smile; ten bucks says this kid loves going to school every morning. "But we can still communicate. Like with the bear we just met— we don't speak the same language, but we both got our points across."

"How?"

"Well, for one thing, your radio really annoyed him."

The glow in his green eyes warms my heart. "It did?"

"Big-time."

"One of the suitcases had batteries." He folds his hands in his lap, and in that moment, he looks like the first grader he probably is. "That's all I did."

"Well, you did a lot, Tim. We'll keep it on so he stays away."

"What if he doesn't?"

"He will."

"Why?"

"Because I told him to."

"You're the boss?"

I nod, even though the last thing I felt like back there was the boss. I felt like bear meat.

"Are you sure?"

"Positive."

"How about Colin? Will they bother him?" He tugs his hat past his runny nose, his quivering chin. He waits for my answer with unfailing patience, and the feeling it stirs in me isn't just an ache; it's a burn.

"Avery?"

"No," I say. "They won't bother him."

"Are you sure?"

"Positive."

Tim scoots a little closer. I pull his hood up again and tie it around his chin. The generous size makes him look like a miniature Eskimo. The fur lining just enhances the effect.

"My mom and dad are dead," he says after a while. The flat, resigned way he says it makes my stomach clench. "Is Colin dead, too?"

I cup his face in my hands. "No," I say. "He's not dead."

"Are you sure?"

This time, I don't hesitate. This time, the trace of doubt in my voice is gone.

"Positive."

•

The boys sleep in a state of oblivion, but I spend the next hour watching the storm cycle through various phases of its natural life. A blowing, gusting snow; the occasional gasps of wind; the silence that follows. In these moments, I find the time and space to think.

Colin would not have made the swim without calculating it from every angle. He would have tried to minimize distance and, therefore, effort. He went at dawn so he would still have time to hike back if it came to that. But the whistles tell me he never even made it into the water.

They sounded close, *too* close. But why signal to us at all? If, in fact, it was a signal. In which case he may be injured, or even lost.

I can't leave these boys for an entire day, but I have to do something. Colin would look for me if the situation were reversed. He wouldn't hesitate. The only difference is, he'd carry all three boys in his arms. I can barely manage one.

I nudge Tim awake.

He finds me holding a toiletry case, its contents stuffed with what remains of our nutrition. In this case, it's a bag of Werther's and a Fruit Roll-Up, which we found stuffed in a slipper. He glances at the Werther's, then back up at me. "Are you leaving?" He looks at me like I've just murdered a puppy.

"I'm going to look for Colin."

"Oh. Well that's okay. Can I come?"

I shuffle over to him. He looks strangely pale, his forehead clammy. "Are you okay, Tim?"

"Yeah," he says. *Would a six-year-old lie to me?* I feel the skin there: It's warm, but not feverish—not quite yet, anyway.

"You sure?"

"Yes," he says, a little disgruntled. I peel my hand away, his sweat clinging to my fingertips. He doesn't look right, but then again, none of us are in prime condition. Maybe he's just cold.

I tuck another scarf around his neck. "Tim, I need you to stay here."

He nods like he expected this. "You need me to watch Liam and Aayu."

"Yes."

"What if they don't listen to me?"

"They will." I zip his coat up to his chin. "They look up to you."

He glances over his shoulder, uncertain.

"Remember what I said. You're the fort master now."

Not sure how I came up with *fort master*, but Tim seems to like it. He gives me a very serious, stern look. I almost smile, but to do so would wound his pride. Instead, I hand him the Fruit Roll-Up and Werther's and tell him he's in charge.

"Don't give any of the Werther's to Aayu, though. I think he's too small. And keep the transceiver on." I squeeze Tim's hand. "I'll be back in one hour. I promise."

"Are you sure?"

This time, we say it together: "Positive."

●

The sky is a muted palette of blacks, grays, and whites. I've seen my share of snow as a native New Englander, but nothing like this. Fine white flakes evaporate into nothing, blending with the swath of gray skies. It's a false calm, the eye of the storm. The mottled clouds tell me Mother Nature is just catching her breath.

I'm traveling light: long underwear, two pairs of pants, a coat, two sweaters, three T-shirts, and a pair of boots from a piece of luggage that washed up yesterday. The boots are at least three sizes too big for my feet, and the camouflage-style gloves on my hands and the hat on my head were clearly designed for a lumberjack. It makes the going slow and cumbersome.

I lick my lips and unleash a long whistle. A flock of birds sweeps the sky above me. I whistle two more times, but the only answer is my own echo, bouncing off the mountainsides until it fades to the same maddening silence.

My first instinct is to follow Colin's likely path, but after ten paces into the forest, everything starts to look the same. Even if the sun manages to penetrate the clouds, I won't have the benefit of daylight. The branches are thick and weighted with snow, obscuring my view of the sky. For as long as I'm in those woods, it will feel like the dead of night.

With this thought, I turn around. The snow, the pale sun, the clouds shifting overhead . . . it all feels like mockery, like a cruel, relentless joke. The snow flutters down on top of me, a dainty dance in the wind. I approach the lake, where everything feels somehow clearer, more possible. While scanning the perimeter for signs of color or movement, I whistle until my lips are numb.

A faint, tinny sound drifts into my consciousness, then fades. I listen to it, let it go. The snow kicks up around me, soft as a caress.

I put my hands on my knees and lean forward, dropping my chin to my chest. My vision narrows until all that remains is my own shimmering reflection. My cheeks are a raw, worrisome red; my skin bears the telltale burn of sun and wind. I see my eyes, too. My father's eyes. Edward's eyes. They would find a way to survive out here. They would make it home.

I lose myself in this thought, searching for comfort in the familiar, for memories that might somehow spur me on. But it doesn't come. My only emotion is grief. My only thought, louder than any other, maybe in all my life, is how desperately I want to find Colin.

Tim. Aayu. Liam. The thought of their innocent, wind-burned faces brings me back again. I can't lose my tenuous grasp on reality, on hope. The boys need me.

Need. As dangerous as hope, as uncertain as the future. I need Colin Shea, and it's a pure, driving kind of need. I understand this now, and it gives me strength; it pushes me onward.

I turn back toward the woods, wading through snowdrifts to get there. North and east and south all look the same, especially now, after two feet of snow. But the answer is out there; it's close.

Where are you?

The tall tree across the lake looms through the haze. Tim's

Tree, as he calls it. The cabin is somewhere nearby, an impossible destination.

Colin would have started at the narrowest distance across, which isn't here. I walk the tree line, just as Colin would have done. The snow is shallower, easier to wade through. Less exposed, and therefore a few degrees warmer, which would have made a difference in preparing for a swim like this.

I spot a small isthmus jutting out into the lake, maybe two hundred yards south of the lean-to. This little strip of land would have saved him fifty meters, a distance Colin can swim in twenty-two seconds on a bad day, but an alpine lake in blizzard conditions isn't an Olympic swimming pool. He would have wanted those twenty-two seconds. He would have fought to conserve them.

Here, too, the cabin is visible—just barely, but part of the roof is exposed. Maybe he saw it, or maybe he didn't. I'm not sure it mattered. He knew it was there.

You shouldn't have done this. It's insane.

I realize this now. The distance is too great, the conditions too poor. Maybe he turned back. Maybe he decided—

There. I whirl around. The sound is so faint as to be almost inaudible: breathy, with a scratchiness that makes my blood hum. It's coming from the woods.

I inch past the first row of trees, despite every spit of good sense telling me to do otherwise. My boots sink into the softer, shallower snow. Shadows draw me into an uninhabitable nowhere. I start reciting Emily Dickinson's creepy poems about death because they are the only words that come to mind. Hopefully it will be enough to keep the bears at bay.

The trees close on me—above, around, everywhere. Lines of poetry turn to breathless chants, and then I'm screaming. *Colin.*

There is no response. No stray sound, no whispers of air. A gust of wind snakes through the trees, and a plume of snow falls at my feet.

I look down at my boots.

And there, half buried in the snow, is Colin's red shirt.

When Colin steps into the cozy lights of the diner, all else slips away. The phone is momentarily forgotten. Lee is forgotten. Everything distills itself to the small space that separates us, a chasm that feels impossible and effortless all at once.

Our eyes meet at the same time. His are that dark, tempestuous blue, intense as ever. Like me, he looks stunned, breathless. I wonder if he's waiting for me to bolt.

"Table for one?" the waitress barks at him like she barked at me, and Colin smiles his shy smile, which softens her up like butter on bread. Or maybe it's the suit—a rich charcoal, tailored to perfection. A slim fit on his lean, powerful frame. The tie matches the flecks of gray in his irises, a subtle, classy color. I've never seen him in a suit before. Never seen him in much other than Speedos, T-shirts, and the army fatigues we salvaged from some stranger on Flight 149. I mean, wow. I just don't know what else to say. He redefines the concept of cleaning up nicely. I pull my dad's coat over my shoulders, suddenly ashamed of my beer-stained dress.

He slides into the booth, holding my gaze the whole time. It is Lee who breaks the silence, his voice coming over the speakerphone. I must have turned it on accidentally.

"Aves? Aves, are you there?"

"Yeah."

Colin glances at the phone with the slightest bit of something—concern? Disappointment? Anguish?—and then it's gone. I hand him the phone.

Lee sighs with great fanfare and continues to express his grievances, oblivious to what just happened. "Aves, look, this is bullshit—"

"Lee?" Colin's voice is quiet but firm. It surprises me how familiar it sounds, as if I'd been listening to it all day long. "This is Colin."

The pause is excruciating. "Colin? Colin Shea?"

"Yeah, it's me. I ran into Avery at a diner in my neighborhood."

This isn't exactly true. According to the address on the menu, we're technically in Quincy, a few streets over from Dorchester. Not like Lee would care about or even understand the distinction. Yesterday, he described Boston as a gravel spiderweb.

"You just ran into her? Was she alone?"

"Yep."

"Huh." Lee muses on this for a while. "You're sure there wasn't a guy with her? Short, hairy, has a chubby face."

"I didn't see one."

"Well, that doesn't change the fact I'm gonna kick his ass—"

I take the phone from Colin. "Lee, don't. It's fine. I got away from him."

Colin's face pales at the same moment Lee asks, "You what?"

"Nothing. Look, can we sort this out tomorrow?"

"No." Lee's voice is tight, controlled. "I'm coming to pick you up."

"In what? You've been drinking."

"A cab. Gruder'll call me one."

"On New Year's? Good luck."

He takes this in, but his grunted response tells me he's not happy about it. I hear Gruder say something along the lines of "You can crash here." Part offering, part apology.

"Put Shea on the phone," Lee says to me. "And take me off speaker."

His clipped tone slices through me, but I do as he asks. Colin takes the phone, rubbing his clean-shaven chin as he listens to whatever Lee has to say. He nods a few times but otherwise says very little.

After a while, he hands the phone back to me. I bring it up to my ear, terrified of what's to come, feeling the sting of sobriety all too soon.

Lee's voice is barely a whisper. "I love you, Aves."

Then he hangs up.

18

The contrast of color slows my ability to form a coherent thought. A moment passes before I realize this streak of red can't be his shirt because he gave it to me the night before. I woke up with it tucked around my neck and under my arms.

No, the red color isn't fabric at all.

It's blood.

I start heaving. Nothing comes up—I haven't eaten anything substantive in thirty-six hours—but it feels as though my body is rejecting itself, turning inside out. Hard, shuddering spasms bring me to my knees. My eyes well with tears, summoned by cold, or pain, or something else.

It doesn't occur to me that the blood could belong to anyone else. I *know* Colin was here; I can feel it in the empty, limitless silence. Some deep, unknowable part of me senses his absence. He's out there somewhere—hurt, lost. Probably dead.

I wrench a branch off the closest tree and hurl it into the void. There is no response. No angry, mocking growl from the bear that lured him here. No shower of snow from the canvas of tree branches. I don't dare look over my shoulder.

Instead, I look down. The blood has left a trail, albeit

mostly buried now, leading deeper into the woods. If I follow it, I may never find my way out again.

In a saner moment, I would forgive Colin for trying to help us. But right then, all I feel is rage. A deep-seated, curdling rage that starts way down deep in my chest and colors every breath I take. *Three boys,* I want to scream. *How am I supposed to choose between you and three little boys?*

I know my hour is almost up. Tim won't last much longer than that.

"Colin!" I scream until the pain in my throat matches the agony everywhere else. "Colin!"

A shadow flits through the trees. I look up. The sun, unbelievably, has broken through the clouds, and a beam of grayish light permeates the gloom. It shines on the specks of blood in the snow, causing a ghoulish but captivating effect. I see where the trail leads now.

And there, in the distance, as far as my vision stretches, I see the stooped wavering shadow of Colin's six-foot-four frame.

I start to run.

●

I find him slumped against a tree, the snow saturated with blood. His eyes are closed, his body still. He doesn't stir in spite of the racket I've made trying to get to him.

"Colin." I shake him hard. "Colin!"

I pinch his fingertips until the skin goes white. "Wake up!"

His eyes flutter open as he draws his hand away. His blue eyes reflect the dazed, glassy look of someone in shock. I put a bottle of water in his left hand because he won't be able to lift anything with his right. The flesh comprising his shoulder is nearly gone.

"Drink this."

"Avery?"

"*Drink it.*"

He does, which rouses him somewhat. I remove all my outer layers—coat, two sweaters, three T-shirts, two pairs of pants—until I'm down to my underwear, no longer caring so much about "modesty." I have to stop the bleeding.

He watches with lidded eyes while I tear the undershirts and wrap them around his arm and chest. I can't begin to estimate how much blood he's lost, but it's significant. There are some major arteries that course through the upper arm and shoulder area, and all I can do is pray he didn't nick one.

I try to ease him onto his feet, but it's a comical effort. He's twice my size.

"Can you walk?" I ask, as gently as possible.

"Yeah." He stands, then promptly topples over. He's barely conscious, and if he passes out, I will have no choice but to leave him behind. It's been an hour. We need to hurry.

"Try again," I say.

My back screams in pain as he leans on me for support. I grit my teeth and power through those first few steps. *It will get easier after this,* I tell myself. He'll find his rhythm, just like he does in the pool.

Nothing about our agonizing trek through the woods is like the pool, but Colin does find a stuttering stride. Every time his eyes drift closed, I rouse him with a hard shove. Blood oozes from his wound, leaving a trail in the snow. My only consolation is that a hungry bear surely would have killed us by now.

We emerge from the trees to darkening skies. Two hundred yards to the lean-to. *One step at a time.* He stumbles, and I catch him. He bleeds, and I do what I can to staunch the flow. We're almost there.

Almost there.

After what feels like a stretch of eternity, we come upon the lean-to. Colin lacks the strength to yell for the boys, and I've lost my voice, but I try anyway. "Tim!"

I scan the shore for signs of the boys—or even little footprints scattered through the snow. They couldn't have gone far. Even so, a blistering panic wells up inside me. *What if they went into the woods? What if—*

"Avery?" Tim pokes his head out. "Colin!"

Tim makes a charge but stops short when he sees the blood. I want to spare him this, but Colin needs to be inside.

"Tim, can you help me with the door?"

He wrenches it open with all the galvanizing force of a six-year-old. Liam and Aayu sit in the corner, their eyes wide. Tim produces the Fruit Roll-Up to distract them. Aayu takes the bait, but Liam starts to cry.

"Colin's hurt," he sobs.

"I'm okay, bud," Colin says. "I'm okay."

"You have blood."

Aayu's chin trembles. "Blood?" He pronounces it *bwud.*

As Colin sinks to the ground, I hand him two more mugs of water. "Drink these."

He does, but his left arm quivers with the effort. My fingers find his wrist to feel for a pulse. Very fast. Too fast. If he's not already in shock, he's damn close.

"Don't look so worried." Colin tries to smile. "It's just a little blood."

A little? Despite this comment, Colin refuses to look at the wound. He's demonstrated his ability to hike a frozen tundra on a bad leg, but for whatever reason, actual blood seems to unnerve him. Like he'd rather feel pain than talk about it.

"Colin, this is serious—"

He peels my hand away from his wrist—gently, reverently, as though he understands why it was there in the first place, but now he wants me to think of other things. His voice is soft, almost intimate.

"It's okay," he says.

I try to breathe but can't. The words won't come.

He draws his thumb across my face, catching my tears on his skin. "It's okay, Avery. Remember?" I know he means the flight, but it feels in that moment as if he is talking about my whole life. Swimming. School. The future. *It's all going to be okay.*

"Now," he says, "I have a confession to make." He cracks a smile—for my benefit, mostly, but for the boys, too.

"What's that?"

"I'm a little afraid of blood."

"A little?"

"Does that make me a wuss?"

"Definitely," Tim says, with the utmost seriousness. This brings a much-needed smile to Colin's face, but it doesn't last. His attention drifts to the supplies Tim has gathered per my request: clean socks, floss, a needle, tiny scissors, and water. Thank God for the career woman's sewing kit.

"I need to take a look at the wound." I keep my voice steady, trying to remember what my dad told me about delivering bad news. Be direct. Don't sugarcoat. Pause for questions. "Based on the amount of blood loss and the mechanism of injury—"

"I haven't told you the mechanism of injury," he reminds me.

"The suspected mechanism of injury . . ." I say, my first attempt at teasing him. "I may have to close the wound with sutures."

"Floss sutures."

"That's right."

He grits his teeth. "Can't I just tough it out?"

"I don't know. I need to take a look first."

"Have you done this before?"

"Once. On myself."

"You gave yourself stitches?"

"Yeah. My dad watched while I slashed my arm from elbow to wrist, threaded the needle, and sewed myself back up."
I act this out in slow motion while describing the steps.

Colin steals a horrified glance at my forearm.

"Kidding."

"Oh."

Tim glimpses the look on my face and grins. "Sarcasm!"
he says, and Colin laughs.

Aayu and Liam gaze at this hastily assembled medical
scene with wonder, their little hands folded together in watchful anticipation. I hope this doesn't scar them for life.

"Okay," Colin says. "Let's do this."

"It'll be fine."

"I know. I trust you."

My dad taught me to suture when I was seven years old.
My first patients (test subjects?) were my brothers. Whenever
one of them came home with a nasty cut, Dad had me assess
it, clean it, and sew it up if necessary. It felt more like punish-
ment than privilege—both for me and for them. For not
the first time, I'm starting to understand why those lessons
mattered.

The first step is assessing the damage. In sum, it's substan-
tial. Deep gashes in the skin and muscle, a lot of blood. Exposed
tendons and shards of bone. Colin used part of his pants as
a tourniquet, and it's worked beautifully; the blood saturating

his sleeves is hours old and mostly dry. I have to admit I'm impressed. Most people don't tie a tourniquet tight enough.

I move quickly. A few snips with the scissors finish off the coat, then the fleece, then two cotton shirts. The layer closest to the skin is some kind of wicking material, and it's caked into the wound, purple threads blending into the gristle. None of the boys—including Colin—are looking at this point; Colin tells knock-knock jokes to distract the younger ones, and Tim has his eyes closed. I'm glad. Now that I can actually see skin, it's clear that Colin was attacked by something. A series of deep, finger-width gashes stretch from collarbone to bicep in what looks like a violent slashing motion.

Colin keeps his head turned while I probe the wounds. His rotator cuff has taken the brunt of the damage—the muscles shredded in some places—the tendons shiny, white, and frayed. The shoulder itself has lost its elegant, complex architecture, such that it barely resembles a joint at all.

In sum, it's bad. Devastating for a swimmer, who needs those muscles to cut through the water, to pull the full weight of his frame with each stroke. This shoulder won't be pulling or lifting anything for a very long time.

"Okay." I take a breath. This isn't just about his swimming career; this is about saving his arm. Maybe his life, if it starts to bleed again.

I go to work the way my dad taught me: slow, steady. Stick to routine. Don't get distracted. Ease off the tourniquet. Apply pressure where necessary. The human body is a machine; all you're doing is helping it repair itself.

"How's it going?" Colin's face is glazed with sweat.

"Good. It looks like most of the bleeding stopped."

He's lucky. The tourniquet did its work—he won't bleed to

death. I unspool the floss and stitch together the exposed muscle and skin.

When the last stitch is placed, I try not to fixate on the messiness of the repair. He could still bleed, which would be catastrophic on top of the amount he's already lost. The wound could get infected. And there is nothing I can do about the damaged muscles, nerves, and tendons. He needs advanced, specialized medical care; he needed it hours ago.

"Can you feel your fingers?" I ask him.

"Yeah."

"Good." Maybe he escaped major nerve damage—or maybe he's just telling me what we both want to hear. "Can you move them?"

He tries to make a fist, but his fingers are slow and clumsy. He barely manages to touch his forefinger to his thumb before grunting in frustration. "That's as far as I can go."

"Don't worry about it." I start wrapping his shoulder in a fresh sock. It takes five of them tied together to reach around his chest. "Give it a little time."

"Am I . . . Will it be . . ."

"I'm not sure." I fasten the last of the dressings, desperate for a distraction. I don't want to be the one to tell him he will probably never swim again.

Some distant emotion passes over his face, then fades. "It hurts like the dickens, though."

"The dickens? That sounds like something my great-grandmother would say."

"I like that expression. Gives me a chance to reference my favorite author."

"I know."

"You do?"

"I mean . . ." It's strange, this sudden scrambling for an excuse. "I saw you reading *Great Expectations* on the plane."

"Ah." He sounds surprised, but the moment passes before I can take it back.

"Anyway, I think I'm done," I say.

He spares a cautious glance at the socks. They're clean and white, a combination that seems to relax him. "Thank you," he says. "This looks much better."

"Much better," Tim says. "Your arm was practically hanging off your body!"

Tim didn't open his eyes until I asked him to hand me the socks, but his good mood is infectious. "Gross!" Liam says. Aayu nods along. "Gross."

"It was very gross." Colin smiles one of those teasing smiles that could thaw a glacier. "But Dr. Delacorte over here fixed me right up."

"Who's Dr. Del-cor?" Liam asks.

"Avery," Colin clarifies. "Her last name is Delacorte."

"A real doctor?" Liam looks at me with skepticism.

"No, I'm just a college student."

"Do you have kids?" Tim asks.

"Kids?"

Tim frowns. "Married people have kids."

"Married?" I feel my face flush. "Who's married?"

"You and Colin."

I'm not the only one scrambling for a response. Colin is doing everything in his power to avoid looking directly at me.

"No, Tim." I force an awkward smile. "We aren't married."

"Oh." Tim thinks on this for a minute. "Why not?"

"Because we're just friends," Colin says. "We go to school together."

"But you're too old for school."

"College." I take a shaky breath. "He means college."

Aayu climbs into my lap and pats my leg. Then he reaches over and pats Colin's. "Married," he says.

"No," I say, exasperated. "We're not married. We're just friends."

Aayu grins. "Married!"

Liam starts chanting it, too. I want to dig a hole and crawl into it, maybe never come out. I never thought a pair of toddlers could embarrass me this badly.

Colin scoops up the boys with his good arm, which sends them into fits of laughter. I shake my head, relieved that the moment has passed but horrified that it even happened. *Did they think we were married this whole time?*

Poor Tim. He lost both his parents and now probably feels like he's lost two more. I take him by the hand and lead him outside, casting Colin a quick glance on my way out.

Once we're safely out of earshot, I crouch down and tilt his head up to mine. "Tim, I'm sorry. I didn't mean to confuse you like that."

He looks down at his boots. "It's okay."

"We should have told you right away that we're just friends."

"I still would've been confused." He pauses. Says *confused* a second time, correcting the lisp that tends to sneak back in when he's not concentrating.

"Why?"

He gazes up at me with those pale green eyes, a mysterious blend of innocent and wise. "Because Colin loves you."

I love you.

It's the first time Lee has ever said those words to me. Becky Wilson, my best friend growing up, always believed this was the most important milestone in a relationship—more important than being exclusive or even having sex. And I suppose now she's right because those three words feel important. They feel huge. Like the axis I'm spinning on has suddenly shifted.

The waitress comes by to check on my progress. She *pfts* and looks at Colin. "How 'bout you, honey? You hungry?"

"I'd love an orange juice," he says. "Thanks."

"That all? Come on, you look like you could eat a goddamn cow and still be hungry." She appraises his towering frame and smirks.

"All right." He hands her the menu. "I'll have bacon and eggs. Bacon crisp, eggs over easy. Wheat toast."

The waitress grins—at least as close to a grin as this curmudgeon probably gets. "See," she says, glaring at me, "here's a man who knows what he wants."

She makes a note and clops back toward the kitchen. The interruption has eased the tension, or maybe that's just the alcohol making its way through my liver. I reach for my coffee.

"Sorry," he says. "I'm just used to this place."

"I think she likes you."

He sips his glass of water. "Nah."

When he puts it down again, I find myself bracing for a lecture, but there is nothing hard about his expression, nothing remotely judgmental in the way he looks at me. "So," he says, "Happy New Year."

Relief sweeps through me. "Happy New Year."

He loosens his tie, which strikes me as a nervous habit. Well, good. That makes two of us.

"Food's good here." He nods at my plate. "Great pancakes."

"You come here often?"

"Used to. I grew up a few streets over."

The waitress takes another order behind us, and the conversation stalls. I don't know what to say to him, or even where to begin. So I sip my coffee, hating myself for having to self-medicate with caffeine. Colin isn't even tipsy, despite the formal attire and the lateness of the hour. He smells delicious, too, like he just stepped out of the shower.

"Did you go out?" I ask.

"Just to dinner," he says.

"Dinner with who?"

He arches an eyebrow. "Why do you ask?"

"Because you . . ." I put my mug down to get a decent look at him. Still bald, but with a freshly shaven jaw. Lovely eyes, even bluer than usual in the muted lights. I must be making him uncomfortable because he loosens his tie again and reaches for the orange juice that hasn't yet arrived.

"Because I what?" he asks.

"Because you look like a million bucks."

A faint blush creeps up his neck. "Try a couple hundred."

"The suit?"

He nods. "I only own one. Fortunately my next-door neighbor's a tailor. Best in the city, you ask me."

Best in the city, best on the block—doesn't matter. Colin would look good in a bedsheet. *Or is that the booze talking?*

"You're blushing," he says.

"So are you."

He smirks. "Well, thanks for the compliment on the suit. My sisters would be pleased."

"Your sisters?"

"My dinner companions." The waitress comes by with his orange juice, and he reaches for it like a lifeline. "A very generous neighbor insisted on it, said we deserved a fancy night out."

"You do, Colin."

He shrugs, forces a smile. "So, what brings you all the way out here?"

"Gruder had a party."

At the sound of Gruder's name, his smile vanishes, and his eyes go dark. "Who tried to hurt you?"

"No one." My face flushes. "I exaggerated what happened."

"You said you 'got away from him.'"

"I don't need a hero, okay? You've already got that box checked." He sighs as he stares into his orange juice. Guilt swims through me. "Sorry."

"No, you're right." He looks up. "It's none of my business."

I sip my coffee to wash things down. "I didn't even get his first name. He's Gruder's older brother."

"And he lives in Southie?"

"Colin, I'm serious. Don't go all vigilante on me. Gruder's your teammate—"

"Was."

That word lands in the air, smoldering. "What?"

"I'm not coming back."

"Ever?"

He turns toward the window, and for a long moment, he just watches the empty street. "I can't swim anymore."

"That's bullshit!" A few old men crane their necks to glare at me, but I'm unmoved. "Get a surgeon who can fix your shoulder."

The waitress brings his bacon and eggs. Colin thanks her, then proceeds to shower his eggs in salt and pepper. He eats with painful deliberation, studying his food like it holds the secrets to the universe.

"Colin—"

"It's not that easy, Avery." He shoves his plate aside. "My rotator cuff was destroyed—nerves, tendons, everything. I can barely lift my arm, much less swim." He tries to maneuver his right hand out of his lap, grimacing as he fails to reach the table. He's not wearing a sling, but he probably should be. "Impressive, isn't it?" he says bitterly.

"Look, my dad knows tons of orthopedists. He can help you."

"No."

"No?"

"I'm not spending the next year of my life in operating rooms." He sighs, resuming his usual volume. "I have other priorities."

"I know you do, but—"

"I should have stopped swimming a long time ago." He looks me in the eye as he says this, his irises dark as ink. "This is where I need to be."

I stare at the tabletop, counting the little nicks and scratches that have accumulated over the years. How many difficult conversations have taken place here? How many first dates, how many good-byes? Maybe we aren't so unique after all.

Colin's gaze drifts once more to the window. A group of

revelers in wool coats and dress shoes amble past, stumbling over chunky piles of shoveled snow. One of them tosses a beer into a bush. We both watch them for a while, afraid to look at anything else—especially each other.

When they disappear around the corner, Colin reaches for his fork. The eggs have gone cold, but he doesn't seem to notice. The waitress swings by and tops off his orange juice, saying, with a wink, "Free refills on New Year's."

"Thanks," he says with a smile, but it fades as soon as she's gone.

When he finishes his meal, it suddenly feels very late. I fumble for Lee's wallet, but of course the pockets are empty because he keeps everything on him. Colin pays the bill before I can cough up an excuse. "I'm a mess." I look up hopelessly. "I'm sorry. I'll pay you back."

"On me," he says, even though the implications always feel tremendous when a guy pays for a meal. Colin slides out of the booth and reaches for my coat. Thanks to a full liter of caffeine, I'm nimble enough to get there first. I zip it up and pull on the hood. "Nice coat," he teases.

"It's a little big."

"Lee's?"

"My dad's. Long story."

"I bet."

His car is a nineties-era Honda, but the paint still shines and the interior smells like fresh lemons, as if he's got a box of them under the seat. Like the diner, his car has a sense of pride about it, older but well cared for. Colin's legs barely fit under the wheel, but he's never had a problem with tight spaces. He releases the clutch like it's a natural extension of his left foot.

"So," he says, "where to?"

I crack the window to taste the air, though it isn't the cold that invigorates me. Even my mind feels clearer. Not just clear but alive. Like the air itself is humming.

"Is your house close to here?" I ask.

He glances over at me as he shifts into second gear. The engine purrs despite the cold, or maybe it's just because Colin knows how to handle her. "Pretty close."

"Can we go there?"

He grips the wheel a little harder, the muscles tensing from shoulders to hands. But the look on his face isn't indignation or even surprise; it's more like curiosity. "Do you want to?"

I don't know where the words come from, or why it feels so right to say them. "I want to meet your mom."

20

While Colin minds the boys, I sit at the water's edge, recording events and emotions and mistakes that will forever haunt me. But the truth has become my duty. This is their story; if we survive, this is part of who they will become.

I hope—*pray*—that this is the most trying chapter of their lives. Their parents are gone, their way of life lost with them. No wonder Tim misconstrued Colin's survival instincts as love. These little boys need a family, and they're mine now. Mine, and I'm only nineteen, with no experience in child-rearing. No sense of what's right, what's wrong, and what we need to do to give them hope.

My gaze settles on Tim's Tree and, to its left, the slanting roof of the cabin. I will never know how he even saw it; the woods are endlessly thick, an army of sameness. The cabin itself roosts in shadow.

"Mind if I join you?"

Colin stumbles as he wades through the snow but rights himself before I can intervene.

"Are you crazy? You can't be out here."

"A little stir-crazy, yeah."

"I'm serious."

He grimaces as he kneels in the snow, holding his right arm close to his chest. The T-shirt bandages and socks have held up well, but nowhere close to well enough.

"I think we should talk about what happened," he says.

"We can talk inside, where it's warmer."

"No." He adds, "Not around the boys."

He dips his left hand into the water, and flakes of dried blood turn the lake a filmy red.

"My plan was to swim it," he says.

I wait for him to go on, to explain. A rush of resentment and shame fogs my thoughts. Unlike me, at least Colin was willing to try.

He would have made it, too. Now he never will. *No one* will because I simply can't swim that far in these conditions.

"So what happened?" I ask, though a part of me doesn't want an answer. The deep gashes in his skin, the trail of blood through the snow—these can only mean an encounter with something awful.

He shifts his weight and skims his wet hand over his head. "I heard a noise," he says.

"What kind of noise?"

"Sounded angry. Large. I'm a city kid, and I've never seen a wild animal in my life unless you count Jimmy Ricks, the nastiest kid on the block back home." He pauses at the memory. "In any case, it was a bear. Huge, too. Smelled like rotting meat."

"So you *attacked* it?"

"Hardly." He sighs, like he's ashamed to admit this. "I tried to run it off. Scare it a little. The lean-to was only, what, a couple hundred yards away? I couldn't just stand there and wait for it to find you."

It already had, I thought, but waited for him to continue.

"Anyway, it snuck up on me. I wasn't fast enough to dodge the first hit."

"And then you . . ." I struggle to form the words without summoning a bizarre image of man versus bear in my mind. "You used your stick to fight him off?"

"I tried. I got a few good blows in, but I dunno. I worry . . ."

I worry, too. I worry about the boys, and creatures tearing us limb from limb, and endless nights in an endless wood. I worry about the trail of blood Colin left for whatever's out there. I worry about the bodies we buried.

"Avery?" His voice tightens. *He knows.* He knows because he reads my silences as well as my words, just like he did the day we met.

He waits for me to meet his gaze. When I finally do, he asks, almost desperately, "Was anyone hurt?"

"We're all fine." I want to lean into him, but maintaining a certain distance feels more necessary now than ever. "My dad taught me how to deal with bears."

"How?"

"Talk a lot. Let them know you're there. Don't run. If a bear confronts you, show it you're not afraid."

"Well, I failed in that regard," he says.

"So does everyone."

He rubs the stubble on his jaw until the skin reddens under his fingertips. His beard is coming in sandy blond, a shade lighter than the fuzz on his head. "Maybe I'll get the chance to redeem myself to you and the boys."

"Redeem yourself? Colin, you've done everything for us."

"I just . . ." He breathes out—long, slow, anguished. "Are you sure you're okay?"

"Are *you* okay? Because we're fine."

"Yes," he says, which I know is a lie in some ways, the truth in others.

I submerge my hands in the water, a kind of baptism on the shores of nowhere. He must know what I'm thinking: We have to find some other way to survive. Some other twist of nature, or fate, or luck to pin our hopes on.

Instead, we hear a scream.

●

Colin can't run, so he lets me go on ahead. The twenty paces to the lean-to feel like a million miles.

I nudge open the door, careful not to knock anyone out in the process. "What's wrong?" I scan the cramped interior. Aayu clutches a pink glove as he cries in the corner. Liam points to Tim.

No.

"I'm sick," Tim says.

The dirt at his feet is covered in bile. As he starts to apologize, he vomits again, his thin body contorting in pain as he tries to catch his breath between retches. While Colin distracts the other boys, I scoop Tim up and carry him outside.

I hold his hand and wipe his chin, but beyond that, all I can do is watch. His eyes are red and watery, his skin a deathly white. His muscles quiver with the effort it takes to reject whatever it is he ate, or has.

After a while, the retching stops. He sags into my arms, but now he's shivering and his skin feels hot. He tries to smile.

"I feel better."

I want to cry, but my father would have forbidden it. When you see people at their worst, you need to be at your best—or at least better than them.

"Tim, what happened?" I tuck his bare hands in a pair of

gloves. "Did you eat something from the woods? It's okay if you did—"

"No." He frowns. "I think it's 'cause I don't have my needles."

Needles? "What needles?"

He shrugs helplessly. "My mom knows."

But she's not here.

I pull him close, close enough to discern the scent of something sweet on his clothes.

Sweet as sugar.

●

The boys are all back inside, including Tim, who felt better after four cups of melted snow. We had no choice but to remove one of the side panels to cycle the air, but I'm not convinced it will do much. With five people cramped in such a small space, the air was bound to go bad, and it has. It's only a matter of time before someone else gets sick.

"How long can a diabetic go without insulin?" Colin asks.

"Depends," I say. "Maybe a week, if you do everything right."

"And if you don't?"

I shake my head. "I don't know." And it's true, I don't. I've seen these kids in my dad's ER, and they turn right around with IV fluids and insulin. Unfortunately, we don't have either.

"What happens now?" he asks.

"We hydrate him as best we can. That's all we can do."

"That's not enough."

"*Of course* it's not enough. He needs a hospital, just like you."

Colin steels his features into tight, controlled lines, smothering a pent-up frustration that has nowhere to go. He stares at the snowy haze for a long time.

"He'll be fine," he finally says.

"Colin—"

"He will, Avery." The hard intensity in his eyes is enough to silence me, but not quite enough to convince me. I wish it were. I wish I had his conviction, even though it should have wavered by now; it should have failed him.

I follow him into the lean-to. The boys look like snowmen, every surface of their bodies covered except the whites of their eyes. Aayu looks snug. Liam's cheeks are red, and Tim's hair is beaded with sweat. The little ones run into Colin's arms.

"Here," I say, reaching for Tim's coat. "Take this off for now." I pull his arms through the oversized holes, inhaling the sugary sweetness that clings to him like a disease. It *is* a disease, of course. A dangerous one. I lay the coat at his feet.

"How do you feel?" I ask.

"Okay."

"Drinking water?"

"Uh-huh."

"Good."

"I have to go to the bathroom a lot."

"I know. That's okay. Don't try to hold it."

He dips his chin to his chest, shamed by this small theft of dignity.

"I'm sorry I lost my needles," he says. "My mom told me never to do that."

"It's okay, sweetie."

Sweetie. My own mother used to call me that; then I grew up. *I want you to grow up, Tim. I want you to have it all.* I rub his hands until the skin goes pink again. His skin is on fire— wet, slick, feverish. I wish it were me instead of him.

As Colin distracts the other boys, I slip a hand under their hats, feeling their foreheads to get a sense of body temperature. It's an imprecise test, one my father loathes, but the only thermometer we found was snapped in half.

Colin manipulates the holes in the ski mask so it's one big hole instead of three. He slips it over his head so his eyes, nose, and mouth are still visible. Liam laughs. "You look funny," he says.

Colin makes a face. Aayu and Liam giggle.

"Okay, time for dinner," I say. As before, Colin and I distribute snacks and cups of melted snow.

Liam frowns. "Do you have milk?" he asks.

"No, Liam. I'm sorry."

He nods, seems to accept this. Colin makes sure Aayu gets enough food, while Liam eats like a champ. Tim gives his pile away.

"I'm not hungry," he says, so I pour him more water instead.

As the other boys devour their meager meals, Colin reaches over their heads and touches my shoulder. He doesn't say anything but instead just leaves his hand there, a steady, calming presence. A gesture of solidarity, an acknowledgment of all we've been through. We've lost so much: the plane, those people. So many people. And yet here we are, fighting for another day, another hour.

Unconsciously, I find myself leaning into Colin's touch. Liam and Aayu crawl into Colin's lap, and Tim nestles into mine, and with a repositioning that feels insignificant and huge all at once, our bodies are touching like they were right before we crashed.

Colin is so *warm*. Even through all the layers of shirts and coats, a furious heat rolls off him in waves. It isn't malignant or worrisome—not like the fever Tim has. No, it's simpler than that. It's *life*. Raw, resilient. Pulsing in his blood like a flame.

"I'm not strong like you," I whisper.

His thumb traces the curve of my jaw, his touch softening with each pass. "You're stronger," he says.

I try to look away, but the intensity of his gaze holds me there.

"I'm terrified."

His fingers linger on the span of my neck. "Why do you think I held your hand when we went down?"

"Because I was on the verge of a breakdown."

"No. Because *I* was on the verge of a breakdown."

Without the penlight, it's impossible to see if his eyes reflect the same desperate vulnerability that colors his voice. It makes me ache, for some reason. Makes me want to know him better, to know *all* of him—who he is, who he wants to be. A thousand thoughts pinwheel through my mind, but one in particular overshadows them all: *I'm glad it was you.*

He lets his hand fall, but my skin still smolders with his touch.

"You built us a strong shelter," I tell him.

"Well, it's not pretty, but it'll do."

"Build a lot of teepees as a kid?"

He smiles. "My dad used to take me to all kinds of construction sites."

"Oh. Right. Your dad's a roofer." It wasn't meant to sound patronizing, but despite the best of intentions, it does. "I mean, I've always admired people who build things."

"He loves his work. On clear days, he says it's like being on top of the world." He seems to ponder something. "What do your folks do?"

"My dad's a doctor, and my mom's a tax attorney—or

something like that. I once asked her to explain it to me and literally dozed off as she was talking."

He laughs at this. For a moment, I think he might volunteer something about his own mother, but he doesn't.

"They're good parents," I say. "I'm lucky."

"I'm sure they feel the same."

My belly warms with the compliment. I *am* lucky. I *was* lucky. My dad never treated me like his dainty daughter; he raised me to be strong and capable. My mom balanced his no-nonsense mentality with gentle words and constant reassurances. They established a path for me, but it was always mine to take. And it brought me here, to a mountainside in the middle of nowhere, with nothing but my wits and Colin Shea to sustain me.

"Do you ever cry?" I ask him.

He shifts his weight but keeps his left arm wrapped around my shoulders. I hope he keeps it there, even though he's probably losing circulation to his fingers. "Sometimes," he says.

"I only ask because . . . I dunno, this feels like the perfect time."

He looks at the boys as they scramble for real estate in his arms. Aayu wears multiple layers of T-shirts, undershirts, onesies, sweatshirts, and on top a pink parka. Liam was reluctant to give it up at first, but he's developed an unlikely little friendship with Aayu. He looks like a little grape in his purple coat, purple hood, purple pants. Even his boots are purple. And Tim . . . Tim looks just like Colin. Same colors, same black pants and green jacket—even a hat with a single, mangled hole, which he poked his face through.

When Colin speaks again, it's barely a whisper. "I cried when my mom got her diagnosis."

Diagnosis? That word has always carried a certain weight

in my father's house, evoking clarity, and answers, and truth. In many cases, a diagnosis means treatment. But for others, it means the end.

I can tell by the wet, spiraling blue of Colin's eyes which of these it was for him. "I'd been back at school less than a week," he says. "We all knew something was wrong last summer— she'd get these awful headaches, and she'd never had those before. She fell a few times, just kind of lost her balance."

He takes a breath, conceding some deep, internal battle. "She's only forty-two, you know? Always been healthy. Never did anything to deserve what she got." He steels himself before going on. "I try not to think about life that way, but it's hard. Some people get cancer. Some don't. We all die—I know that. And she's accepted that. I just wish I could."

Colin never mentioned any of this to anyone on the team. I would have known, too, because this is the kind of information that gets people's attention. When Kai Landon's dad had skin cancer last year, she told the whole world. We all signed Get Well cards and sent them out en masse, even though he wasn't really that sick. He had a straightforward procedure and was cured the same day. Meanwhile, Colin has been suffering in silence, bearing his burden alone.

"The night before the Fall Qualifiers, my sister called me." He puts his free hand on Aayu's back, tempering the rhythm of his shallow breaths. "She said Mom had wandered off that afternoon. When the police found her, she was way over in Quincy, completely lost and confused, asking, '*Where is Colin?*'" His voice falters. "'*Where is* my son?'"

"Colin . . ."

"I booked a flight that night," he says. "I know it was bad for the team. I know it was selfish. But I wouldn't even *be* in college without her. I love my mom. I just wanted her to feel that, right up to the end." He stumbles on that last word. "Whenever that may be."

"I misjudged you," I say. "Everyone did. If people knew . . ."

"It wouldn't have mattered." He puts his head in his hand, his elbow on his knee. For the briefest of moments, it looks like he might cry.

I put my hand on his shoulder. Despite all that muscle, he feels fragile under my palm, a formidable structure on the verge of collapse.

"I hope she knows I didn't abandon her."

And then I understand why he took my hand and willed me to survive, why I believed him when he said we'd be rescued. The false promises of survival have plagued him for months, the certainty of death right on the horizon. *This* he can control. *This* he can face.

"She knows, Colin." I put my hands on his face, my thumbs tracing the trail of his tears. "She knows."

It's after two when we pull up outside a pale blue house with white shutters. It's a small colonial-style home, with an aura of age and experience that radiates from its core like a beating heart. The thinning lawn is patched with snow, and the roof appears to be missing a few eaves. A crooked dogwood tree leans over the porch. In spite of its winter weariness, Colin's home exudes a warmth that overwhelms all its physical shortcomings. When he opens the door, it feels as though another part of him is letting me in.

We go in through the back, the hinges creaking to high heaven despite Colin's best efforts to quiet them. The kitchen offers a sprawling view of the backyard, spotted with snow. An old, noisy clock ticks over the oven.

"My mom's an early riser," Colin says. "But, ah . . . she's probably still asleep now."

"I can just wait in the kitchen . . ."

"No!" He flinches, peeking at the floorboards overhead, waiting for them to creak. "I mean, you should sleep. The thing is . . ." He shoves his hands in his pockets. "We don't have a guest room or anything."

"Oh." I look toward the living room. "I can sleep in there."

"My dad sleeps downstairs now, so . . ."

I didn't realize this was going to be so much trouble for him. Then again, what was I thinking, asking to meet his mother in the middle of the night?

"You can take me home if that's easier. I can meet your mom another time."

"There won't be another time." For a long while, he just stares at his shoes, wet with melted snow. He's right, of course. I go back to California tomorrow.

"I mean, if you want to go home, I can definitely take you . . ."

"Can I sleep in your room?"

My voice echoes in the predawn stillness, magnified by the intimacy of the room and the delicate inches that separate us. Maybe it's the cold, or maybe it's him or me or us, but we're standing just inches apart. I don't dare look up. I don't know what would be worse: the cold finality of a rejection, or the complicated, irrevocable implications of him saying yes.

After a while, when the silence starts to transform into something almost painful, he says, "If you want to."

Of course I want to. Every cell in my body wants to. He takes my gloved hand and guides me around the framed pictures of little girls; of Colin, their big brother, at baseball games and birthday parties. Each one captures a slightly different emotion—a playful wink or a probing smile. In none of the photos is anyone posing. This is Colin's family unfiltered, unembellished. His father looks like he did in the news clip: astoundingly tall with a grizzled beard and a shock of prematurely gray hair. His mom is her husband's opposite: petite, with a warm, lovely smile, and those familiar stormy-blue eyes. She loves her son dearly. I can see it in the photos, in the way she's glowing in each and every one, even when it's clear she has no idea she's being watched. The camera found her smiles because they were always there; her happiness was always real.

Colin's bedroom echoes the same spectrum of emotion, but in a different way. The walls are a pristine white, adorned with amateur watercolor paintings signed by his sisters. They provide a stark contrast with the hardback books on his desk, most of them old and weathered, as if tossed out on the street by some disgruntled librarian. But there is no sign of dust, no indications of long periods of disuse. In fact, two of them sit with their pages flapping open, waiting for their reader to return. Colin catches me studying them and gives a sheepish shrug. "I'm old-school, I know."

"Dickens?"

He smiles. "You remembered."

I walk over and inspect the flap: *A Tale of Two Cities.* An older, dusty edition, its pages a dry yellow. This one, too, has an "If found" message inscribed on the title page.

"Anyway," he says, palming his bald head. "Anything I can get you?"

"A shower would be great, actually."

He gives me an awkward look. "Uh, sure . . ."

"I mean, just me, you know . . . in there . . ."

"Sure." As he hands me a towel, he has the decency not to acknowledge the blush raging on my face. "Anything else?"

"No." I accept the towel with shaky hands. "Thanks."

The bathroom is smaller than a closet and encased in linoleum, but like every other room in this house, it feels homey. The door sticks on the frame, and I have to muscle it closed. The interior evokes a decidedly pink theme: a pink curtain, pink seat cover, pink rugs. Three varieties of shampoo bottles, body wash, and pink razors crowd the shelves. On the windowsill, apart from everything else, is Colin's corner: a razor, a toothbrush, and floss. I smile, recalling the NO BOYS ALLOWED theme of Colin's childhood. Apparently he's made a few small strides.

As for me, I'm a mess. I can't meet Colin's mother like this: hair all over the place, dress damp with alcohol. I strip everything off and climb into the tub. It takes me a solid two minutes to figure out the showerhead, but the temperature's perfect—a rush of heat and steam. Booze and sweat and Old Gruder's grunge leak out of my pores and circle the drain. I steal some pink shampoo and rinse the gunk out of my hair. By the time the water starts to run cold after four, maybe five minutes, I feel like a new person.

Panic sets in when I see the towels without an accompanying pile of clothes. I can't change back into that dress. I never want to see that dress again.

As if on cue, a quiet knock comes at the door, followed by the slow fade of footsteps down the hall. I crack open the door and peek out. There's a change of clothes sitting on the floor—Colin's sister's, from the looks of them. Flannel pants, a high school sweatshirt. Nothing too skimpy or feminine. Then again, I can't imagine Colin would want me prancing around his house in lingerie, that's for sure.

Dressed, clean, and totally refreshed, I make my way back to Colin's room. The hinges creak with the slightest pressure, announcing my presence.

"I'm just, uh, making the bed for you—" He falls silent as he turns around, his gaze sweeping over me. He doesn't look away with apology or shame, nor do I want him to. He lets the moment linger, as if held there by long-denied desire, a kind of giving in.

My skin is already flushed from the shower, beads of sweat trickling down my forehead. I thread my fingers through my hair, suddenly desperate to pull it back. It's soaking wet.

"Thanks for the clothes." I give up on my hair as it falls in wild strands across my eyes.

He clears his throat, manages a smile. "No problem."

For a long time, we stand there in a different kind of silence, new and indefinable. He doesn't resume the task of making the bed; he seems to have forgotten about it altogether.

I don't understand his silences, but I feel like he knows mine. Conflict. Longing. Fear. Fear of the unknown, fear of the unfamiliar. Fear of interpreting the afterglow of tragic events as the real thing. Because isn't that what this is? Isn't that what *we* are?

I point to the thin swatch of carpet near the window. "I can just sleep there."

"I don't think so." He finishes stacking the bed with blankets; there must be a dozen layers, enough to warm a whole family of Eskimos.

"Colin, I'm not sleeping in your bed."

"You can't sleep on the floor. I'm sorry. I just . . ." He skims his head again. "I don't feel right about it."

"I don't sleep anyway," I say, staring at my bare feet.

He looks up. "What did you say?"

"I can't . . ."

He crosses the room in three swift strides. Although we're closer now, so very close, he seems hesitant to touch me. Is it wrong that I want to feel him again? That I miss it more than anything?

"Avery, tell me."

He uses the pad of his thumb to tilt my chin up, but it's enough. Enough to remember the longing in his touch, the fevered heat of his skin. I don't know how he can feel so *warm* all the time. His heart must be three times the size of a normal person's. Even now, it pounds in the silence.

"Nothing." I manage a smile. "Just a light sleeper is all."

"You still have the dreams." He draws his hand away, and his sudden absence feels emptier than hunger, sharper than physical pain.

"No, not really . . ."

"Avery."

"I don't want to talk about it."

"That's fine, but don't lie to me." His throat catches on that ugly, ugly word. Yes, I lied. I've been lying to everyone. Lying to survive.

Panic bubbles in my chest, images of fire and water and empty skies searing through my consciousness. I close my eyes, bracing myself against the force of those memories. Sometimes it brings me to my knees; other times, I wake up scratching at my own throat, gasping for air.

But this time it rears up, peaks . . . and simply fades away. I feel Colin's strong arms around me, his heartbeat thundering in my ear. He's lost weight, but he's still so solidly built: his chest, his shoulders, his back. Like he could withstand anything—wind, snow, plane crashes. The death of a loved one.

The memories come flooding back, a rush of experience and unresolved emotion. My mind doesn't know what to do with them, so it just gives in. I don't wither and die. I don't shatter into a million pieces. I'm still standing. I'm okay.

In the next room, something crashes to the floor. An alarm begins to sound—a low, melodious beep, which steals Colin's attention.

"I'll be back in a minute," he says, glancing over his shoulder as he starts toward the door. "Would you . . ." He stops, breathing the question like it means the world to him. "Can you come with me?"

"I . . ." For a moment, I can't find the words. "Of course."

We go down the hall together, my trepidation increasing with each step. Colin doesn't seem to be in a huge hurry. He walks at an easy pace, taking one stride for every two of mine. None of the other doors in the hallway are open.

The floorboards creak with our weight, but then I realize it's just me causing such a racket; Colin knows exactly where to step. I like that he knows his home so well. It grounds him somehow, gives me a place in which to picture him.

The master bedroom is only slightly larger than Colin's— a very modest size, the bed tucked against a sprawling bay window that looks out onto the street corner. A second dogwood tree obstructs part of the view, providing shade in summer and a burst of pink flowers in spring. It must be his mother who loves those delicate trees. I know it for certain when Colin turns on the light, and the woman sitting up in a lovingly made bed finds my gaze. Her eyes are an inquisitive, vibrant blue, two pools of life in a disease-ravaged body. Even from across the room, I can see all the bones in her hands, the ridges in her skull. She must weigh seventy pounds.

Colin turns off the alarm and picks up the oxygen tank that has fallen to the floor. The room is otherwise sparse, at least in terms of medical supplies: just a few pill bottles on the dresser and a commode in the corner, which is draped in a white sheet.

Colin sits on the bed and fixes the cannula so it's resting perfectly under her nose. She doesn't flinch, though her gaze drifts from me to Colin, a smile flickering in her eyes.

"Mom, this is Avery." Colin takes me by the hand and pulls me a few steps closer. "Avery, this is my mom." He studies her face, perhaps seeing the woman she used to be. "Her name is Caroline."

Her hand is cold and slightly damp, mere bones and skin. She doesn't respond to my touch. Her hand hangs limply in my own, but it's okay, because I know she'd give me a firm shake if she could. "It's a pleasure to meet you, Mrs. Shea," I say.

I wonder how long it's been since she's spoken. I wonder what she told her children when she realized that day had come; her voice all but gone, her final words spoken to those she loved the most. I imagine she had a beautiful voice, enriched by a lifetime of deep, genuine emotion. It's strange to think we've never met. I feel like I've known this woman a long time.

We sit with her until the sun comes up, a red dawn feathering the residential grays and blues of Dorchester. The only sound is the thin wheeze of the oxygen tank, but it calms me somehow, giving me the strength to face the day.

To face a future without the man who gave me one.

Friday. Snow.

Saturday. Snow.

Sunday. Total and utter despair.

We ran out of food yesterday. It's too cold to even think of scavenging the lake for more washed-up snacks. Our only hope is that a benevolent gust of wind will bring them to us. My fingers and toes are changing colors, succumbing to frostbite. My face feels as though it's been whipped with rawhide. And I'm in the best shape of everyone.

When the storm hit Friday night, it drove us inside for thirty-six hours. Cabin fever took many forms, first a restlessness that tanked the collective mood, then a frenetic urge to get outside and breathe. The boys' tantrums became less frequent, slowly transforming into lethargy. Now they sleep through fitful dreams, choking on damp, stale air. I've taken to shaking them awake every thirty minutes—especially Tim, bribing him with melted snow.

"Hey," I say, giving Colin a nudge. It's more like a shove, which is what it takes now to rouse him. "Hey, wake up."

Colin's eyes flutter open. A mixture of emotions cast a pall on his drawn features: Panic because he never knows where he is at first, anger at himself for falling asleep. Then, finally, worry. Always worry.

"Is it still snowing?" he asks, his voice like sandpaper. I hand him a mug of melted snow. His fingers are ice-cold, but the rest of him is a wet, sickly warm. This is new.

I lay a hand on his forehead, but it's unnecessary; I can feel his fever from here. "Here, let me see your shoulder—"

"It's okay," he says. "Doesn't hurt."

"Of course it hurts." I start unwrapping his bandages with frantic fingers. The first layer comes away damp. The second, third, and final layers are saturated with a yellowish, pungent liquid. It looks and smells like pus.

Oh god oh god oh god.

He glances at the wound for the first time, as if finally accepting that it exists. Almost pleadingly, he says, "Don't let the boys see it."

I bunch up the soiled layers and stuff them in a corner— for now. As soon as I get the chance, I'll go out and bury everything.

"I think we should let it air out for a bit." To appease him, I lay a fresh T-shirt over his shoulder.

"Is it contagious, though? With the air in here—"

"No. It's just a wound infection."

"Sure it is," he says, forcing a weak, heartbreaking smile. He must sense the fever raging in his blood, the telltale fire of sepsis. He could die from this.

He *will* die from this.

I turn my head before he can see me cry. Colin—our strong, massive, and seemingly indestructible hero—won't last another day out here. Barely another hour. The boys might make it through another night, but only if the little ones stay healthy. Tim stopped throwing up, but he sleeps all the time now. His fever has morphed into an ominous chill. At night, he shudders in my arms, his breathing rapid and raw. I urge him to drink sips of melted snow, but he barely has the energy to swallow.

As if reading my mind, Colin says, "Focus on Tim. I'll be fine."

Focus, in this case, means *watch him die.* I can't wait for that to happen, even though it *will* happen, because there are no planes, no hope.

I scramble toward the door anyway. "I'll be right back."

"Avery—" Colin says, grasping my arm.

"Five minutes," I say, and he lets me go.

Under overcast skies, it's impossible to tell what time it is. Midday, maybe, judging by the depth of shadow in the trees. Time in this place seems to alternately race and stand completely still. The hours achieve a certain monotony, the mornings blending into afternoon blending into night. It feels inevitable, this dutiful passing of the hours, this endless cycle of day and night. We're on a runaway train, racing toward the brink.

The winds shifted with the storm, carrying the floating luggage even farther away. The orange duffel bag must have snagged on something because it hasn't moved in days, but it's still at least a mile offshore, which means a two-mile swim. And the cabin . . .

Forget the cabin.

Colin never had any doubt that he could make it there, but then again, he's *Colin.* Bigger, stronger, faster. He doesn't swim so much as glide. He doesn't doubt his abilities because he has no reason to. He saw that cabin and saw hope. I see defeat.

Which reminds me, in some strange, nostalgic way, of the day we met. For the whole of my freshman and sophomore years, I've swum the 200 and 500 freestyle, the standard middle-distance events. I'm not the best on the team, but I'm not the worst. Coach appreciates my ability to "go where I'm needed." There are no real expectations, no pressure. I swim because I can, and middle distance is my event now, and the team needs me there.

But I miss the 1500, the closest thing swimming has to a mile. A mile to find a rhythm, to become one with the water. I miss everything about it.

The cabin isn't much farther than that, maybe two thousand meters. I tell myself it's too far, too cold, but it isn't.

The truth is, I'm afraid.

Colin hasn't asked me to attempt it since that night he broached the subject, but I wonder if he's thought about it. I wonder if he remembers that conversation on the golf course; I wonder if he hasn't asked because he doesn't want to hear me say the words:

I can't do it.

The wind swirls around me in lazy gusts, mocking me with its unpredictable power. I thought being outside would restore some hope for rescue, or at least encourage it. Instead, I find myself hating this place we've come to know: the sky, the grizzled peaks, the lake's teasing calm. The awesomeness of nature no longer inspires me; it infuriates me. Fighting back tears, I walk along the shore with my gaze trained on the ground, seeing nothing but a canvas of white, blowing snow.

It's for this reason I almost miss it, a buzzing in my brain that becomes a whir.

A plane.

It looks like a red bird circling the north end of the lake. I gaze at it, too stunned to do anything more than just stand there, admiring the blur of color in colorless skies.

Then, a different thought: *rescue.*

I start running, falling on hands and knees in a desperate scramble to be noticed. The pain in my lungs explodes with every breath. I wave my arms, ignoring the ache in my shoulders, the drain of energy on my tired muscles.

Then, like the curtain coming down on a one-act play, the plane crests a peak and disappears. The roar of its engine fades to a low drone, then to silence.

It's gone.

Physical pain surrenders to an acute sense of loss. This was our only chance for rescue, a last-ditch effort by the authorities to find a few lucky souls who *might* have survived a sinking airplane, who *might* have swum to shore, who *might* have lived through five straight days of storms with no real shelter. They saw the debris, took a good look at the lake, and assumed what any logical person would have: No one survived.

Our tiny lean-to stands proud in the distance, its red logo glinting in the grayish light. Impossibly, I see Colin waving his left arm. At me, at the plane—I don't know. He must have heard it, too.

The trek along the shore was difficult before, but now it's torture. Every step reinforces the void I'm walking toward. There is no goal, no purpose. I'm going to lose them. Colin. Tim. Liam. Aayu. I can't do this alone. I can't do it at all. My knees give out along with every urge to keep moving forward.

What would Edward say? Or my father, who has devoted his life to saving people's lives? It wouldn't be so bad if they expected me to die, like any reasonable human would. But the thing is, *I don't know.* And the not knowing means I can't just assume they've stopped fighting for me. The not knowing means my dad may be out there somewhere, hounding the Search and Rescue operators because his daughter knows a thing or two about survival, dammit.

I get up, rubbing my palms to ease the pain of new bruises. My first step is unsteady. The second is better. I look up and see Colin in the distance, still waving. But not up, not at someone or something that streaked across the sky and disappeared.

He's waving at me. Not good-bye. Hello. Come back. We need you.

And that, for now, is enough.

23

When Lee calls at seven, Colin insists on picking him up and driving us both home. I overhear this conversation from my comfy perch in his bed, which smells so much like Colin it makes me light-headed. Light-headed in a good way. In a confusing way, too.

On my way out of the bathroom, he hands me Lee's cell phone, along with my freshly laundered dress. "It's not perfect," he says, "but I've learned a thing or two over the years."

I mumble a thank-you. *Colin knows how to launder a dress?*

He looks good—tired, but a healthy tired. He's wearing jeans and an old baseball T-shirt, his last name stitched across the shoulder blades.

"You played baseball?" I ask.

"You look shocked." He laughs. "Am I that uncoordinated?"

"No, it's just . . ." I sit on the bed and fold the dress across my lap. "I figured you were just a swimmer."

"In this neighborhood? I'd be laughed off the block."

He's right, of course, another part of his history I've neither considered nor explored. It's so much easier to slot people into neat little boxes.

The phone buzzes with a new message. It's from Lee: *Where are you?*

"I'll get the car warmed up," Colin says. A few seconds later, he's down the stairs and out the door.

I let the dress flutter past my hips, stunned by its transformation. It looks brand-new—creased in all the right places, the hem restored to its threadless glory. It smells like fabric softener and lilac, like a spring morning.

My throat tightens as I think about his mom, dozing peacefully down the hall.

She would have been proud.

●

When we pull up to the house in Southie, Lee is sitting on Gruder's snow-covered porch. His eyes are bloodshot, betraying a sleepless night. When he sees us pull up, he strolls over and heaves a sigh. "Dammit, Aves. You scared the shit out of me last night."

"I know." I try not to look at him. "I'm sorry."

"Turns out Gruder's brother has a criminal record." He snorts as he climbs into the backseat. "Asshole."

"Gruder, or Gruder's brother?"

"Both. They're both assholes." He nods at Colin. "Thanks for, uh, filling in here." His voice sounds strained, and I start to wonder if the dinner at Anna's was more about reconciliation than reunion.

Colin responds with his usual grace. "No problem. I'm just a few blocks from here."

Lee says nothing, appraising the narrow, snow-dusted streets and tight-knit houses. Older-model cars line the shoulder, parked at haphazard angles to avoid the snow. The occasional bundled-up individual braves the early-morning chill.

"Anyway," Lee says, "hope Avery didn't kill your New Year's." Lee's implication settles in the air, hovering like deadweight.

Colin eases to a stop at a red light and cracks the window. "Not at all."

"No hot date on New Year's?"

The light takes years to turn green. I try to sink down in my seat, but the area between my knees and the dashboard is only marginally bigger than a shoe box.

"No." The tension in Colin's voice is almost undetectable, but it's there. Probably not enough for Lee to notice, but obvious to me.

"Huh." Lee meets Colin's gaze through the rearview mirror. "Can't say I'm surprised. You always were evasive."

"Lee—" I start, but Colin quiets me with a look.

"I was at dinner with my sisters," Colin says.

"Uh-huh."

"He *was*, Lee," I snap. "His mom's sick and has been for a long time. That's why he missed Fall Qualifiers." Colin winces. Guilt whirls in my gut, but I keep going. "You need to get over it."

"Get over it? Avery, that meet was everything I've ever worked for."

"More important than someone *dying*?"

Lee looks away. Colin's grip tenses on the wheel.

"Sorry about your mom," Lee says.

Colin glances my way, but I can't bear to look at him. "I'm sorry, too," he says. I wonder what, exactly, he's sorry for, though I suppose it doesn't matter. The apology is out there, a kind of peace offering.

"So, how did the party end?" I ask, falsely cheerful.

Please answer. Please work. Please let them just get along. Fortunately, Lee has a blessedly short attention span.

"Eh." Lee shrugs. "I punched Gruder's brother in the face."

"What?" I whirl around, meeting Lee's hard stare.

"He deserved it, and you know it."

"Yeah, but he's Gruder's brother. You'll never race again if Gruder hates you."

"I don't care what Gruder thinks. Far as I'm concerned, he's a dick, too."

At this, a tiny smile curls on Colin's lips.

"See?" Lee says. "Shea gets it. You don't let a guy treat your girlfriend like that without repercussions."

"This isn't the 1800s."

Lee sweeps away strands of hair that have fallen across my face. His breath smells good—like cinnamon, as always. "I'm not a vigilante, Aves." He lets the wisps of blond settle on my shoulders. "But I'm not a pussy, either."

"Yes, but there are consequences." I look at my hands, embarrassed by how dumb this sounds but knowing it's also true. "Gruder can make life a lot harder for you."

"Let him."

"Lee, listen to me. I made a mistake, okay? Why don't you let me talk to Gruder?"

"No."

Colin turns off the highway near Fenway, putting us within a mile of my house. He's probably only been to Brookline a few times, but Boston is small enough to navigate once you understand the nonsensical arrangements of the streets. Colin drives like a local: confident but a little unpredictable. Avoiding one-way streets where there probably shouldn't be one. Ignoring the intersections where three out of four of the intersecting streets have the same name. Dodging surface trains and random crosswalks.

"Still going the right way?" Colin asks me.

I manage a nod, and five minutes later, we're there. The car hasn't yet come to a complete stop when Lee climbs out of the backseat. He opens my door with semifrozen fingers.

"Come on, babe." His teeth are chattering. "I need a hot shower ASAP."

He reaches in to take my hand, but every bone in my body resists him. I shouldn't say anything to Colin—not with Lee scrutinizing me, not with that damning question left unanswered. But then the words are out of my mouth, and it's too late.

"Are you ever coming back to school?" I ask him.

He stares at the empty road ahead. I want him to look at me. I want him to say, *Yes. As soon as I possibly can.*

Instead, he murmurs, "No."

Lee finally manages to pull me out of the car, my heel catching on the curb in a foolish attempt to turn around. I want to say something. I do. I should—

But Colin is already gone, the sounds of a weathered engine fading in his wake.

Lee takes my hand, warming it in his own. We trudge along the shoveled sidewalk toward the porch. I used to count my paces when I was little, used to know where I was going without seeing the world in front of me, savoring the confidence of each step. The knowledge that my two-hundred-year-old house was still there, buried in its foundation, aging slowly enough for me to feel like it would never change, was enough to steady my stride.

But now, every step, even with my eyes wide-open, feels like a blind leap.

Coach Toll's office is a chlorinated hovel. Thanks to years of sweaty swimmers and poor airflow, it reeks of polyester, body odor, and moldy concrete. A random assortment of trophies proclaiming various triumphs lines the shelves: league champs, division champs, national champs. Brass figurines loom over his desk with outstretched arms, condemning the state of chaos. Because it truly *is* chaos: Papers strewn about. Ribbons hanging on nails. Pens scattered on the floor. No sign of a computer unless that boxy antique in the corner turns on.

He twirls a pen in his thick fingers while he looks at me with deep-set eyes. I've come to believe his intimidating presence is just part of his shtick. It takes a special person to control a bunch of college jocks.

"You sure you're ready to get back in there?" The daily calendar over his head displays the date: January 15. After a week on a cross-country train and another back on campus, I'm prepared to swim again—or so I tell myself.

"I think so."

"You *think* so?"

I try to sell my enthusiasm with a smile. "Absolutely, Coach."

"But?"

"But what?"

"You've got something on your mind."

I never took Coach for an empathetic individual—or maybe I'm just that transparent. It's true that the water makes me nervous; it's also true that I've avoided pools since the day we were rescued. But this is *my* pool. *My* team. I don't have to go out there and muscle through the 200 anymore. I just need to get in the water and swim. The rest will fall into place.

"Well, I see this as a chance to start fresh," I say. "Maybe break out of my routine a bit."

He stops the pen twirling. "How so?"

"I'm not sure yet."

"Fair enough," he says, and I let out a breath.

"I know I'm out of shape, but I'm ready to work really hard—"

"Of course you're out of shape. That'll change."

"Great." I try not to think about the eight-thousand-yard beatings sure to come in the next days and weeks. Coach Toll will whip me into shape, all right. And I'll endure it, and savor it, because I'm not fighting a career-ending injury. I still have a future in the pool.

"I'll need medical clearance from your doctor," he says.

I hand it over. It's signed by three different doctors: my family physician in Boston, the internist in Denver, and my dad. The first two had no problem clearing me to do whatever I liked; my dad, however, wrote an addendum three paragraphs long.

Coach waves the forms. "What's this about mental health issues?"

"It's not an issue," I mumble, feeling the sting of shame. "My dad is just paranoid."

"Says here he insists you see a psychiatrist on campus."

"I already did." Which is true. Last week, I visited a meek, turtleneck-loving woman who struggled to be heard over the hum of the noise machine. She was technically a guidance counselor, who specialized in things like homesickness and binge drinking. Even though my dad wrote "PTSD" all over his addendum, she never mentioned it and I didn't ask.

"Can you get me a note from this person?" he asks.

I hand this over, too. Her signature is indecipherable scrawl, and so are the letters after her name. Coach doesn't seem to notice. I doubt he really understands the difference between a psychiatrist, a psychologist, and a guidance counselor.

"Hmph," he grunts. He leans back in his ancient desk chair and folds his arms across his chest. It's a wonder he can reach: Everything about him is huge, taut, and wound extremely tight.

He extends a hand, which is the closest he gets to a grin. "Welcome back, Ms. Delacorte."

●

My first day back starts like the hundreds that have come before it. Alarm goes off at 4:30 A.M. Hit the snooze once. Now 4:39. I roll out of bed, relieve my bladder, brush my teeth, and throw on an old Speedo—usually with my eyes still closed, but today I'm wide-awake. Even the snooze was unnecessary. I pull on my heaviest tracksuit and brace for the blitz of January weather that never comes. Without that awful arctic blast, it's actually a lot harder to wake up. But today, alertness is not an issue. Today, every cell in my body feels like a live wire.

The boys are practicing later on, so it's just the girls out there now. The locker chatter is minimal. A cluster of freshmen wave hello; one even manages to squeal, "Welcome back!" I do my best to ignore the attention and make my way to lane 2, my home base. It shimmers in the overhead lights, the clear waters pulsing with a surrealist energy. I have always savored this moment, before the water swells with the furious rhythm of windmilling arms and fluttering ankles.

But today, my usual sense of calm is overwhelmed by a deafening roar. It's coming from within, building and swelling despite my best efforts to push it back down.

A wet hand lands on my shoulder. "Avery?" Marjorie Kline comes into focus. "Are you all right?"

"Yep." I inch closer to the water. "Great."

She answers with a confused stare. "Okay. Great. Do you wanna jump in?"

I usually go first in lane 2, which means I'm fast enough to swim in lane 3 but don't really want to. I've never strayed from the comforts of my "medium speed" lane. Coach doesn't push me on it; I guess he figures I'll make the move when I'm ready—which, of course, is never. But today, lane 1 (for "the slackers") looks appealing.

"Avery?"

"Yeah. Sure." Everyone except me, Marjorie, and the three other girls in lane 2 is already in the pool. Coach sits under his chalkboard, staring at me. The sun's begun to rise, creating a searing glare through the glass. The temperature bumps a few degrees. Sweat slinks down the back of my neck, pooling in the groove between my shoulder blades.

"Why don't you go ahead?" I say. "I'm out of shape."

"Oh." She wipes her goggles for the thirtieth time. "Sure. Right. Okay."

She dives in—a smooth, graceful motion. The others follow. A steady beat of swimmers, all muscled shoulders and tanned legs, disappearing under the surface. Everyone starts with freestyle. Smooth, reliable freestyle. It all looks so easy. Mechanical, even.

I'm alone on deck, teeth chattering from the cold. There is nowhere to hide, no excuses worth offering. Coach caps his felt-tipped marker and heads in my direction. His eyes are narrowed and questioning, his pale lips set in a thin line. He parts them to say something—

And I dive in.

Cold. *So cold.* It worms its way into my blood through every pore, every imperfection in my windburned skin. It steals the oxygen in my lungs and dulls my senses. Liquid ice flowing in my veins. My heart skips out of rhythm, beating in frantic defiance of what I've done.

The agony of drowning hits me like a jolt of electricity, a wretched tightening in my throat. I don't fight for the surface; I just breathe, inhaling water instead of air. Soon, the quietude returns. The fire and fear and cold just slip away, releasing me into some strange, soundless in-between.

I'm not strong like you.

Then: pain. God, it's awful. A tearing through my chest, the bones splitting open at the hands of some invisible demon. My lungs fight to expand against it, but someone is pushing down on them. Breaking them. Breaking *me.*

I can't breathe. *Can't breathe.*

"Sit her up. Sit her up!"

The water in my lungs hits the deck with a sickening splash. My tongue tastes like chemicals and blood, a stinging fire. Someone rolls me onto my side and waits until the coughing stops. Pain begins to mingle with the sting of humiliation.

I finally open my eyes to see a dozen ankles and feet, then legs and hips and shoulders, then stunned faces. "Paramedics are on their way," someone sobs, and I know it's Marjorie Kline. Her ankles disappear from the group into the locker room.

Coach waves everyone else away, but it doesn't matter. It's too late. Now everyone knows my secret. Everyone knows that I'm not ready; I'm not even okay.

I'm still in that lake, searching for rescue.

25

That night, after a battery of tests, Lee takes me back to the dorms. He usually drives with the seat pushed back, music blaring, one hand on the bottom of the wheel. Tonight he drives in the ten-two position, in silence.

At least the dorms are quiet. It's a Tuesday night, and the campus has settled into its usual, industrious calm. Lee carries my bag and scans us into the building. A dozen other swimmers live in my dorm, and two of them pass us by, their heads down as they race down the stairs. Shame floods through me. Shame, and embarrassment, and the dreaded realization that this episode will change everything. Coach will hire a lifeguard for practices. I'll be relegated to the diving well, forced to swim with a chaperone. In meets, I won't even compete. I'll serve Gatorade and orange slices to the people who do.

The logical part of my brain tries to argue that it was just a bad day. It wouldn't have happened yesterday, and it won't happen tomorrow. A weird moment. Maybe it was Marjorie Kline's awkward smile, or the way the lights hit the pool, a scattering of shadow that felt wrong. Maybe it had nothing to do with those things; maybe I just swallowed a ton of water and blacked out. It could happen to anyone.

Except it doesn't. It never has. In my fifteen years of

competitive swimming, I've never seen someone drown—or even require the services of a lifeguard. People don't break their necks while walking down the street. It's the same thing. Swimming comes as naturally to me as breathing. The fact that this happened isn't just shocking; it's pathetic.

Lee scans me into my room and flips on the light. The state of disarray is astonishing. Clothes hang on windows and lamps and the TV. Useless textbooks and paperbacks litter the floor. My laptop is frozen in a state of abrupt abandonment. I used to be better than this. More organized. I used to have a little pride.

Lee, thankfully, doesn't acknowledge it. He ignores the piles of clothes on the bed and sits on top of them. He waves me over, patting the bedspread. I shuffle toward him. My throat still burns and my ribs are sore, but it's nothing compared to the anguish of letting him down. Lee tried to talk me out of getting back in the water so soon, and I ignored him.

He sweeps a wisp of hair out of my face and takes my hand. He sighs, but his expression isn't angry or judgmental. It's pained. Like he saw this coming, watched it happen, and now somehow feels responsible for it. "Can you stop tempting death, Aves?" He tries to smile. "I'm really struggling over here."

"I don't know what happened." I attempt a deep breath, but my lungs feel like they've been power-washed with a garden hose. "I'm so embarrassed."

"Embarrassed? Come on. This isn't about your reputation."

"Of course it is!" I turn to face him, braced for an argument. But it's all gone out of him—the anger, the defensiveness, the bravado. He looks wounded.

"I just want you to be okay again," he murmurs.

"I *am* okay."

"No, Aves." He looks up. "You're not."

I can feel it shift, then: the axis I'm turning on, the ground under my feet. Even the ceiling feels like it's tilting away from me. "I'm trying. I've *been* trying."

His gaze latches on to a crescent-shaped stain in the carpet, which is what remains of a Jell-O shot that never quite solidified the way we'd intended. That was freshman year, just two days after we met.

"I talked to your dad," he says.

"What?" It comes out like a hiccup.

"I called him." He puts his hand on my arm, and I feel the tension everywhere. Like a coiled spring compressed to the breaking point.

"Why?"

"He wants you to see someone," he says.

"I did see someone."

"Someone with actual credentials."

I glance at the window and imagine myself hurtling out of it. Anything would be preferable to this topic of conversation.

"Your dad is a doctor," he says. "I don't get it. Are you afraid of mental health people?"

"Psychiatrists?"

"Look, I don't know what they do. I'm no expert. I'm just trying to figure out how to help you."

"I don't need your help." Again, the open window draws my attention. The night is quiet, the campus wiling away the hours of the midweek doldrums. There are always some people out, of course. Groups of friends walking back from dinner in town. Intense pre-med, pre-law, pre-whatever gunners making the trek from library to dorm and back again. Couples talking or fighting or kissing, or maybe one couple accomplishing all three. I can't see faces in the dark, just shapes, passing by my window in a great collegiate march.

"Your dad said he's going to pull you out of school if you don't get help." He says this as gently as possible.

"So? He's always making threats."

"This sounded legit."

"So I leave school. Who cares?"

His muscles tense as his arm grazes my side, rustling my shirt. "Is that how you feel about it?" He takes a breath. "About us?"

A light from outside falls on his face, accentuating his sculpted features and perpetual stubble. I reach out and touch it, savoring the feel of something so predictable. "No," I whisper. "It's not how I feel."

"Then let me help you."

"You can't—"

"I can." The edge in his voice surprises me. I look up, expecting to see signs of Lee's short-fused (and completely benign) temper, but whatever anger he brought into this room has long since dissipated.

"How?"

He smiles. A true, unconstrained Lee classic: more mischievous than polite, his eyes dancing with it. "I've got a few ideas."

●

My father delivered on his threat. He showed up on campus the next day, dragged me back to the hospital to review my discharge plan, and coordinated a deposition with Coach about "my future in this organization." After an agonizing ninety minutes in that mildewy office, an agreement was reached, a contract signed. I committed to weekly sessions with Dr. Linda Shin, a psychiatrist who specializes in post-traumatic stress disorder and specific phobias. Dad knew her from medical school (of course—who *doesn't* he know?), but this time, I had veto power. If the first appointment didn't go well, Dad would round up someone else.

Two days later, I'm sitting in Dr. Shin's pristine office downtown. So far, our future together doesn't look promising. Her office has too many potted plants. The paintings are bland, the carpet an overly enthusiastic yellow. The window looks out onto the street, and I sit as far from it as possible, terrified of being recognized by passersby.

At least the magazines are up to date. *People* provides mild, mindless entertainment while the clock ticks toward two o'clock. I flip through the pages, wondering when my face will pop up with the caption *Whatever Happened to . . .*

"Avery?" The door opens and Dr. Shin pokes her head out. She's a petite Asian woman, with sloping cheekbones and a gaze that misses nothing.

She extends a hand. "I'm Dr. Shin."

I shake it, maybe a shade firmer than my usual. "Hi."

"Please come in," she says, gesturing toward the cozy office. For such a small woman, she has a surprisingly deep voice.

The tidy room offers several seating choices: two chairs or a stiff-looking couch. I opt for the chair. It's a little closer to the door, a little farther from the window.

She takes the other chair. "How are you?" she asks.

"Fine. You?"

She gives an infinitesimal nod. "I'm doing well, thank you."

I hand her the questionnaire she asked me to fill out prior to our appointment. It's pretty much a blank sheet of paper except for my name. No to *depressed mood,* no to *hallucinations,* no to *flashbacks* and *nightmares* and *history of trauma.* It's all relative, after all—my little episodes are nothing compared to the full-on psychotic breaks she probably manages on a daily basis. I've seen those people in my dad's ER, coming down from manic highs or talking to imaginary government agents. I've seen failed suicide attempts and successful ones, too. Teenagers, veterans, professors. All of them going about their daily business, hiding their demons.

I'm not like them.

She flips through the pages and tosses them onto her desk. A queasy feeling blooms in my stomach. I left too much out; I left *everything* out.

And she knows it.

She uncrosses her ankles and studies me for a long moment. The bland reassurance in her eyes is gone. "Avery, what exactly do you hope to get out of these sessions?"

The noise machine whirs its toneless tune, an idle static that heightens every other sound. I put my head in my hands and let it wash over me: the silence, the expectations, the weight of Dr. Shin's question hanging in the air.

"I'm not sure," I say. "A free pass from my dad?"

She doesn't smile. "You know, I can tell a lot about someone from this form."

"Seemed pretty standard to me."

"It is standard. And meaningless, at least in terms of understanding someone. But the people who actually *want* to be helped? They check all the boxes and answer all the questions. They're honest. Maybe a little too honest."

"Well, maybe I don't fit into a neat little box."

"Maybe you don't. Or maybe you *really* don't want to be helped."

My gaze drifts to the window, to the careless throngs of people walking through town. Kids laughing. Dads pushing strollers. Women on their lunch break, talking business strategy. "Maybe I don't *need* help."

"I think your coach and about twenty-two other swimmers might disagree there."

"I had a bad day."

"Is that all it was?"

Of course not, I want to scream. That day was all of my worst fears wrapped into one harrowing moment of fear, pain, and loss. It was about my old life and the new, the *before* and the *after*. Before I watched two hundred people scream and cry and pray to a god that had deserted them. Before my trust in air travel crashed and burned in an icy lake, shattering my ability to feel safe anywhere. Before Tim and Aayu and Liam lost their parents, before they became orphans in the span of minutes. Before Colin grasped my hand, told me everything was going to be all right, and it wasn't. It hasn't been all right since that night, and in my darkest, quietest moments, I'm convinced it never will be.

I know she can't hear my thoughts, but her slate-gray eyes and sleek professionalism make me feel like I'm under scrutiny, although scrutiny is a far cry from judgment.

"Are you familiar with post-traumatic stress disorder?" she asks.

My gut cramps in response. I hate those words, their calculated ambiguity. I wonder if it's possible to experience symptoms of PTSD just from saying its full name.

"I've heard of it," I say, choosing my words carefully.

"It's become fairly common vernacular in today's culture, which is unfortunate in my opinion. PTSD is a severe anxiety disorder that requires careful, focused, and longitudinal treatment. I'm not saying that's what you have, Avery—although your father seems to think so."

"He's an ER doc."

She allows a small smile at this. "Yes, well, I imagine that's why he called me."

"And you're an expert?"

"I work with a lot of patients with the disorder. I've devoted my entire career to it—conducted clinical studies, taught hundreds of residents, met with experts all over the world. I've spoken at a number of conferences." Her voice lacks the haughtiness I've come to expect from some doctors. "Does that make me an expert? I don't know. But I like to think I'm qualified."

"So how do you, uh, make the diagnosis?"

"I ask you about your symptoms. Psychiatry is unlike other fields of medicine in that I have to rely on your insights and experiences to make a clinical diagnosis. I can't really do that if you don't talk to me."

"What kinds of symptoms?"

"Well, there are a number of them, and no one experiences them in the exact same way. Nightmares. Flashbacks. Avoidance of triggers that stimulate memories or feelings associated with the traumatic event." She lingers on that word: *event.*

"Is that all?" I ask.

"No. Some patients experience hypervigilance—they scare easily, have difficulty sleeping. It's really a spectrum. PTSD requires individualized treatment because individuals are different. That's what makes it challenging for me as a provider. For you, the challenge is internal."

I look at the clock. So much time left—an eternity, really. Dr. Shin leans forward, her wrists on her knees. "So," she says. "Second chance."

"For what?"

"For you to tell me why you're really here." She nudges the clock in my direction. "You could have walked out ten minutes ago."

The noise machine continues to whir, but it feels quieter now, the static in my head less intrusive. "I want to swim again."

It's hard to imagine this tiny Asian lady hurling me into the pool, but maybe she has other ideas. I don't want to experience them in all their psychoanalytic glory, but I'm desperate.

"All right," she says.

Her answer startles me. "Seriously?"

"Yes. We can work on that."

"Okay, great." I reach for my coat. No matter the hourly fee, I've had enough for one day. Dad will just have to understand.

"So," she says. "Let's plan on the same time next week."

"Wait a second."

She stops, her neutral expression replaced by a knitted brow that suggests real concern. "Absolutely," she says. "What's on your mind?"

"I don't want you talking to my dad after these appointments."

Her brow relaxes a bit, but her eyes maintain that fierce intensity. "Our conversations are confidential. Your father is paying for these sessions, so he'll receive the bill, but that's it."

Something about my father getting billed for a completely confidential service makes me smile—almost. "Okay."

"Okay?"

"Okay meaning 'we'll see.'"

"Fair enough," she says as the clock chimes with the passing of the hour. "See you next week."

●

Six weeks later, after a rare evening appointment, Lee intercepts me outside Dr. Shin's office. My usual routine is rushing in, running out, trying hard not to be seen—so this is a surprise.

"Hey," he says.

"Hey."

"It's March first."

"Okay . . ."

"National Pool Day."

"Is that a real thing?"

"No, but it should be." He kisses my cheek. We've talked about National Pool Day, or at least some version of it. Dr. Shin encouraged it, thought it would be good to set goals. For me, National Pool Day is the first step toward swimming again.

It's after nine by the time we reach the steps of Naudler Natatorium. The layout of the facility never ceases to amaze me: a sprawling, glass-enclosed feat of architecture, with polished brick steps leading to a light-infused atrium. It's like stepping onto an indoor beach, with sand-colored floors and sky-blue walls. The ceilings are lofty and sloped, a transparent cathedral.

But the central focus, the grand finale, is the pool. A crisp, transparent blue filling the space like a shimmering sea. A strange blend of awe and terror grips me as we stand before it.

"We don't have to go down there," he says. "But we can if you want to."

"But you already spend so much time here—"

He turns toward me, never letting go of my hand. "Then I'll spend more."

"But it's so . . ." I trail off, unsure how to complete the thought.

"Hard?" He gives my knuckles a squeeze. "I know. It's gonna be really, really hard. But you want to swim again, right?"

"More than anything."

He watches me process the sight of the pool, devoid of swimmers for the first time in recent memory. Moonlight streams through the glass, scattering as it hits the water. I have to admit the pool looks hopelessly romantic at this time of night. There are no screaming coaches. No whirring kicks or thrashing arms. No exhausted co-eds stumbling out of the locker rooms and into the deep end. This is just a pool. A safe, sweeping, glorious pool, three times the size of the one I learned to swim in but otherwise just the same.

He squeezes my hand and pulls me into him. He smells good, like soap and spice, a blend that reminds me of early-morning practices.

The squeeze turns into a caress; the caress becomes a kiss. My hands find the scruff of his neck as he works his way through my hair, sweeping the wisps from my eyes. I have always liked the way Lee kisses me: freely and fiercely, like he's going on instinct. It's a little rough, a little wet, and then it's a frenzy. We don't stop until we're gasping.

"You know," he says, trailing kisses across my collarbone, "we can tweak the plan a little bit. Add skinny-dipping to the mix if you prefer."

"Uh-huh," I say, smirking. "Let's start slow, shall we?"

"Yes, ma'am." He takes me by the hand and tugs me toward the pool. A low hum betrays the presence of the overhead lights and filtration system. Lee breathes it in with the gusto of a springtime frolicker.

"Nothing like it," he says.

"Come on. You hate it sometimes."

"Damn right. I hate it at five A.M."

"But now's okay?"

"Yes." He leans in, whispering against my lips, "Because now I'm with you."

The words flood through me, warming me, bringing me to a place that feels altogether different, and wrong, and unexpected.

Colin.

I think of him then, those storm-blue eyes that seemed to reflect all the world. The team doesn't talk about him, which makes it easier. Forgetting about Colin and our five days on that mountain makes *everything* easier. And so, when his memory surges through me at the very moment I should be thinking of someone else, I push it away.

"Aves?" The wetness of Lee's lips on my skin tingles as he pulls away. "What is it?"

"Nothing." I try to smile. "I'm just happy to be here with you."

We step onto the pool deck, which, for the first time in months, doesn't fill me with instant dread. Instead, it's calming, almost restorative. I step out of my shoes, peel off my socks, and savor the cool dampness of the tiles underfoot.

"Still okay?" Lee asks.

"Great." And it's the truth. Being here feels natural, like an unexpected homecoming.

Together, we take our time circling the perimeter of the pool. It's a first for both of us. My recruiting visit was rushed and pressured. Practices are always an exercise in efficiency and time management. Meets are crowded, chaotic affairs, with packed decks and swimmers scurrying from place to place. I never thought about how purely functional a pool could become, almost like a workplace. It's no wonder so many of us burn out after college.

"It looks different at night," I say as we round the third corner. Above and beyond us, the moon and stars and California sky loom over the bay.

"I know." He stops and looks up. "I feel like I'm on a lake." He flinches. "I mean, not like . . ."

"It's okay." I lean into him, finding sanctuary in the crook of his arm.

"Aves," he says, turning toward me. "The sessions with Dr. Shin . . ."

"Are helping."

Which is true. They *are* helping. The flashbacks are less frequent, the triggers less random. Some nights, I don't dream at all.

"It was her idea to try the conditioning therapy, and I thought maybe I could help . . ." He rushes on, "Was that out of line? I swear I didn't ask about—"

"No, no. It's okay."

"You sure?"

"Totally okay."

"I know I don't have much training—"

"Much training?"

"Okay, *any* training. But I told her you trust me." His smile falters. "You do trust me, right, Aves?"

"Of course." I loop my arm through his and sit down on the deck. We dangle our bare feet in the seventy-nine-degree water, a temperature that feels just right when you're swimming hard. Even now, it's a luxury—brisk but refreshing. Designed for human comfort, tuned to the finest degree.

I lift my feet, watching the water stream between my toes and return to the pool. A ripple of unease courses through me, as unwelcome as it is fleeting. It's gone before Lee can see the tension in my jaw, the smile struggling to stay there.

"Aves?" he asks. "You okay?"

I drop my head on his shoulder and close my eyes. When I open them again, the world isn't spinning anymore. The pool glistens and hums, and the humidity warms me everywhere. It all feels so safe, and natural, and right.

So right, in fact, I almost forget about the dangers lurking beneath the surface.

26

Dr. Shin waits until the first of April to ask about Colin. It's our tenth appointment, the middle stage of a relationship that starts to feel like it needs to *go* somewhere. And Dr. Shin isn't the type to stall out. So I start with a tidbit about my family (one of her favorite subjects), which I'm hoping is enough to sustain her until the appointment ends. Next week, I'll think of something else to blabber on about.

"My brother offered me a job," I say, picking at the tuft of gray threads under the armrest.

"Which brother?"

"Edward."

"The professional baseball player who lives in LA? You've never mentioned him by name."

"That's Edward."

"I thought you said he was moving back to Boston."

"He is." I return my hands to my lap. "The job is in Boston."

A long pause.

"I see," she muses. Dr. Shin doesn't like to prompt me with too many questions. Sometimes we sit in silence for ten or twenty minutes while she waits for me to say something.

"Anyway, I said no."

"May I ask what the job is?"

"He's trying to rejuvenate athletic programs for inner-city schools." I pick at the threads until three more of them give way. Maybe she stocks these couches because she knows the crappy fabric is therapeutic.

"You told me once you didn't think he'd actually leave professional baseball."

"Well," I say, looking up, "I was wrong."

Her intense stare makes me want to rush on, to say more than I probably should. This is part of her effectiveness as a psychiatrist, more a weapon than a tool of the trade.

"I can't go back to Boston," I say.

She doesn't even bother to express the long *mmm* that usually follows such a statement. With no more threads to unravel, the only thing left to focus on is her eyes, reaching into me like a pair of hands.

"Why not?" she asks.

"Because my life is here. I've got the team, and Lee, and swimming . . ."

"But you're not swimming," she says. "The conditioning therapy hasn't worked."

She's right, of course. I'm sure Lee has been hounding her with e-mails, begging for advice. After that first "lesson," I wore my favorite suit for the second one, all decked out and ready to swim. I couldn't get in past my knees.

"Did Lee tell you what happened?"

"A bit." She folds her hands together as she gathers her thoughts. "He couldn't speak to what it was like for you, though."

"Well, I can't really describe it. It's like some other part of my brain takes over."

"Similar to the episodes you've had before?"

"Yeah."

"So you feel afraid when you're in the water. Not around it, but in it." She directs her gaze upward for a moment, thinking. "What else do you feel?"

"Helpless. Fragile." My voice trails to a whisper. "Out of control."

"Have you ever been able to regain control?"

I shake my head, conceding the obvious. "The feeling passes after a few minutes, and it takes a while for me to feel like myself again."

"How so?"

"I just feel lost."

She crosses her ankles and studies me for five, maybe ten seconds. It feels like an eternity, but in the scheme of our frequent drawn-out silences, it's really not that much.

"How do you feel about spending the summer in Boston?" she asks.

"I'm indifferent." I look up, registering that telltale frustration in her eyes, colored with disappointment. She always seems to know when I'm lying.

She waits patiently for me to revise my answer.

"I'm uneasy about it," I admit.

"Why is that, do you think?"

"Well, they all live in the Boston area. The boys, I mean."

"Have you seen them?" she asks.

The answer comes haltingly, guilt welling up as I say, "No."

Their voices. The lilting sounds of their laughter. The details of who they were under those merciless gray skies have faded, but my mind still wanders. Sometimes it finds them sitting under the stars, begging for candy canes. I've dreamed about seeing them again, and each time, I wake with tears on my face and a lurch in my throat.

"And Colin?"

"What about him?" I choke out.

"Have you spoken with him at all?"

The sudden change in tack takes me by surprise; only in rare cases will Dr. Shin go straight for the jugular. It throws me off my game. Makes me less likely to bend the truth. At least this time, I manage to suppress the first thought that comes to mind.

"I don't want to talk about him," I say.

She leans back in her chair but doesn't look away. Her hair is tied into a tight bun, which accentuates the tautness of her features, the depth of her eyes. The truth is, I *never* want to talk about Colin. Because if we don't talk about him, maybe he won't haunt me in ways that confuse my emotions and sabotage my attempts to move on. Maybe the truth will never come out.

I put my head down and inspect the tiny knots in the carpet, as if willing myself to sink through it. "I just want to forget about him."

Her voice is gently inquisitive. "Why?"

"Because he reminds me of everything that happened out there."

Shit. I walked right into it.

"I thought you said you got separated early on."

"We were. We did." The media refused to accept the "I don't remember anything" excuse when they got wind of Colin's floss sutures. I told them we'd been together five hours instead of five days—just enough time for me to stitch up a wound. "That's what I meant."

"You said 'everything.'"

"'Everything' is a vague term. I meant Colorado. The plane. Whatever."

"I'm not sure that's what you meant."

"Of *course* it's what I meant." I don't realize I'm screaming until someone knocks on the door and asks if everything is all right.

"Yes, fine," Dr. Shin says. She waits for me to go on, but I can't. I won't. The person at the door gasps as I wrench it open and burst into the waiting room.

As it turns out, my abrupt exodus from that office isn't as freeing as I'd hoped.

It's damning.

●

The media wanted a hero, but more than that, they wanted to know about Colin and those three little boys. They wanted to know how we'd ended up so far apart, a logistical anomaly given the fact that there were no other survivors. The only reasonable answer was to say nothing—and later, when the floss sutures called into question the whole "amnesia" story, I came up with an abbreviated version of the truth. I told the world we'd gotten separated early on, which made for a very bland story.

The boys were never interviewed; the media assumed they were too young or sick or traumatized to remember anything. And then, of course, there was the question of taste. No one wanted to torture little kids by dredging up bad memories. *Avery Delacorte, though—she could handle it.* Except I couldn't. So I lied about what happened, and the interviews stopped.

By the time Colin recovered enough to speak to the media, he didn't challenge the details I'd provided, sparse as they were. He did this for me, of course, just like he did everything else.

For some reason, the world was kinder to him. Headlines

painted him as the quiet hero. The photos recycled by all the media outlets over and over again were actually flattering. Most were taken in and around Boston, after his discharge from the hospital. And then, of course, there was that parking lot footage. The tabloids had a field day with that one: *Has Avery Delacorte been holding back about what* really *happened out there?* For weeks, life felt like a reality show.

But I could cope with the media firestorm. I learned to navigate it in my own way, sheltered by the cocoon of a college campus. The public has a short memory. People forget. They move on. Other stories, other tragedies, steal their attention. And I let it happen because being *normal* meant more to me than being *me.*

Colin never said anything about the notebook in our brief hours together on New Year's, though I sometimes wondered if he intended to. The recovery personnel never found it, not like I made any effort to track it down. I didn't want to relive those harrowing five days, nor think about them at all.

The truth was, the boys deserved better.

"Aves?"

I look up to see Lee sitting on the steps of my dorm. He has flowers in one hand and a brand-new Nike suit in the other.

"Hey."

"What's wrong? Did something happen?"

The silence expands until it's everywhere, all at once, torturing me in ways that words never could. I've exhausted my ability to lie. There is only the truth, embedded in memory. Haunting memories, beautiful memories.

This is who I am now.

"Yes," I say, wishing the answer were different.

27

distribute another round of melted snow, which fails to rouse any enthusiasm from the boys. Aayu barely has the energy to sit up, and Liam has a cough now, too. Tim's toes and fingers have gone a disconcerting purple. No one feels like drinking anything.

Colin rubs Tim's hands and feet while I change the other boys' clothes. Everything is damp—clothes, blankets, hats, gloves. I don't know if it's because they all have fevers or because we failed to dry things out this morning. What seemed practical two days ago now feels like an exercise in futility.

People die because they panic. My father's words—repeated on every ski trip, every white-water rafting excursion, every adrenaline-infused expedition he ever took us on—rattle around in my brain. *Take it easy,* he'd say. *Relax.* He never panicked, even when his own kids were in danger. But he's not here, and I'm not my father.

"I'll go out." Colin pulls on his hat, the one with the enlarged hole for his face. "The boys need to eat."

"Colin, you can't."

He sinks to his knees beside me. He's laboring to breathe— shallow, raspy breaths that sound like a rusted engine. His mind wants to keep going, but his body can't oblige. It's excruciating to watch.

"Maybe you're right," he finally says.

Hearing him admit this is worse than the damning thump we heard right before impact, worse than the angry roar of the bear. He's giving up. *He knows.*

"Listen to me." His hands cup my face, warming me everywhere. "You aren't going to die."

"*We* aren't going to die." I grasp his wrists so his hands stay on my face. Everything around us falls away. There is only him, just like we were on the plane. Arms wrapped around our knees, heads turned toward each other. *Only you.*

"Avery—"

"Don't say it. Not now." I whisper against his lips, "Not ever."

"I won't," he says, his voice breaking as he removes my gloves. He fumbles with them—the left, then the right, and then his own, until it's just us, skin touching skin, my hands in his. He's warm, so warm. He rests his forehead against mine, and for a rare, stolen moment, it feels like we're breathing for each other.

●

Some time later, the gray walls in my dream turn black, then red, and suddenly there is nothing in front of me but a wild, consuming flame licking the plastic curves of the cabin. All the passengers are eerily silent, their ankles and wrists and necks strapped into seats. I go to them, one after the other, yanking on seat belts that have no buckle. The fire moves in from everywhere, consuming them as I struggle to set them free. Water rushes in, mingling with the flames. Their skin peels off in thin strips, revealing charred bone underneath.

They don't say anything to me, but their chests rise and fall with the exertion of staying alive. Their breaths are hot on my face. They're dying, and I can't save them. . . .

I can't save them.

I snap awake to the sound of new horrors banging on the walls: hail, snow, wind. The assault whips the trees into a frenzy and transforms the lake into a frothing sea. Waves thrash the shore, and it feels almost personal—the lake's rapid metamorphosis from docile companion into a vengeful monster. The bear that caused us so much grief is probably asleep in a warm den, sheltered from the elements it knows so well, while we freeze in a hulk of metal.

While the wind pounds the walls, I gather up every scrap of clothing and wrap the boys up like mummies. This includes ties, shawls, pashminas, stockings . . . everything. I make little slits for their eyes, noses, and mouths, careful to cover every inch of skin. The boys are too dazed to protest—even Aayu, who always cries when the sun goes down. Tim is no longer conscious, but his chest rises and falls with each breath, and that is all I can hope for.

"I'm cold," Liam says, and I hug him and tell him everything's fine, we beat the other storms and we'll beat this one, too. Colin sings to Aayu, rasping the words because it's all he can manage. The lyrics don't make sense: oceans and kings and butterscotch candies, not that it matters. He never stops singing, even though he must feel those boys dying in his arms, succumbing to the circumstances that betrayed them.

His voice is husky with fever, his face windburned, but he's still Colin—strong, kind, and fiercely loyal. He finds my gaze and smiles that soft, lovely smile, and even though it summons every shred of hope left in my body, I can see the truth there, too: This is the end.

I squeeze his hand and see our fingers intertwined, the way they were on the plane, the way they should have been months ago. Did he know what would happen when we met? Did he think, in some strange, tragic way, that the world would bring us together again?

He stops singing to catch his breath, to kiss the tiny sliver of skin between the boys' eyelids. My acceptance turns once more to sorrow, then to rage: I hate that these boys will never be men. I hate that Colin will never be a father.

"Colin."

He looks up, no longer hiding the longing in his eyes, now tinged with regret. I see Colin Shea standing outside that locker room on my first day of practice, rescuing me from paralyzing insecurity. I see his kind smile, his inquisitive blue eyes; I see someone who understood me.

"Do you remember the day we met?" I ask him.

He smiles—a soft, lovely smile that reminds me of that first afternoon. "Of course," he says. "Best day of my life."

I discard my gloves, using my bare hands to trace the steep curves of his features, the thick stubble on his chin. It's the first time I've ever touched him this way. Intimate, exploring. His breath catches, his left hand finding mine as he holds my gaze in a moment of pure, aching recognition. The thrum of his heart fills the silence, fills me everywhere.

"I'm glad it was you," I whisper.

I kiss him softly at first, a whisper of gratitude, of loss. But it doesn't feel like good-bye. It feels like a first kiss, electric and wanting and tragically overdue. Every ounce of me roars to life again—lips, fingers, toes. The numbness in my veins turns to fire, more intense than anything I've ever felt, anything I ever thought I was capable of feeling. I breathe him in. He tastes like peppermint—*How does he do that?*—but his lips are warm and wet, and he responds with a hunger that matches my own. There is no shyness, no holding back. He draws me into him, and I no longer feel hopeless anymore, or angry. I feel loved.

When he pulls away, the storm continues to rage all around us, but the world is different now.

I fall asleep on his shoulder, dreaming of clear waters and blue skies, Brookline streets and chocolate-covered doughnuts, baseball games and gondolas. Bug. People I've known my whole life; strangers who pass me by.

Tim, Liam, Aayu.

Colin.

28

Lee takes me by the hand, leaving us suspended in some hazy in-between. It reminds me of the *before* and *after* that has followed me since the crash, relentless as a shadow and just as intangible. The rest of the world—the occasional late-night straggler, the dorm, the California sky—dissolves around us.

I wait for him to unfurl a barrage of questions, but he never does. Those memories aren't his. They aren't ours. And yet they're still relevant.

They're everything.

"I didn't want to do it this way," I say.

"Do what, Avery?" The way he says my unabbreviated name makes my stomach clench. "You said something happened. Are you hurt? Was it something Dr. Shin said—"

"I lied about what happened after the plane crashed."

There.

The silence gives my confession the weight it deserves.

"Avery?"

"I lied about so many things."

"What kinds of things?"

So many things. But the words won't come because they aren't for him.

"Aves, you need to talk to me."

"I don't know what to say."

"You *do* know. Tell me."

"I left them behind," I whisper.

"Left who behind?"

"The boys." I breathe his name. "Colin."

"After the crash? I thought you weren't even together——"

"We *were* together. For five days, we were together."

"But you said . . ." He trails off.

"I lied about what happened because I wasn't strong enough to tell the truth." I release his hands, and he folds them over his chest. "I loved them, Lee. I loved them, and I left them behind. And now I have to face that."

"How?"

"I'm going back to Boston."

His cheeks are glistening and wet. He doesn't reach for me; he doesn't even look up. The red swimsuit he'd planned on giving me dangles from his fingers.

"Do you still love him?" he asks.

"I don't know," I say, because to say no would be a lie.

"Then I'll wait for you," he says. "And I'll be here when you get home."

Home.

The truth is, I don't know where that is anymore.

29

Dr. Shin doesn't act surprised to see me when I show up on the last day of the semester, but I know that's just her infallible stoicism. After two months of total silence, she was probably wondering what happened to me.

"Good to see you again," she says, and seems to mean it.

"I wanted to thank you."

"For what?"

"For asking the tough questions."

She allows a smile. "That's my job."

"I'm going back to Boston for the summer."

"I see," she says, betraying no emotion whatsoever.

I look out the window, at the scores of people walking by. The last day of the semester. An ending, but also a beginning. I've decided it depends on how you look at it.

"I need to talk to Colin about what happened because you're right, he was there," I say. "He was there the whole time."

There is no telltale lift of the eyebrows, no *mmm-hmm* that sounds in any way like an *I told you so*. She simply waits for me to go on, her gaze attentive but nonjudgmental, her hands folded primly in her lap.

"Well," she says, "let me know when you start swimming again."

"I can't swim." Even now, after all these months, it wounds me to admit this. "The conditioning therapy hasn't worked."

"Of course it hasn't." She hands me my New Patient questionnaire, the pages so blank they shine. For maybe the first time ever, she smiles openly. *Knowingly.*

"Good luck in Boston," she says.

●

An hour later, Edward picks me up outside my dorm, his Jeep packed to capacity for the cross-country move. He could've shipped everything like most millionaires do, but that's not Edward's style. He likes to do things old-school. Be resourceful.

So it's no surprise to see boxes of all shapes and sizes cluttering the backseat, fighting their way to the front. The passenger seat has about fourteen inches of free space, barely enough to accommodate my butt. His yellow Lab glares at me from the floor—*Sorry, buddy, we're gonna have to share.* It's a good thing I'm somewhat small and narrow.

"Hope your suitcase is a reasonable size," he says, "or we may have to tie it to the exhaust pipe and drag it along."

"Very funny."

Edward follows me into my dorm, finds my suitcase packed to the gills, and carries it down the stairs. I don't even offer to find a place for it in the Jeep. He's got the whole thing planned out, a testament to the organizational zeal he inherited from our mother. My suitcase fits snugly into the left side of the trunk like a missing puzzle piece.

His skills in car maintenance, however, leave something to be desired. He knows how to repair a transmission, replace an exhaust pipe, even hot-wire the engine—but car washes are beyond him. In this way, he's like our dad.

He rubs the windshield with his bare hand, pinching the dust between his fingers. "Probably should've taken care of this a little earlier," he says.

"Nah. Perfect way to see the country."

He flicks the dust at me and revs the engine. It's slow going at first, with Bay Area traffic and summer travelers clogging the freeways. The sun sets behind us, casting its furious orange sheen on the Pacific. Ahead of us, green hills and sloping valleys stretch toward an infinite horizon. It's a magnificent landscape, a place that rightly deserves all the poetry, songs, and literature espousing its beauty.

"Missing it already?" Edward asks.

"I'm easily seduced by sunsets."

"Ah." He fiddles with the radio. "Nothing quite like a Boston sunrise, though."

"You're awake for those?"

He laughs, but a serious note finds its way into his voice. "I try to be." He settles on a song from the nineties, one of his favorites growing up. "They're worth it."

●

Three thousand miles and a week later, we hit the Mass Turnpike. For a Friday evening, the traffic flowing into Boston isn't as terrible as I remembered. It's all stop-and-go, narrow ramps and careening corners, unlike the monotonous drag of a California freeway. Windows down, city air flooding my lungs, I watch it all pass by: the skyscrapers in the distance, the river on my left. When Fenway comes into view, its fairy-tale lights glittering on the horizon, I finally feel like I'm home.

My parents are there to greet us when we pull into the driveway. Dad grunts a hello, mutters something about us not calling often enough, and pulls me into a very awkward hug—the first I can remember since childhood. He takes my suitcase and rolls it up to the house.

"Oh, honey" is all my mom can manage.

"Hi, Mom," I say, which brings actual tears to her eyes. I give her a hug, inhaling the familiar scent of her favorite lotion, a citrusy smell that reminds me of spring.

Every time I come home, the house looks the same but somehow different. Family portraits from years gone by line the mantel in reverence of the past. Newer photos sit in the kitchen, where my mother likes to "test-drive" things for the house. Growing up, we always used to congregate here, which drove her crazy. For one thing, it's hot in the kitchen, in spite of the multiple A/Cs installed in the windows. She goes over to the biggest one and puts it on high.

"So darn hot," she says. "Sorry, sweetie. You're probably not used to it." She gives the struggling appliance a shove. "Dinner's in thirty minutes."

"Don't be late," Edward teases as he reaches for a stack of plates and silverware. Setting the table was his designated chore growing up. Because I'm not ready for a full-on family discussion about my life, I head upstairs to regroup.

My suitcase sits outside my bedroom door, right where my dad left it. The bulging compartments remind me just how much I took to California, and how little I left behind. Or maybe it's just the accumulation of *things*, the dutiful progression of time marked by the dutiful collection of meaningless possessions. I roll it over the threshold and close the door.

In those first few seconds of being here, being *home*, the burden of what I've done weighs on my shoulders. I haven't thought about the logistics of being here, especially since

Edward exaggerated the time commitment. On the trip home, he admitted he's barely got a sign-up sheet, much less a whole program going. He's a skilled negotiator, especially when it comes to his little sister.

I lie on the creaky mattress and stare at those familiar yellow stars. Still there, still peeling. I find myself blinking away tears. *How am I supposed to do this?* I don't even know where to begin. Colin? The boys? What if they refuse to see me?

Some time later, my dad knocks on my door.

"Busy tomorrow?" he asks.

I wish the answer were *yes*, but it's not.

"Not really."

"Good."

Somewhere down the hall, Edward snickers.

●

Saturday mornings in an emergency room are usually quiet, representing that rare reprieve between the two wildest nights of the week. Today, though, the waiting room extends to the parking lot, triage is overwhelmed, and occupied gurneys line the walls. My dad instructs me to start with these unfortunate folks: take a history, get an updated list of meds, try to tame the crazy. I'm rounding the corner in pursuit of a shrieking heroin addict when a tentative voice calls my name, a flash of clarity in the chaos.

I slow to a stop. The little voice repeats itself, each syllable pronounced with quiet authority: "Avery." I know who it is long before I turn around, but even so, the sight of Tim in my father's ER takes my breath away.

He's sitting on a plastic chair intended for adults, his legs dangling as he clutches his arm to his chest. Grass stains and blood defile the pristine white sleeve of his baseball jersey. In spite of this, he doesn't seem at all frightened, and why would he be? He's seen much worse.

He leaps off the chair, oblivious to the dangers of running wildly through an emergency room. The smile on his face is luminous. He slams into me, forgetting the bloody arm as he wraps them both around my waist.

"I knew it was you!" He trips over the words, so excited he can barely speak. In that regard, he's better off than me—I can't manage a sound. Tim was so sick for all that time, it's a shock he even remembers me.

"Do you work here?" he asks.

He's so strong now—taller, too, with a sunburn that isn't raw or worrisome. It's a boyhood baseball burn, and it makes his skin glow.

"No, not really . . ." I steal a glance at my borrowed scrubs. "I mean, yes, sort of."

"Oh," he says, still beaming. "Well I hope so because then you can fix my arm!"

His confidence floods through me, wrenching me into a memory that isn't altogether bad—just raw. Even now, after all this time, those details tend to surface with the softest prompting.

An older man approaches us, his trimmed hair flecked with gray. His collared shirt is buttoned almost to the top, and his smile is warm and proper, echoing his wardrobe. He holds out a hand. "Joe Caldwell," he says. "It's a pleasure to finally meet you."

"Mr. Caldwell," I mumble, recalling all those letters signed in his sturdy hand, his countless invitations to come visit. All were either deferred or denied, though I had an endless number of excuses. "I . . ."

"You don't have to explain," he says, then takes my hand in both of his own. He holds it there for a while, diffusing all those feelings of guilt and inadequacy through one simple gesture.

I smile at Tim, and this time, it comes easily. "So, how's baseball season going?"

"It's good." He drops his gaze to his grass-stained pants. "I bat eleventh."

"That's not bad. Everyone has an equal chance for a hit, no matter where they are in the lineup."

He nods, acknowledging the logic.

"Playing any infield yet?"

"He's played shortstop a few times," Mr. Caldwell says, mostly to comfort Tim. "He's improved quite a bit since the spring."

Tim gives a sheepish shrug. "Thanks, Granddad."

The way he thanks him fills me with my own sense of gratitude, though it's difficult to express such a thing to a seven-year-old. I hope these last six months have been good to him; I hope he's found his own way of moving on without completely letting go. I think his parents would have wanted it that way.

"You and Colin should come to a game!" he says.

"Oh." I adjust the clipboard in my lap, as if that will distract him somehow. It doesn't. "Well, maybe sometime. I haven't really talked to him—"

Tim nods. "I know."

"You do?"

"You've been at school."

"Oh." Relief sweeps through me. "Well, that's true."

"He comes to games all the time."

The lump in my throat is monstrous. "He does?"

"He's helped me a lot. You should come. Sometimes I feel kind of sorry for him sitting in the bleachers all by himself."

"Tim, Avery's a very busy lady." Mr. Caldwell puts his arm around Tim's shoulders. "Let's not put even more pressure on her time."

"Oh." Tim frowns. "Sorry, Avery."

"I'm not that busy." I shift my gaze to Mr. Caldwell, whose smile is so imperceptible it may just be my imagination. He has Tim's eyes, a pale, dreamlike green, deep with meaning.

"Where's Tim Caldwell?" A resident in blood-specked scrubs barges into the conversation, his pockets loaded with pens and other shiny apparatuses.

Tim nods like he's going to the gallows. "That's me, I guess."

The young doctor pulls up a stool and plops himself in front of Tim. Most of the residents treat me with some semblance of respect because of my father, but this guy isn't one of them. His name is Kyle, and he ignores me with the same condescending air he ignores all the alcoholics camped out front.

"So," Kyle says, addressing Mr. Caldwell. It's as if Tim, the patient, isn't even there. "What happened here?"

"I fell on a rock," Tim says before his grandfather can answer.

"Playing baseball?"

"It was in the outfield. There was a broken bottle in the grass."

Mr. Caldwell produces the piece of glass, which looks like the remnant of a beer bottle. The mere act of handling it seems to pain him, as if Tim's injury were his fault—which of course it wasn't. Some stupid kid probably left it there after stumbling home drunk from a party.

Kyle gives it a casual glance. "Yeah, happens all the time."

"Shouldn't we do a tetanus test or something—"

"Nah." Kyle peels back the sleeve of Tim's shirt to inspect the wound. Tim grits his teeth but makes no sound as Kyle pokes and prods with angry-looking instruments.

"You okay, Tim?" I ask him.

Tim nods. Kyle finally acknowledges me with an angry glare.

Mr. Caldwell keeps opening his mouth to say something, only to close it again like he's afraid of interrupting the doctor's work. I give him a reassuring smile, which seems to calm his nerves a bit. Meanwhile, Kyle ignores the distress on Tim's face as he reaches for a syringe.

"Wait!" Tim screams.

Kyle sighs. "It won't hurt that much. I'll spray with anesthetic—"

"I thought Avery was gonna do it."

"Avery?" He looks me up and down, eyebrows raised. An arrogant grin plays on his face. He spins back around to face Tim. "She's a volunteer," he says. "Doesn't know how to fix things like this."

"She fixed it with floss last time."

"Uh-huh." Kyle smirks as he pulls his gloves on. "She tell you that?"

"No." Tim stiffens and pulls his arm back. "I was there."

"Uh-huh," Kyle says again as he threads the needle.

By then, my father is standing over us, his arms folded as he watches this sad display of arrogance, followed swiftly by mortification. "Take the gastroenteritis in 2," he says, pointing Kyle in that direction.

"Look, Dr. Delacorte—"

"I said, gastro in 2. Put on a gown, though—mask, too. Poor guy's got it coming out both ends."

Kyle trudges down the hallway, stripping off his gloves as he heads for a gloomy arrangement of rooms. The choked sounds of someone vomiting fill the hallway as he opens the door and goes inside.

"Hello, Tim." Dad extends his hand for Tim to shake, then does the same for Mr. Caldwell. The introductions are brief but professional, colored by mutual respect that was so sorely lacking a few minutes ago.

"She really did it," Tim says. "She saved our lives."

"That's not true, Tim," I say.

"It *is* true. She helped Colin with the big lady and made me feel better when I was sick, and she told us everything was gonna be okay, and it was."

Before I can manage a word, my dad says, "Well, I can't say I'm surprised." He holds my gaze as he preps the sutures. "Avery is the toughest kid I've got."

I start to say more, but my father shakes his head, lets it go. Tim doesn't seem to care about my total aversion to the truth. Maybe Colin doesn't care, either.

Maybe it's *me*.

30

Tim doesn't leave the ER until I've promised to come to his next baseball game. Mr. Caldwell gives me the details: Friday night, seven P.M. Under the lights. In Newton, a ten-minute drive from my house in Brookline, and therefore way too close to use traffic as an excuse. I know I should go. I'd even *want* to go if it weren't for Colin.

I leave the hospital feeling a strange mixture of fatigue and nerves, savoring the heat as it yawns over the city. In the two hours it takes to walk home, I've considered every excuse, fiction, and fake "accident" within the realm of possibility to explain my absence to Tim. Nothing sounds even remotely reasonable. He'll know, and it will hurt him. That's something I'm simply unwilling to do to a boy who watched his parents die.

The rest of the week proceeds in slow motion until finally Friday dawns, springlike and mild. It's the longest day of the year, the first official day of summer. I spend the morning indulging in warm sunshine, reading one of my dad's old medical textbooks on our front porch. In the afternoon, I go for a run—something of a routine since my brisk adventure with Edward, although never quite the same as that first one. When

I return, the day has lost its slow, languid pace. The hours rush forward. And then, suddenly, it's after six. Time to catch the train.

I steal one last glance in the mirror before heading out. The cowlicks around my forehead have begun to curl, conceding to the humidity. At least the color is right again: a wistful, almost translucent blond, as close to white as hair gets on the blond spectrum. The chlorine used to give it a greenish sheen, but that, too, has grown out. It's a truer hue than it's been in years.

My mom pokes her head in my room, a frequent event because the door is always open. After waking up a dozen times to find her watching me sleep—*Just wanted to make sure you're still breathing, don't mind me!*—we made a deal. I promised to keep the door open at all times, but no more creepy nocturnal visits. The dreams won't kill me, although it took a while to convince her otherwise. But last night was a good night, a dreamless night, and I'm feeling wide-awake now—on edge, my blood humming with frenetic energy.

"Need a ride?" she asks. The hopeful look on her face never falters. Guilt swims through me. How many times have I said no since middle school? A hundred? A thousand?

"Sure." I smile, really meaning it this time. "I'd love one."

"Really?"

"I miss your driving, Mom."

"No, you don't," she says, laughing. For the first time in many months—in years, maybe—it hits me: She misses me. She misses me so much, she doesn't want me to leave.

"And you," I say. "I mean . . . I miss you, too."

Her laughter fades to a soft, knowing smile as she pulls me into a hug. "I know."

Because moms always do.

She drops me off near the snack bar, where I spent most of my time during my brothers' games. "Call me when you're ready to come home," she says.

"I think I'm good with the train," I say. "But thanks."

"Have fun." She sends me off with a pat on the arm and a reassuring smile. It helps. Being here sparks a tangle of nerves that have been brewing since that day in the ER.

Aside from the spiffier uniforms and electronic scoreboard, it hasn't changed much: Three Little League fields sit under a dome of white lights, the outfield walls blanketed in local advertisements and kid-friendly green mats. It's the energy, though, that evokes so many memories, that makes me miss those long, lazy afternoons watching my brothers play while my parents bought me my fill of hot dogs and candy.

I gravitate toward the third-base line, searching for Tim's familiar face in a swarm of orange-and-black jerseys. When I finally do find him, he's waving at me from the dugout with a blinding grin on his face. I wave back, warmed by his unabashed enthusiasm. Still waving, he dashes out onto the field with his friends, stumbling over the pitcher's mound as he takes his position at second base.

Tim's grandparents are sitting in the very first row, munching on Cracker Jacks like it's 1952. They call out friendly hellos, and I wave back. They don't seem the least bit surprised or insulted when I head for the top of the bleachers, which feels less threatening than the crowded front rows. I always liked it up here—no crowds, breezy but warm, with a spectacular view. After settling into my chosen seat, I lean back and whistle the way my dad taught me: low and sonorous, carrying above all the others.

Until someone behind me does the same.

Behind me? There is no one behind me; this is one of the advantages of the top row. The players' families are all clustered up front, chewing on sunflower seeds and snapping photos and texting relatives every time the ball is hit or caught or even completely missed. And then there's me, the random girl in the nosebleed section, rooting for a boy who's too old to be her son and too young to be her brother. No, our connection is different. Unique. And it's mine, only mine, until Colin climbs over the seat next to me and sits down.

And then it's ours.

"Good spot," he says. "No one throwing sunflower seeds at your head."

He smiles, eyes shining as he settles in beside me. My first thought is that he looks good, *really* good. Healthy, the sheen of sunburn glowing on his skin. He doesn't favor the right shoulder as he did months ago, though the scars remain.

My second thought is *hair.* Most of it is hiding under his baseball cap, but still, the change is obvious. Beautiful, sun-blond hair cut close to his scalp but well past the domain of bald. He must catch me staring because his face reddens.

"It's . . ." I find myself grasping for words. "You look great."

"Thanks," he says, his gaze sweeping ever so subtly over the rest of me. The sudden, unapologetic attention gives me butterflies.

"You look lovely," he says, and the butterflies turn frantic, the hollowness of our separation suddenly filled. It's such a sweet, Colin thing to say. Nothing embellished about it. A single word, exactly as he intended it.

"I, uh, thanks."

"You're welcome."

As before, it takes me a while to reconcile the memory of

Colin Shea to the reality of him. I always expect the worst: flashbacks, regret, unbearable tension. Instead, it's relief that sweeps through me—relief and a strange sense of groundedness.

"Better weather up here?" He watches me for a moment, perhaps gauging my reaction to his teasing tone, his shy smile. I see then that he's changed in other ways, too—he seems relaxed, eased of some terrible burden. I don't know if that burden is the crash, or expectations, or even me, but its absence plays on his face.

"Safer from foul balls," I say.

"I don't know about that." He gestures to the boy in the batter's box, who wears his uniform like a second skin. "That kid can crush it."

I smile, thinking of Edward back in his Little League days. He was all finesse: a perfect swing, flawless mechanics. Never the biggest kid on the team but a natural talent. In that way, he reminds me of Colin.

"I hear you come to a lot of games," I say.

"I try to." He salutes Tim, who grins as he responds with a salute of his own. It's a curious connection, one that seems developed rather than instantaneous. Colin hasn't spent the last six months writing letters that he never sends, that's for sure. He's been here, in Tim's life. Probably in Aayu's and Liam's, too. Shame floods through me.

"You okay?" he asks.

My vision blurs. "I'm so sorry, Colin." In spite of the electric energy of the night and a hundred people screaming at seven-year-old boys, the only thing my sensory system can process is him. I put my head in my hands, stealing a moment of calm.

"For what?" he asks.

"For a lot of things."

There is no anger or blame in his gaze, only sorrow

reflected back at me in pools of blue. He's always been this way, but I can sense a change in him now, a kind of letting go. Mr. Caldwell wrote to tell me about Mrs. Shea's death not long after I went back to school, and though I called Colin to give my condolences, he never returned the message.

The crack of the bat reverberates through the stands, and Tim ducks as the ball sails past him into the outfield. His coach gives a whole-body sigh while four players chase it down.

"He's a little afraid of the ball," Colin says.

"He's not afraid of blood, though." I keep my eyes on the field, hiding a tentative smile. "Unlike some people I know."

Colin laughs as he stretches out his legs, inhales a breath of summer. "So." He pulls off his Sox cap and folds the brim in his hands. "What brings you out tonight?"

"Tim." I pause to catch my breath. "Saw him in the ER."

He furrows his brow, worry swimming in his eyes. "The ER?"

"I was just volunteering for the day. Tagging along with my dad."

"Ah."

"I probably should have called." I look down at my bare feet, my flip-flops caked in baseball dust. "You know, give you some warning . . ."

"Nah. Your presence is not the kind of thing you need to warn me about."

He goes back to watching the game, totally content to just sit here and *be*. During our five days of total isolation, long silences were frequent—and necessary. Every breath was something to be savored, every word a small but undeniable expense of energy. Conversation, when it happened, always drifted to the same things: Food. Supplies. Weather.

But everything is different now. *We're* different. All the

pertinent topics are potential land mines: Family. Lee. Recovery. Nothing feels safe, except maybe Tim's baseball career.

And maybe that's the secret—maybe we don't have to talk
about anything. I came here for Tim, for no other reason than
to support him. Yes, there was always the possibility of seeing
Colin. Yes, I took the time to blow-dry my hair. But once it
dawns on me that we don't have to talk, that we can sit together like normal people and be okay, the overhead lights
aren't so intrusive and the silence feels more natural. After a
while, I'm cheering for Tim the way I used to do for my
brothers—with silly songs and rhyming chants that only
"stupid girls" use. Edward waited until last year to admit that
he actually liked those cheers; the whole team did.

The game ends with a mercy ruling, but the players barely
notice. After shaking hands with the victors, all fifteen of
Tim's teammates make a mad dash for the ice cream truck—
but not Tim. He waits for us behind home plate as Colin and I
climb down the bleachers.

"Thanks for coming, Avery!" Tim goes in for a hug, then
reconsiders when he remembers where he is. The other boys
are acting tough, high-fiving one another and kicking up dirt
at any and every opportunity. Tim's uniform is the cleanest of
the bunch.

I offer him a high five, which he giddily accepts. "Great
game, Tim," I say, meaning it more than he can possibly know.

"Thanks." He blushes. The lisp is still there, but less pronounced. The ache of a familiar memory grips me, then fades.

"Um, I have to talk to Colin for a minute," Tim says. "For
our postgame chat."

"Oh. Of course."

Colin tips Tim's hat as they walk over to the ice cream
truck, a playful gesture that reminds me of the bond that used

to exist between my brothers. Before any baseball discussion can take place, they get in line behind a rowdy group of boys. I'm not sure which is the priority: baseball tips or the post-game dessert. Either way, they both seem to savor it.

While Tim debates his options, his grandmother spreads her arms wide as she makes her way over to me. "Oh, Avery, we're just so glad you could come," she says, and pulls me into a hug. "Tim loved your letter. He reads it every night."

"I'm glad," I manage. There should have been a hundred letters. A *thousand*.

As this thought takes hold, Colin and Tim rejoin our tiny circle. Both their hands are covered in the goopy remains of ice cream sandwiches.

Mrs. Caldwell wipes Tim's fingers. "Goodness, this is going to wreak havoc with your sugars. Did Granddad remember your insulin?"

"*I* remembered, Grandmom. Don't worry." He looks up at her with one of his warm, endearing smiles, and all she can do is sigh.

Colin offers me an orange Creamsicle. "It's a little melted," Tim explains.

"Oh, that's fine." I make a complete mess of myself as I dig in. It's a mild night, almost springlike, but the ice cream doesn't stay solid for long. A part of me wonders if those ice cream trucks are kept at warmer temperatures because everything tastes better semimelted. Or maybe it just feels better, a child-hood memory that everyone shares.

"Did you have fun?" Tim asks me.

"*Me?*" I can't help but smile. "How about you?"

"Yeah." He thinks about this for a second. "I had fun."

"That catch you made in the fourth inning . . . wow. Everyone gasped." Which was true, although it might've been because a collision seemed imminent. Fortunately, the beastly first base-man tripped over his own ankles before mowing Tim down.

Tim beams. "Thanks. That one was tough."

"All right, Timmy," his grandmother says. "It's getting on to your bedtime."

"Grandmom!" He bristles, but it's mostly for show. "It's Friday night."

"Yes, well, you're seven, not seventeen."

"Okay," he mopes. With a final lick of his fingers, he hurls himself into Colin's arms and hugs him tight enough to leave arm prints in Colin's shirt. Watching them, I realize this un-encumbered display of affection hasn't changed at all since those days on the mountain. Colin hugs him right back, tip-ping the brim of Tim's cap as they go in for one last high five.

Then Tim turns to me, his smile slightly shy, like Colin, in a way. Shy but knowing. When he hugs me, it feels as though *I'm* the one holding on to *Tim*. He holds on for a long time—or maybe it's me, maybe it's always *been* me—and pulls away as gently as he dares. His cheeks are flushed, bits of ice cream sandwich sticking to his lips and chin. "I miss you, Avery," he says, four of the most beautiful words I've ever heard.

His grandparents take him by the hand, leading him un-der the haze of baseball lights and summer stars. He turns around twice, waving with the same unwavering enthusiasm, and then he's gone. His sudden absence leaves me reeling.

Colin, sensing this, puts his arm around my shoulders. There is nothing intimate about the gesture, nothing to sug-gest more than a connection shared by two good friends, if that's even what we are.

"It's a long season," he says.

31

Colin drives me home in his aging Honda, its interior packed to capacity with swim gear. Fins, paddles, kickboards, pull buoys. A pile of Speedos, drying on the front seat. The interior smells like sunscreen and summer, like humidity and open windows.

"Yeah, uh . . ." Colin hurls the Speedos into the backseat. "Sorry about that. The seat shouldn't be wet or anything."

The question burns on my lips: *Are you swimming again?* But he doesn't look my way, skirting any discussion as he shifts into gear. He handles the stick with ease this time, no longer grimacing or favoring his right side. A series of raised scars— some ragged, others clearly surgical—track up his arm to the base of his neck. He looks strong—not in the exact same way he was before but getting there. His massive hands grip the wheel like he's been doing it for years.

"How's the shoulder?" I ask.

He shakes it out a bit. "Oh. Better. Bug's been whipping it into shape."

"Bug?"

"My unofficial physical therapist."

I can't quite imagine what those sessions entail—probably hours upon hours of stretching, strengthening, and gritty determination. If Colin works as hard at PT as he does at practice, it's no wonder he's come this far. "Looks like you had an operation," I say.

"A few, actually. Rotator cuff repair, labral repair, bursectomy, a few debridements . . ."

"Wow."

"I came around a bit on the whole surgery thing."

"Got over your fear of blood?"

He smiles. "That, and my dad told me to stop feeling 'damn sorry for myself.' "

"Sounds like good advice," I say, careful to avoid any tonal hint of *I told you so.*

"It was. I should have listened to you months ago." He reaches for the dash and adjusts the air vents. "You okay, temperature-wise?"

"I'm fine."

He fiddles with the knobs until I have to put his hand back on the steering wheel. "I'm okay, Colin," I say gently.

"All right," he says, but he continues to glance over at me, ready to blast the A/C at the first sign of perspiration. Or heat, if I spring a goose bump.

I turn toward the window, finding solace in familiar scenery. Soon the college kids will be back and the cycle will start all over again. Summer, fall, winter. Humidity, amber sunsets, snow. Tourists, students. The change from year to year is subtle but enough to notice, enough to miss when it's not a part of your life anymore.

"I stopped swimming," I say.

Colin tenses, then coasts to a stop as the light up ahead turns red. We're alone in the intersection—no other cars, no distractions. No escape from a conversation I haven't had with anyone. "I almost drowned at practice."

The light turns green, but we remain there, idling. It's a quiet night, almost lonely. The sidewalks are deserted; the narrow streets leading to and from the local hospitals have taken on the appearance of late-night alleyways. Everyone's gone home.

After another cycle of light changes, Colin shifts into gear. He still hasn't said anything, but the tension in his jaw tells me he wants to say quite a bit. Maybe he wants me to elaborate. Maybe he isn't sure where to even begin.

The last stretch of the ride brings us through a sparsely wooded park, onto a bridge that overlooks the T. The platform is already swollen with young people, their workweek over and their weekend just beginning. I watch them, and I wonder, *Will it ever be like that for us?*

He makes the final turn onto my street. Up ahead, my house beckons with its sultry, summery glow. Colin seems to sense my inertia, his hand hovering over the ignition as he puts the car in neutral. I know what he's thinking: If he leaves the key in, it means the night's over, time to go. If he takes it out . . . well, I don't know. Usually if a guy takes the key out of the ignition on a night like this, it means he wants to make out. There isn't much middle ground.

As the debate rages (or maybe it's just in my head), my mom pokes her head out the bedroom window, sparing Colin the agony—and implications—of that choice. She beams at us, waving both arms. Colin laughs.

"Sharp eyes up there," he says.

"Very."

He waves at my mom, then puts his hand back on the ignition. "Well . . ."

"Well." This shouldn't be an awkward moment. It shouldn't be a moment at all.

"You free tomorrow morning?" he asks.

I steal a glance at the upstairs windows, but my stealthy mother has disappeared. "I think so. What time?"

"Six?"

"Wow. Okay."

Do the buses even run that early? Doesn't matter; I'll find a way to get there.

"What's wrong?" he asks.

"I, uh . . . I don't have a car . . ."

"I'll pick you up."

"No way, it's too far—"

"Too far?"

I exhale long and slow, conceding the stupidity of that logic. "Okay."

"Great." Colin leans over to my side, his T-shirt grazing my thighs as he pushes open the door. I inhale deeply, but it does nothing to temper a sudden gasp of nerves. "By the way, whatever happened to that purple suit of yours?"

"Why?" My stomach flips. "Are we going swimming tomorrow?"

Before he can answer, a bedroom window slams shut. Colin laughs. "I think your mom's up there with a telescope."

"Wouldn't shock me."

"Anyway," he says.

"Anyway."

His foot stays on the clutch. His gaze stays on me.

"I had a good time tonight," I say.

"Good."

"Did you?"

"Of course."

His hand is still on the keys, a bottle opener dangling from the key chain. "Well . . ."

"Well——"

"Wait!" My mom runs down the porch with a tray of peppermint bark, which she makes twelve months out of the year. "I made this."

"Mom, it's summer," I say, laughing.

"Well, I don't see your friend complaining."

"Not at all." Colin selects a healthy chunk. "Looks delicious."

"Why, thank you," she says, utterly charmed. Then I realize they've never met before.

"Uh, Mom, this is Colin Shea." I make the necessary introductions, remembering how he did the same for me all those months ago. "Colin, this is my mom."

"Pleased to finally meet you," she says, emphasizing the *finally*. She puts her elbows on the window frame and leans inside.

"So," she says, settling in for a long conversation, "how was the game?"

Sometime later, Colin takes the key out of the ignition. He stays for a long time, longer than I ever imagined he would. It's wrong to think it, but sometime over the course of the night, it happens anyway:

I wish he would stay forever.

●

Six o'clock in the morning comes after a sleepless night, but not the kind that warrants a psychiatrist or troubles my parents. By the time Colin pulls up in front of my house, dawn has announced itself, the sky fraught with glinting reds and yellows. A cool breeze whips through open windows. I put on shorts and a hoodie, the sleeves pulled down over my fists.

Colin opens the passenger door, always the gentleman.

The interior is surprisingly toasty, just as I suspected it would be. Toasty but empty. "What happened to your mobile swim business?" I ask, laughing.

"Yeah . . . I took care of that." He palms his head, a telltale sign of nerves I remember well. "Are you warm enough?"

"Perfect," I say, though he still fiddles with the vents. This habit may never change, but I kind of like that he cares so much.

We drive in the direction of Fenway, then on toward downtown, navigating the streets in a natural silence. Long before we get there, I know exactly where we're going.

The sky is a sultry blue by the time we pull up to the Dorchester community pool. Although the parking lot is empty, the neighborhood pulses with activity. People are already out and about, heading to weekend jobs, tending to tidy gardens, chatting with neighbors. The corner store across the street teems with early risers, the hearty scent of pastries and coffee drifting through the car's open windows.

Colin fishes a bag out of the trunk and slings it over his shoulder. He gives me a gentle nod. "Ready?"

"Colin . . ." I stare at the cracked blacktop. "You don't understand. I can't swim—"

"Who said anything about you swimming?"

I fumble for a response, but he's already walking toward the gate. To unlock it, he uses a set of keys with a fake Olympic medal as its key chain.

"Issued by the pool," he explains.

"You work here?"

He smirks. "When they let me."

After a tense walk through a narrow hallway, the pool unfolds before us in all its urban glory. The water is a magical, silken blue bordered by cracked cement and a haphazard display of lawn chairs. The lane lines are a faded, tired red, and the lifeguard stands look about forty years old. A lonely diving board looms over the deep end. It's nothing like the pools I've been swimming in for the last two years, embellished with bleachers and electronics and endless banners proclaiming past achievements. The Dorchester community pool doesn't even have starting blocks. It's just water glistening under a familiar summer sun. It's *safe*.

He escorts me over to the shallow end, a warm-up area for children just learning to swim. The pool here is only three feet deep, which would make any college coach squirm. Shallow pools are notoriously slow, which is all that really matters at the elite level. Deep water means fast times, and fast times spell championships. Anything else is considered subpar, barely deserving of "pool" status.

Colin peels off his shirt, careful to do so with minimal fanfare. I'm so used to seeing him in sleek Speedos at practice that I can't seem to get over the sight of his floral-print swim trunks. Not that I linger very long on his swimming attire; his bare chest steals my attention for a full minute. He was always so lean and toned. So natural. The only thing different now is the array of scars tracking down his right shoulder.

I force myself to look south—not that this is a stellar idea, either. "Nice swim trunks," I say, trying to sound casual.

He blushes as he shoves his hands in his pockets. "Christmas present from my sisters."

"I like them."

"Thanks."

His breath hitches. Maybe I'm not as alone as I thought. Being so close to the water, so close to him, brings me to the brink of memory, of fear. Even here, even now, thousands of miles and thousands of hours removed from the source of all the trouble, I'm afraid.

But unlike everyone else—my parents, the doctors, even Lee—Colin doesn't look at me like damaged goods, frustrated by my inability to confront something so benign. He doesn't coax me to the water's edge. He doesn't ask me how it feels to look at a pool.

"I'm not getting in," I say, though he doesn't ask. I just want to clear the air. Admit my failures before he has to learn about them the hard way.

"I know."

"Then why did you bring me here?"

"I dunno," he says, though the gleam in his eyes tells me he does.

With that, he jumps off the ledge. The crisp, rain-chilled water splashes my legs, reminding me of my earliest days learning to swim: the agony of getting in for the very first time, the pressure of watchful eyes, the bite of cold water. Other memories—the plane, the lake, the taste of melted snow—retreat to the back of my mind.

I sit on the wet cement, savoring the sun as it warms my back. Colin slices through the water, swimming with the kind of smooth, languid magnificence that so few creatures can claim. It's mesmerizing. I could sit here all day, all summer, just watching him swim.

After a while, he coasts into the wall, filling his lungs with a giant breath as he surfaces in front of me. He rests his elbows on the concrete and gazes into my eyes. When he frowns, it takes me a second to realize what's wrong.

I'm crying.

"Avery . . ."

"I left you behind."

He takes my hands, and pool water drips down my wrists and onto my legs. It reminds me of a dozen childhood summers, the happiest days of my life.

I say it again. "I left you behind, and then I lied about what happened."

"You didn't lie. You didn't want to talk about it. I understand that."

"I *lied*, Colin. I made it sound as though those days never happened."

"*I* know they happened. *You* know. The boys know." He climbs onto the deck beside me. "Who else matters?"

"The boys don't know," I say. "I only wrote one letter after the crash. A good-bye letter, for each of them." It takes me a moment to choke out, "I never told them anything."

"You will." His voice is kind, his eyes a vibrant, telling blue. In that moment, he looks so much like his mother it takes my breath away.

"I will?"

"Avery, we all grieve on our own time line. We all have our fears and failures. My shoulder, for one thing. I was tempted to twist it off my own body for months." He tries to smile. "I gave up on it."

"But you're swimming now."

"Yes," he says. "Today."

"Today?" My eyes go wide. "Today is your first day back in the pool?"

"That's right."

"But your mobile swim business . . ."

"Small steps."

Still, his weaknesses seem tiny compared to mine. Three little boys were counting on me, and I let them down.

"I should have been here," I say.

"Then stay."

My response is automatic, a denial that feels like a vow. "I can't."

The fact that he doesn't argue makes it worse, a thousand times worse. I pull my legs onto the deck, sensing the absence of water as intensely as a physical loss. It pools in the grooves of my fingers, the shallows of my soul.

●

The Saturday swims turn into Saturday lessons at nine o'clock. Colin has been teaching the neighborhood kids since he was fifteen, and it shows. The younger ones clamor for space in his classes, while some of the eight- and nine-year-olds are now formidable swimmers on the local team. Colin was there when they took that first leap, when they swam their first strokes. If this pool had a mascot, it would be him.

While Colin teaches, I sit in one of the lawn chairs and watch. It surprises me how easily I'd forgotten the familiar sounds of kids learning to swim: the cries, the protests, the whimpers; then, inevitably, the laughter. Some have no fear whatsoever. They just march toward the edge of the pool and tumble in, their parents gasping as Colin scoops them into his arms. Others hate everything about the water: the shifting surface, the coolness, the depth. But even for them, there always comes a moment of sudden, breathtaking awe—the moment they learn to trust it. Not just the water but themselves.

I'm processing this utter transformation when a little girl tugs on my shorts. Her bathing suit is a faded, beloved purple, with orange swirls. Her hot pink goggles match her crooked cap. She looks like me at six years old. She could be me.

"Are you the other teacher?" she asks me.

"I, um . . ."

"With Colin. You're here every week."

Colin smiles from across the deck but makes no move to join the conversation. The girl studies me, her goggles fogging up even as she talks.

"I just watch," I say.

"Why?"

"Because . . ." I take a breath. "Because I'm scared of the water."

"Oh." She seems to think about this. "Why?"

Because it's so cold, and foreign, and hopeless. Because I thought we were going to die out there. Because it's everything I ever loved, and now it's everything I've ever hated.

"I don't know," I whisper.

"Come with me," she says, and gives my hand a tug. Colin watches as she leads me to the water's edge, our bare toes curling around the sun-beaten cement. This isn't the shallow end; it's deep, and blue, and fraught with uncertainty. It's where people drown.

"I can't—"

She tightens her grip. Colin comes up beside us, his familiar, summery scent washing over me as he takes my other hand. The fluttering in my chest subsides. The ripples of panic in my throat sink back down.

"I won't let go," he says to me.

And then we jump.

32

Dawn over the lake breaks with a hum, soft and musical.

Every summer, the town of Brookline hosts outdoor concerts a few blocks from our house. The sound of their revelry was always just within range, though the finer details were lost, swallowed by the street noise. Only the echo of something faintly instrumental ever made it to my window.

This sound is like that, but couched in blackness. It grows louder, building and building until it fractures the silence, this dark, eerie hour—everything. The cold snaps up my spine like a jolt of electricity. My face and fingers are numb. My nose is crusted in ice. I try to lick my lips, but my tongue feels fat and dry, and my muscles won't respond to the command.

The hum is now a drone. A roar. An engine.

A plane.

My vision takes an agonizing moment to clear. Colin's eyes are closed, his lips tinged blue. The boys are still curled up in our laps, their bodies warm—*warm!*—to the touch. I don't have the time or forethought to rouse them. I just go.

I try to kick open the door, but snow is everywhere. Four, maybe five feet high, surrounding us on all sides. My first thought is an avalanche—*How else could there be so much snow?* Then I remember the storm's final phases: the lightning, the hail, the violent gusts of wind. We must be buried in a snowdrift.

Placing both hands on the roof, I push upward with my back, legs, and shoulders. The fuselage barely moves. I try again, fighting the electric pain in my hands and arms, the relentless ache in my ribs. For what feels like hours, this process continues. Finally, something shifts and one of the slabs gives way. I clamor up and out and into the snow.

Dawn. Calm, scarlet skies, the snow-capped peaks casting shadows on the valley below. Everything is breathlessly clear. Not a cloud in the sky.

In this scene of perfect stillness, the hum has gone silent.

No. *No.* I want to cry. Scream. Hurl myself into the abyss of this godforsaken lake and succumb. After all we've been through, how much we've survived . . .

I drag myself toward the water's edge, no longer knowing why or how or for what purpose——something simply draws me there, an invisible force tugging at my soul. My body doesn't feel like mine anymore. I'm so cold and tired. So utterly spent after days in a wilderness that hasn't shown a shred of mercy.

Then, of course, I see it. The orange duffel bag floating an impossible distance from shore. The blowing ice and snow scratched my corneas, and it's hard to see much of anything. But I know it's out there. That stupid bag and the unreachable cabin are the only constants in this savage, ever-changing place.

Cold, clear water laps at my feet. I'm not the teenager who swam across Otsego Lake, a placid but solid nine miles. I'm not the eighteen-year-old who swam to Alcatraz on one of our family vacations out west. I'm weak, and exhausted, and as close to death as I've ever been.

But as Colin would say, I'm still a *swimmer.* A distance swimmer. And there is a distance before me now, a deathly stretch from here to there.

I *have* to do this. For the families we left behind, for the one I found out here. Tim, Liam, Aayu.

Colin.

The air smacks my bare skin as I peel off my heavy layers: gloves first, then hat and boots and everything else. The stinging lashes don't affect me as much anymore. I'm numb. My legs wobble as I shuffle toward the water's edge, my knees giving way as the icy water meets my toes. For so many years, this sensation was entirely different; getting wet was like coming home. Now it feels like my final act. A battle waged against a cruel mistress who doesn't care about all those years, all those memories. I never belonged in the water. I never belonged *here.*

My brain squeezes like a fist as I dive in, recoiling against the cold. The first few strokes are a desperate, ugly effort. Shoulders aching, chest splintering with each breath. It's more than pain; it's agony, visceral and electric. An icy blackness encroaches my vision, stealing my ability to form a coherent thought. My first and only urge is to sleep—how sublime it would be to sleep.

Somehow, I find my rhythm: arms reaching, hips rolling, the two-beat kick. These motions sustain me onward, across a body of water so expansive it seems never to end. I'm nearing the limits of my reserves when the orange bag floats into my grasp.

The bottom is charred black, but the label is somehow intact: EMERGENCY. I loop one of the straps around my ankle, but it must be snagged on something because it resists me after a few strokes. I pull hard, thrashing and yanking and treading

water, trying to set it free while staying afloat in frigid temperatures. Numbness gives way to fear. A vacant sky littered
with distant stars and a crescent moon mocks my efforts. I
want to scream, but my muscles are numb, my lungs cold and
raw and failing.

You're going to make it.

Colin's voice sweeps through me, and although it's just a
memory, it feels real, heightened somehow. It reminds me of
the last time he made that promise—and the fervor with
which he kept it. It makes those thoughts of giving up a little
less visceral.

So I keep fighting it, until finally, finally, the strap gives
way—

And the bag rips open.

I'm too clumsy with cold to catch the contents: Bottled
water, packets of food, medicines. Something plastic and angular that feels like a flare gun. I will never know for sure. All
that matters is that hope, once again, is lost.

I tread water for a precious few seconds. My head throbs,
my muscles ache, and it feels, impossibly, like I'm burning
alive. Another ten minutes out here, and I will freeze to death,
then drown. A swimmer's worst nightmare—and certainly
mine, since that day fifteen years ago when my father sat me
down at the kitchen table and explained what it meant to die.

Ahead of me, the opposite shore looms in all its impossible,
terrifying mystery. I never thought I could make it, but I'm
halfway there now. Three-quarters of a mile to that damn
cabin, maybe a little less. Fifteen minutes if I swim to the
point of exhaustion. If it takes me longer than that, I won't
make it at all.

Every stroke is harder than the last, and my rhythm deteriorates into clumsy, disjointed movements. My legs float behind me like deadweight, a motor with no engine. I can barely breathe. The frigid water fists my heart, hard, and takes hold. I wait for my lungs to give out and my arms to stop working.

In the meantime, I keep swimming.

The shore draws closer, but not fast enough, because the cold finally wins, and my body sighs with exhaustion, and my legs sink—

And hit stones. Soft, polished stones.

Land.

Then: music. A soft hum cresting the mountains and rolling into the valley like an approaching train. Or no, not a train—a *plane.*

My legs refuse to carry me, so I crawl through snow to the tree line. My blood must have frozen because my fingers are a stony white, my skin dusted with ice crystals. And yet my heart keeps beating and my lungs keep breathing, which gives me purpose. The cabin is just ahead. Reachable. *Real.*

I punch open the tiny window and crawl inside. A brief search yields flares—a dozen of them stacked in piles like orange cigars. I carry the box back down to the water's edge and into the open. It takes only a second to set the first flare, and a second more to let it go.

It rains across the sky in a dusting arc, a blaze of color that reminds me of Boston's epic fireworks display. I set off another flare, and another, even after the plane—or no, it's a helicopter—changes course. It sails over the black surface of the lake, suspended in boundless skies as it accelerates in my direction. Its approach fills me with a strange sense of undeserved accomplishment. It doesn't feel real, like I'm dreaming someone else's dream, imagining someone else's rescue.

As it lands, the world in front of me starts to break apart. Distant shouts, then voices, filter into my consciousness, but everything seems so far away. I know this feeling; I've experienced it many times before, in what feels like a hundred different lifetimes.

I'm underwater—drowning, drifting.

Gone.

●

I wake sometime later to the sound of churning propellers and shouting. A team of people are unloading me off the helicopter onto the roof of a building.

"Wait." I manage to grasp someone's arm. "Wait!"

No one hears me. I palm the oxygen mask and rip it off my face.

"The others," I rasp. "The others, please . . ."

The gurney I'm lying on jerks to a stop. A female doctor with startling gray eyes and a midwestern accent leans in close, her ear nearly touching my lips.

"What did you say?"

"The others."

She gives me a blank look that haunted me then; it haunts me still.

"What others?"

T he chlorine stings the whites of my eyes, but it's nothing like the icy burn of a glacial lake. It's familiar. Normal. Everything is blurred but somehow heightened. The little girl with pink goggles grins at me, then kicks her way to the surface.

Colin's eyes are open, too, but he doesn't go anywhere. He grasps both my hands, holding on to them as he promised he would. We sit on the bottom of the pool, our legs stretched in front of us, bubbles rising to the surface.

Thank you, I say, mouthing the words so he can understand.

As we float to the surface, everything suddenly comes into focus. Our story isn't about two star-crossed lovers who survived five days in the wilderness.

It's about two people who found their way home.

34

With the exception of Tim's baseball games, my interactions with Colin are limited to the Dorchester community pool. His days are busy, with work and classes and family obligations. We live from Saturday to Saturday, until one day, the routine changes.

I'm on the porch, listening to the drone of the late-summer cicadas, when Colin arrives just after dawn. He opens the car door, stealing a glance at my shoulders as I climb in. He's looking for swimsuit straps, which he does every time he picks me up. As usual, he sees only my bare, freckled skin.

After fiddling with the vents—"Are you warm enough?"—and being chastised—"It's eighty degrees outside!"—he focuses on the road. He taps the steering wheel as he drives, a rare display of nervous energy. Every minute or so, his phone beeps with a message.

"Someone really wants you," I say, angling for a view of the display.

"My sisters," he says. "They're wondering where I am."

"At six thirty on a Saturday?"

"I'm on breakfast duty every Friday, but I missed yesterday. Had to go to work early because one of the guys had chest pain."

"Oh."

"He's okay, don't worry—back to work in the afternoon," he says, like this kind of thing happens all the time. "But it really devastated the Shea breakfast routine."

"You must be a good cook if they're texting you at the crack of dawn."

"Terrible, actually." He glances over at me again to see if I'm shivering. "You cold?"

"I'm fine, Colin."

He will never accept this, but at least now it's a bit of an inside joke.

"We can skip the pool today, if you want." I roll down the window, suddenly desperate for air.

Colin's response comes before the words are even out of my mouth. "We'd love to have you," he says. Then, a little embarrassed: "I just hope you're not hungry."

"Why? Is there not enough food? I could run to the store—"

"Because I've yet to cook an edible meal."

I give him a look that says, *Yeah right.*

"I'm serious."

"You used to make a delicious chip soup."

He smiles, and the tension in my belly—wherever it came from, whatever it means—blossoms into something almost like warmth.

●

Breakfast at the Shea household is a spirited affair. There is no real order to it, despite Colin's role as chef, cook, waiter, etc. His sisters spend most of the prep time sprinting from bedroom to bathroom to bedroom again, getting ready for their various activities. A household of teenage girls—*whoa*. My mom could barely handle one.

Colin explains their various obligations: The youngest, Corinne, has summer camp. Elizabeth failed gym ("a total scam," she explains), so she's on her way to Saturday classes. And the eldest, Lauren, volunteers at a nursing home down the street. They offer sporadic details at a rapid clip, their Boston accents so thick it sometimes requires clarification. Colin tells me they're just hamming it up; they like to mess with folks from "Snobsville."

Corinne, though, is shy and deferential, like her big brother. Once we're sitting down, she asks me thoughtful questions about my interests and listens with rapt attention. She looks about thirteen, a startling image of her mother.

"You're so pretty," she says. "Just like Colin said you were."

The other girls glare at her, as if she's just spilled some terrible secret. Colin's short hair does nothing to hide the blush creeping up his neck as he flips the pancakes.

"Thank you," I say. "You know, you look just like your mom."

She beams. "Really? She was so beautiful. Even when she lost her hair." She stares at her empty plate for a long moment. "Did you know Colin shaved his head to make her feel better about it? I know the team only does it for big meets and stuff, but he kept it that way for a really long time—"

"Done!" Colin announces, clicking off the burners with an air of finality. Sweat trickles down his brow, which he wipes with the back of his arm. His collar is damp, his skin glistening. He smells good, though. Somehow, he always smells good.

If he heard Corinne, he doesn't show it—nor does he comment on my silence. He says nothing as he serves a heaping stack of pancakes, a pile of eggs, crisp bacon and toast, and an impressive assortment of accoutrements. The eggs are a little runny, and the bacon is on the charred end of the spectrum, but no one seems to notice.

Colin and the girls mutter a lightning-fast prayer, barely a mumbling of the lips. "My mom's tradition," Corinne explains via whisper. Then we dig in.

The food is gone in minutes, attacked by a crowd of hungry teenagers. Colin returns to the stove twice to replenish the plates, and by the time he finally sits down for good, the girls are already out the door, yelling good-byes and telling him to pick them up at such and such time.

A draft of cooler air sweeps inside, melting into the heat. Even the walls look like they're perspiring.

"You do this every Friday?" I ask, as the door slams behind them.

"Used to do it every day." He samples a helping of cold eggs. "After my mom died, I tried really hard to keep some of her traditions going. But doing this on a daily basis wore me out. Now it's just Fridays and whatever other day I can manage—like today."

I wait for him to say more about his mom—about those last few days, the sacrifices he made to make things easier for her. But Colin never was much of a sharer. He sips his orange juice in a contemplative silence.

"Do you miss her?" I finally ask.

He nods, the smile on his face wistful but not sad. "All the time."

For just a moment, he closes his eyes and breathes it in: the hum of the ancient, wheezy air conditioner, the absence of chatty girls and all their obligations, the quiet of a weekend morning. Then he sees the aftermath of a family meal, and it's back to reality again. He gets to his feet.

"I'll clean," I tell him. "You rest."

He gestures to the huge stack of dishes. "I didn't bring you over here to clean up after five people."

"The cook never cleans."

"This cook does," he says.

I glare at him before heading over to the sink. The truce lasts for about a minute before Colin joins me, dish towels in hand. It's even hotter over by the stove—or maybe it's just him. His body heat has a languid, seductive effect. I just want to lean into him.

Hot water from the faucet fogs the glass, obscuring the view of the neighbors' small but tidy yards. I turn it to cold—ice cold, as far as it will go. I try to focus on the dishes. The homey, flowery china. The old jelly jars substituting as glasses. The pots and pans and . . .

He reaches over me, his hand grazing mine as he turns off the faucet. The sudden contact makes me dizzy. The way he lingers—a shade of a second, just enough for me to notice—makes me feel something else entirely.

Something like wanting.

I put the plates down and turn, slowly, to face him. My hands are dripping wet, my skin slick with sweat. It's a strange, luxurious feeling—a kind of reckless abandon. There is no hope for propriety in hundred-degree heat. I back up against the sink and run my wet hands through my hair. It doesn't help much, not like I expected or even wanted it to.

Colin clears his throat. "Hot?" he asks.

"Hot as hell," I murmur.

He smiles, but there is nothing soft or shy about it. His mind is elsewhere—on my hands, my hair, my soaked shirt. His voice sounds deep and husky. "Good thing my sisters aren't here to chastise you."

"Good thing."

His eyes turn a shade darker as the teasing smile fades. He takes a step closer, and my shoulder blades hit the cabinets above the sink, arched and waiting. I wait for him to touch me again, to say everything I'm feeling, but he doesn't. He seems suspended in a lonely in-between—the place we've occupied for months.

So I just say it. "I fell in love with you."

I take a step forward, indulging in the heat and charge and mystery of him. He holds my gaze with a feverish intensity, but he otherwise stands very still. I look up into those glorious blue eyes, wondering how I ever doubted the conviction there. How I ever doubted *him.*

"I love you, Colin." My voice breaks, but I don't care. I want him to see me cry. I want him to know I was wrong, I was weak, I was terrified. "Colin, say something—"

Then he kisses me.

●

It isn't like our last kiss. This one is all heat and fire, bare skin and sultry sweat. An exploration that takes place in ways that are new yet familiar, this coming together of need and desire that never had a chance in a frigid nowhere. He tastes like mint and oranges, like a summer morning. I give in to it, breathing him in, dizzy with the scent and feel and taste of him. The kiss deepens. Frantic, fast, everywhere. I love the roughness of his hands, the ease with which he pulls me close. He's so strong. I can feel his muscles working against me, his hips driving into mine. He lifts me up like I weigh nothing at all.

He carries me toward the living room and up the stairs, careful to dodge the haphazard array of backpacks and textbooks littering the hallway. He knows this house. Knows its secrets, its quirks. There is no uncertainty in our hasty trek from kitchen to bedroom.

We're barely over the threshold when he stops. "Fuck, it's hot," he breathes, and continues down the hall. He's kissing my neck when we bump into the bathroom door, stumble over the raised tiles, and end up in the bathtub. He turns on the shower and a sheet of deliciously cold water rains down on us. The change in temperature surges through me like an electric charge. My back hits the tiles, my legs still hiked around his waist. I open my eyes to see him breathing hard, his eyes swimming with desire. Water snakes down his face, his neck, his shoulders, until finally finding its way to his soaked T-shirt. He never even bothered to take it off.

So I do it for him. Slower now, fingers grasping fabric. I love the way he feels; I *remember* the way he feels. Strong. Warm. Vulnerable in ways that go so much deeper than physical scars. The water from the showerhead roams his shoulders and pools in my hands. I let my fingers wander up to his chest, a flutter of movement against his skin. He tenses. His heart thrums to the beat of rushing water.

"Don't stop," he whispers.

I kiss his hands, his wrists, his bare, beautiful chest. He says my name and it reaches, somehow, across months of memory and pain and regret, and it finds me in a place that feels safe, and whole, and right.

I'm glad it was you.

He lets me linger, then kisses me again. The newness of it makes my blood hum, but Colin isn't like anyone I've ever kissed. He seems to know me. My wants, needs, desires. Our tempo has a duality to it, a naturalness that goes beyond mutual understanding. I'm not trying to breathe right, or turn my head the right way, or kiss him the way he wants me to. I don't think about those things at all.

When I'm with him, I never have to.

"Stay," he breathes against my hair. There is nothing polite about the way he says this, no tentative gentility in his hard, needful gaze. *Stay.* As if the word itself has physical power.

He leans back, hands sliding from my jaw. When he sees the gooseflesh on my skin, he turns the water off, but instead of losing its magic, the moment gains a surreal, tangible sadness. I feel as though my very soul is separating.

"Stay," he says again.

Stay.

Swim.

Breathe.

I never doubted him when he willed me to survive. His conviction carried five people from the wilds of Colorado to the comforts of Boston; in so many ways, he brought us home.

And now, here, at *my* hand, it ends. I can't stand to look at him as I shake my head, stumble out of the tub, and leave him behind.

This time, there won't be any going back.

35

I spend the fading weeks of summer at my old desk—laptop cast aside, hands cramping despite the stress ball on the shelf. Two pens have already run out of ink. The stack of paper next to my weathered paperbacks dwindles by the hour.

I write until dawn breaks over the city.

I write until it feels like I can't possibly write another word.

I write until my sorrow turns to pain, and then I know I'm getting somewhere.

On the last Saturday of the summer, I ask Edward to drive me to a tidy house in Newton. He owes me one for the schoolyard disaster yesterday, where a sword fight (with baseball bats) at one of his elementary schools ended with stitches over my left eye and a bloody nose.

I tried some makeup, but the skin is still inflamed, the sutures obvious. Edward closes the mirror on the sun visor with a decisive thump.

"You look great. The stitches add character."

I take a breath, but my nerves are frayed beyond physiologic repair. The stack of pages in my lap suddenly feels like it weighs a hundred pounds. I tried for a decent presentation, but some of the papers are crinkled, and quite a few have cross-outs. A number of pages look like they went through a washing machine—stiff with dried tears, emotions laid bare.

I should have written less. More. Fewer details. Richer details. I should have left out the part about the pregnant woman, or the bear, or the way the snow sounded right before dawn. What if they read this when they're too young to process it? What if they *never* read it?

"Edward . . ."

He lays a gentle hand on my shoulder. "This story was never meant for anyone but them," he says. "It doesn't have to be perfect. It just has to be *yours*."

Mine. *Ours.* I wonder if Colin's version of events would play out any differently. *What would Colin think about Tim saying he loved me?* Our story, in this sense, is incomplete. I suppose now it always will be.

"Thank you," I say.

"Don't thank me," he says. "You did all the work."

Recounting those five days in all their harrowing detail *was* work—harder, in some ways, than getting back in the pool, or going back to college, or even swimming across that desolate lake under hopeless skies. Dr. Shin knew how hard it would be. Colin knew. And Edward . . . Well, Edward's my big brother, and he knows everything.

We approach the quaint, colonial-style home that sits under a swath of maple trees. The sun shines warmly on its red brick walls, and its bright, lived-in feel reminds me of my own house in Brookline.

I don't have to ring the doorbell. As it turns out, I didn't have to worry about the neat stack of pages under my arm, or even the walk across the lawn, which felt like a journey of a thousand miles. The boys know I'm here. As Edward says, they've probably been up since dawn, waiting for me.

Liam tackles me first—stocky arms and a big grin, which grows even wider when he recognizes Edward. Four years old, and he could probably name every player on every team in the American League. Maybe the National, too.

Aayu approaches us with more reserve. He watches me for a long moment before letting go of his grandmother's hand. His amber eyes soften. He knows who I am.

He remembers.

"Pretty," he says, and smiles.

My heart soars.

●

Unlike Edward, my father lacks the subtlety gene. I had planned on spending my last night in Brookline adhering to the same routine of dinner, Internet, and sleep, but it takes a turn when Dad offers to take me out for ice cream. He hasn't blown off work since I was eight years old, and only then after a particularly brutal afternoon in the ER that, even now, he refuses to talk about. My mind considers all sorts of reasons to explain this strange behavior. Does he want to propose additional psychiatry appointments? A stint in an institution? Maybe he wants to talk about "my future" (ugh). Or maybe he just has a craving for ice cream.

I climb into the front seat and buckle myself in. He's a seat belt nazi, always has been, and he won't start the car until he hears it click. Tonight, though, he barely glances my way. I don't know if it's because he trusts me or because he's preoccupied. He grips the wheel in his usual ten-two, white-knuckled position and fixates on the road ahead.

For a while, we coast along in silence. I find myself admiring the prim, regal homes, the lush gardens and crooked maple trees. The echoes of Brookline's weekly concert series float through the open windows. I close my eyes, hearing the dissonant sounds of conversation as it mingles with the melody. I think about Tim, and Liam, and Aayu. About their new families, their new lives. I wonder if they will remember me five, ten, twenty years from now.

When I open my eyes again, a different scene plays out in front of me.

A pool. *My* pool.

We pull into the lot. Every space is occupied, so Dad has to park on the grass. A sign hangs from the front gate: POOL CLOSED FOR MEET. The cheers of parents, kids, and coaches float over the hum of cicadas. This is nothing like the white noise of my entourage back at school. This is swimming for the love of the game, as Edward would say.

We stay in the car, windows down. The fence that separates us from the pool grounds is moderately nicer than the one in Dorchester but still a little grungy, a little used. I remember wrapping my hands around the links as a kid, my fingers sticky with ice cream and Popsicle juice. Maybe the residue is still there, buried deep.

I steal a glance at my dad. "You want to get ice cream here?"

"Why not? I'm sure there's a snack bar in there."

Of course there's a snack bar. Half the swimmers are only there for the food—the homemade sweets, the hot dogs, the ice pops and candy bars. Our coaches always told us to hold off on pigging out until after the meet, but it's hard to explain delayed gratification to a nine-year-old. I swam with stomach cramps more times than I'd like to remember.

"You didn't take me here for ice cream, did you?"

He doesn't say anything as he stares straight ahead, lost in the sights and sounds of a distant memory. My dad was never a swimmer, and baseball consumed much of his free time, but he made every effort to watch me swim. For years, he sat in the same spot on the bleachers with a stopwatch and a clipboard. My friends called him crazy; their parents preferred *eccentric*. I didn't care. I always swam my best when he was there.

He folds his arms, as if steeling himself to say something. "Look, Avery," he finally says, "I'm no good at lectures. And to be honest, lectures are pointless. I can't tell the bad residents how to be good doctors. They've got to learn it on their own. Make mistakes. Give patients bad news. Realize their own shortcomings." He finally looks over at me, and I can tell this isn't easy for him. "You know, when those folks finally got their shit together and found you on that mountain, I wasn't the least bit surprised. You're a survivor. Stronger than all your brothers put together."

He puts his hands on his knees because his hands, steady as ever, have begun to shake. He hasn't spoken this many words to me since the day I left for college.

"Dad—"

"I'm not done."

"Okay," I say, sinking a bit in my seat.

"But sometimes we need a little help along the way. Doesn't matter if you're freezing your ass off next to some glacier or just trying to get your feet wet. Don't be afraid to ask for it, Avery. And don't feel like there's any shame in needing it."

I nod, still unsure what to say to all this. My dad, the tough survivalist. The epitome of independence. The cutthroat ER doc who intimidates even the most senior surgeons when he has to—whatever it takes to help a patient. I'm not a patient anymore, but maybe he still sees me this way. Maybe he sees all of his children this way.

"We like having you home." He puts his hands back on the wheel. "You're always welcome here."

He sighs, like he's searching for the right thing to say. "You know, when I was your age I went halfway across the world to study glassblowing for a while."

"Glassblowing?"

He waves this off, but something in his expression softens at the memory. "Yeah. I went to some crazy hut in the jungle and made vases that looked more like bedpans. After that, I finagled my way into an Ivy and chugged beer for a few years. Then I got a job—all kinds of jobs. Finance, research, law. I worked as a park ranger for a while, looking for hawks." He chuckles at this, remembering. "In any case, I did it all. It took me fifteen years to come back here, to realize all that soul-searching was just a great big circular path. Why do you think I work in an emergency room?

"Because it's chaos?"

He cracks a smile. "Because it feels *right* to me. Always has." He watches the pool for a beat. "You need to listen to that."

"Are you saying you don't want me to go back?"

"No." He glances at me, then back at the fence and the pool beyond. "I'm saying you should, if that's the life you want."

"I thought it was," I say, hearing the past tense.

I watch the water for what feels like hours, reliving my childhood in the races, cheers, and nervous energy of young kids experiencing the first taste of pressure and competition. There are other details, too: Coaches on deck, instructing little kids on legal stroke mechanics. Four little girls getting assembled for a relay. Two best friends playing Spit in the damp grass, their cards wrinkled from daily use. I have the sudden urge to go out there and be a part of it. To spit in my goggles and fix my crooked cap and grab the blocks like I know what I'm doing. At their age, I had no idea; I just wanted to swim. The buzzer would sound, and Edward would yell my name, and the water would wash over me like magic.

Then it hits me: *Before* isn't just aquamarine pools and California skies, parties and lush green campuses. A boyfriend with a peculiar but interesting accent. Middle-distance races and Fall Qualifiers and Scary Tan telling me to kick faster than a dead president.

Before is also Brookline. It's this pool. It's my house that groans and creaks and rejects air conditioners like a bad meal. It's my street, always covered in leaves or snow or spring blossoms, depending on the season. *Before* is the ER my father took me to as a little girl, a place where I learned about survival. It's the city bus that delivered me to grade school, and middle school, and high school. It's those eight white letters, glittering on the list of departures: BOSTON, MA.

After is who I am now.

And I think I'm okay with that.

●

My only piece of luggage is a small carry-on. In addition to the standard necessities, its contents include an odd mix of swim gear, sports memorabilia—and, of course, emergency supplies. I'm not just talking a first-aid kit: I've got matches, flares, antibiotics, freeze-dried packets of food, and other items that will surely buy me a pat-down and probably an arrest. I don't care. I feel better having those things with me.

As I approach security, my mind drifts to the same things, in the same order: California. Lee. Boston. The boys.

And always, always . . . *Colin.*

He never told me his plans for the fall, but I saw the envelope on his kitchen table: MIT. He's transferring. His new life begins in an old, familiar place, but it's still new. No one would argue with that. Colin Shea found a way to move on.

Travelers swarm the security lines in a chaotic blitz, anxious to get their licenses checked, their boarding passes verified. It's contagious, this sense of urgency to stand in a series of lines. Unlike everyone else, I'm in no rush. I wheel my little suitcase behind me, ignoring the elbows being thrown in my direction. I keep my head down and follow the signs.

I'm traveling business class for the first time in my life, which means my own private security line. I guess this explains why these passengers are never late. A memory of irritated glares and champagne glasses flits across my mind, of the twelve people who started their journey in the lap of luxury and finished it at the bottom of a lake. I push the thought away.

"ID please." A guy with a buzz cut glares at me. I search my pockets for my wallet, but it's buried at the absolute bottom of my carry-on. It takes me a full minute to find my license. The people behind me groan.

He studies it for a moment, his glare morphing into a curious look. *Oh no.* He recognizes me. As I brace myself for the inevitable comment that can only accompany a plane-crash survivor attempting to board a plane, he holds out my ID. "Have a nice flight."

"Uh, thanks." I stuff it back in my wallet.

Security is a breeze in the priority lane—no sign of little kids or loose pennies. My suitcase sits in the X-ray machine for a long time, which doesn't surprise me given the contents. A woman in oversized pants calls me over to the security bench.

"Are you carrying flares in this suitcase, ma'am?"

"Uh, yes."

"Can you tell me why?"

I'm grateful for the attempt at privacy, but a few eyes pene-trate the back of my skull as she points to my luggage. I stare at my hands, guilty as charged.

"I wanted to have them."

"Ma'am, flares are prohibited in carry-on luggage."

"Why?"

She looks at me like I'm speaking in a different language. "Why? Because they're considered a weapon by the TSA."

"Then how is anyone supposed to find you if your plane crashes?"

She laughs. She actually *laughs*. A part of me crumbles in-ward; another part wants to punch her in the face.

"Ma'am," she says, "if that happens, you won't need to worry about flares."

I reach for my luggage. "Can I have this back, please?"

"Minus the flares."

"Fine."

I grab my pathetic, discombobulated suitcase and sprint for the terminal. Again, I keep my head down. I don't want to be seen, or recognized, or bothered. I just want to *get* there.

Willpower only carries me so far. One second I'm hurrying into the bathroom, and the next I'm sitting in a stall, crying behind the plastic door. Airport restrooms are always loud and frenetic, an unending flow of foot traffic. My vision blurs as I watch high heels and sandals and clogs and sneakers pass out-side the door. The toilets flush in a whirlwind of noise and ur-gency. Sinks click on and off again. Hand dryers whoosh in my ears. I sit there for a full ten minutes, drinking in the sound of humanity—of life—until I'm finally able to walk back out again.

Now I'm late. My flight is getting ready to board, which means I should be at the front of the line along with all the other first-class passengers. But the crowd feels so huge. Strangers jerking for space, waiting to be done with this horrid process. A baby wails. Latecomers sprint for the gate; the over-prepared repack their luggage. I try to remember a time when all of this excited me, but I can't. The only thing I feel right now is panic.

So I imagine, instead, what that November night *should* have been. Colin, coffee in hand, bumps into me outside the gate. His smile is warm, his blue eyes ablaze. I see him and think, *I'm glad you're here,* which is the truth, and always has been, even though I spent months denying it.

An announcement would have sounded overhead: *Now boarding first-class passengers.* As they boarded, Colin would have offered me food, because he always notices the little things, like a missed meal or a growling stomach. And I would have accepted, because seeing him smile is always worth it, even if the snack is stale Doritos or a flat soda.

I'm in 34B, he would have said. *Care to join me in the lap of luxury?*

And I would have balked, because the last row really sucks, but I would have said yes. *Yes yes yes.*

He would have offered me the window seat, and I would have taken it because I love the window seat. *Used* to love the window seat. The sky, the stars, the spectacle of earth 35,000 feet above your natural habitat. Like swimming in that it defies the usual patterns of physics, and nature, and life.

I would have noticed his book, and I would have commented on it, and he would have told me all about his hometown, and his family, and the mother he so desperately wanted to see on her favorite holiday. He would have said, *You need to get the heck out of middle distance,* because he tries hard not to cuss, even though he cusses so well.

I would have said, *You're absolutely right.*

And sometime later, with a pink, familiar dawn on the horizon, we would have reached the city we both call home. Our families would have met us at the baggage claim. After the holidays, we would have been back at school, back in the pool, but things would have been different. I'd be swimming the 1500. Colin would still be the phenomenal swimmer he always was, but I'd support him, and admire him, and maybe even love him.

Instead, our plane went down. And even though these last nine months have been the most trying of my life, they've also been the truest.

And the truth, right now, is that I have to get on that plane.

●

Six hours, two minutes.

I fold myself into 6C, the aisle seat. No window, no shade. The autonomy of controlling the shade is an illusion, after all. I'm not the one dictating my fate—not here, not for the next six hours, two minutes.

I close my eyes, determined to sleep through all of it: the takeoff, the turbulence, the free drinks and stale snacks. Somehow, it happens.

And I dream.

I'm surrounded by water, but the palette is a vivid, skittering blue. The sun burns on a distant horizon, casting slants of pinks and yellows and oranges on a calm, glassy surface. The water is utterly translucent, the sand a pale, snowy white.

I am not alone on this vast, pristine shore. I'm with three little boys and a man who could be their father—tall, strong, distantly familiar. These are people I know well, though their faces are never clear, their voices just shy of identifiable. All I know is that I love them.

The wave that washes over us is warm and gentle, the water smooth as silk. The only sound is laughter; the only thing to fear is a vague sense of an ending. I don't know where this comes from—maybe the burn of the sun on the horizon, or the laughter that fades as it rolls through the silence. Or maybe it's my own mind, hearing the same good-bye as it rolls off my lips, fading into oblivion.

●

It's after nine by the time we touch down in San Francisco. My cell phone confirms eight text messages, all from Lee, his excitement increasing by the hour. *The Shinster misses you! I reserved the pool for skinny-dipping!* His unabashed enthusiasm makes me smile, but it's a sad, aching smile. I know he's standing down at baggage claim, holding up a sign that is almost certainly sexually inappropriate, though only in ways that a full-grown adult would appreciate. He knows better than to steal the innocence of children.

It takes me a few seconds longer than everyone else to appreciate the success of the flight. To everyone else, it's just another long trip. A journey that always starts with a safety video and ends with a mad dash for the overhead bins. To me, it's a gift, a breathless exhale. It's reclaiming a bit of faith in the system.

I grab my bags and make my way toward the restroom. The panic from seven hours ago has begun to fade, left behind in Boston. I try not to think about what else I left in Boston. I try not to think about anything except Lee, and my dorm, and my first day back at practice on Monday. The worst part is over. All I have to do is walk through the terminal.

I roll my luggage all the way down to baggage claim, close enough to sense Lee's presence in the midst of strangers. I can almost taste the cinnamon on his breath; can almost hear the cool, casual sound of my name as he yells it over the din of the crowd.

I lift my gaze for just a second, for no real reason other than to process the cabbies, limo drivers, and air travelers hustling past me. Just long enough to glimpse the list of departures, flashing overhead like a siren.

And there it is: the same flight that crashed almost a year ago, announcing its departure in sixty minutes. Same airline, same time. A red-eye. In the span of a second, my mind considers it, digests it, internalizes it.

The sound of my name—*Aves! Aves!*—floats through my consciousness. My face and shoulders and hips turn toward it, but my eyes won't leave the screen.

Aves!

I am hearing a different voice now. The voice in my dreams, in my memory. A voice I have always tried, so hard, to shut out completely.

Avery.

I'm glad it was you.

I close my eyes and grip the handle of my rollaway. My feet are no longer rooted to the spot; my mind, too, feels suddenly liberated. A certain calm comes over me then, something I never expected to find in an airport, of all places.

I open my eyes and start walking.

EPILOGUE

The boy sits in the sun with his knees pulled up to his chest, his gaze trained on the glistening surface. It's a clear, sun-kissed day, and the pool teems with the wild energy of young children. He seems not to notice them. He simply stares at the water, studying its depth. I'm in the pool, standing right in front of him, ready to catch him when he's ready.

I must admit, I didn't expect this. I've taught hundreds of kids. I taught Tim, who's swimming on his high school team now. And Liam, who took to the water like a fish in the sea, as I suspected he would. Even Aayu trusted me when I took him by the hand and coaxed him into the shallow end.

But this little boy is different. He looks at me with tears in his eyes, the tiny muscles tensing in his jaw. I've seen fear before, especially in children his age. But this isn't fear. This is frustration, a helpless anger bordering on despair. I can see it in his glass-blue eyes, in the way he grits his teeth every time he inches closer to the edge.

I wade over to him, though I know he doesn't want me to. He shakes his head and scoots backward. "I can do it . . ." He wipes his tears hard enough to leave a mark on his face. "I just . . . I'm scared."

Most children get in eventually. Sometimes it takes an hour, sometimes days. But he's been resisting for weeks. I would have stopped taking him to the pool after the third failed lesson, but he insisted we come back. Since then, I've learned to simply stand in the water until he tells me he's done, which can be minutes or even hours. For a three-year-old, he's shockingly patient. Well, maybe not shockingly. I know exactly where he gets it from.

"It's okay to be scared," I say. "I was, too, for a long time."

He shakes his head defiantly. "You're not scared."

"But I was." I rest my hands on his knees. "More scared than you, even."

He finally looks up. His face is devastatingly handsome, with skin that loves the sun and bright, expressive eyes. The freckles on his nose look painted on, the work of a careless, though talented artist.

Of course, I know I'm biased. He's my son.

"When?" he asks.

"Before you were born." I rub his knees with my hands, getting them wet to acclimate him to the water. Sometimes he flinches, but today he seems to relax—just a bit, but it's a start.

"Why?"

"Well, I was on a plane from San Francisco to Boston . . ."

"With Daddy?"

I glance over at the lanes designated for lap swimming, where a small crowd has gathered. It's not every day an Olympian swims laps on a summer afternoon, but I know my husband. He loves the chaos, the clueless swimmers, the occasional kid who jumps in right alongside him and attempts a lap of butterfly like his life depends on it. He loves it because this is home to him—the crowds, the noise, the incessant shriek of lifeguards' whistles. The medals and attention and everything else pale in comparison.

We both watch him for a while, and it's strange, but I think he can sense us doing it. He glides into the wall, pulls off his goggles, and waves.

"Yes," I say. "With your daddy. I had to swim in a very cold lake, and I was afraid."

"And he helped you do it?"

I lean forward so our foreheads are touching, and the world is just us—no pool, no fears, no other kids splashing around. I whisper my answer so only he can hear it: "No, sweetheart. He told me *I* could do it."

He nods, suddenly serious. As I pull away, giving him the space to stand and try again, the surface shifts with sudden movement. And then a pair of strong, loving arms are around me, and Colin murmurs my name, and it *feels* right—him, the water, our family. The transfer to Boston College and four glorious semesters swimming the 1500. Medical school and summer swim lessons and long, painful runs with Edward. Watching the boys grow up. Being there when they asked, some years later, to hear the story of our lives.

Beside us, our son suddenly gets to his feet, his shadow falling on the clear waters beneath him. He looks at Colin, then at me. "I'm ready now."

He takes a breath.

And jumps.

ACKNOWLEDGMENTS

Many thanks to my extraordinary agent, Stefanie Lieberman, for championing this book and its author; and to Denise Roy, my equally extraordinary editor, who elevated it far beyond my capabilities. You turned this writer's dream into reality, and for that I will always be grateful.

I would also like to acknowledge my parents, Bob and Teresa, who gave me every opportunity to thrive; Fletcher, for always supporting my creative pursuits; family and friends, especially Randee and David, who wanted to read this book long before I wrote it; and my medical school classmates and fellow residents, who supported me, believed in me, and made me a better writer, doctor, and person.

This book is for you.

GIRL

UNDERWATER

CLAIRE KELLS

A Conversation with the Author

Reading Group Guide

**BOOK
ENDS**

DUTTON
— est. 1852 —

A Conversation with Claire Kells

What inspired you to write *Girl Underwater*? Where did this incredible story come from?

I think it came from a place of fear, to be honest! I was flying across the country for residency interviews and I started to wonder—in vivid, excruciating detail—what would happen if the plane went down. I decided that I would be doomed, but a tough, competitive swimmer with an ER doc for a dad might actually have a shot. Avery's story unfolded from there.

You are a practicing resident physician, and *Girl Underwater* is filled with gripping medical emergencies. Does your training as a doctor affect your writing?

It does, for sure. Medicine is challenging on many levels but also deeply rewarding. I feel fortunate to have that kind of background to inform my writing, and I hope those details feel realistic to the reader.

Speaking of your day job, how do you balance the demands of your medical career with the demands of writing?

It's hard. I try to carve out time for writing whenever I can, and I'm fiercely protective of that time. Sometimes it's just an hour a week, and other times I can't even manage that. Residency is a tough job, both physically and emotionally, and I don't force myself to write if I'm exhausted. But I look forward to those times when I can set up camp in my favorite bagel shop and write for hours on end.

How did you come up with the setting for *Girl Underwater*? The Colorado Rockies, and the danger they contain, are such an important presence in the book.

A few months after my college graduation, I flew to Colorado to visit my boyfriend at the time, who was an avid hiker. He wanted me to climb an obscure "fourteener" with him, and I had no idea what that meant but it sounded cool. I remember he told me we needed to leave at four a.m. or we'd probably get struck by lightning. We left an hour late, and sure enough, we ended up sprinting down the mountain to escape the huge thunderstorm that rolled in just as we reached the summit. It was such a raw, visceral experience for me. There was no one out there except the two of us and the brutal presence of Mother Nature. We were totally at her mercy.

That the novel unfolds in dual time lines—alternating between flashbacks and the present—is an interesting structural choice. How did you choose it, and what (if any) challenges did it present?

All credit goes to my brilliant agent, Stefanie Lieberman, for that choice. She proposed it on our very first phone call, and I gently informed her there was no way I could rearrange the whole story to fit that format because I simply lacked the skill-set to do that. She told me I could do it and somehow it happened.

A searing love story emerges from tragedy, and Avery must choose between two men who love her. What is the secret to writing an effective love triangle?

I honestly never set out to write a love triangle; it just emerged organically from the story. I might even go so far as to say I tried *not* to write a love triangle because they are so hard to execute well. But Avery's relationship with Lee is important to the story, and I didn't want to neglect that. In the end, I tried to cast each of them—Avery, Lee, and Colin—as unique characters with their own wants and needs and flaws.

Among the most moving passages in the novel are those that follow care that adults bestow on children who are not their own. What is your message on this point?

One of the themes of this story is family, and in Avery's case, family takes many forms. Her complex relationship with her own family, and later, the family she comes to know, play a critical role in Avery's survival and recovery. For Colin, he has a very clear sense of what family means—and it drives him in different ways.

So much of *Girl Underwater* is about the psychological toll that the disaster has on the survivors. Did you research PTSD while writing the book?

Yes, I did a great deal of research. In medical school, I worked directly with PTSD patients and psychiatrists at the Veterans Affairs medical center, and that experience played a role in this story. I am in no way an expert on PTSD, but I tried to portray it as accurately as possible.

Like Avery, you were a competitive swimmer in your youth. Is swimming still an important part of your life?

Yes, definitely. I burned out after high school but started swimming again with a local team four years ago. A bad shoulder injury hampered my return for over a year, but I'm back in the water now, and I love it. Swimming is very meditative for me.

If *Girl Underwater* were to be adapted as a movie, who would you like to see play Avery, Colin, and Lee?

Well, I'm unhealthily obsessed with movies, so this question makes my heart skip a beat. There are so many talented young actors and actresses working today—my only request is that he or she knows how to swim!

What is next for you? Any more books in the works?

I'm working on another book now.

Reading Group Guide

1. When Avery meets Colin, they immediately clash: Colin thinks Avery should push to swim distance—the event she loves best—but Avery is willing to swim an event she isn't passionate about for the sake of the team. Who do you think is correct? How do their stances affect how they see each other? What helps them change that initial impression?

2. Avery intentionally tries to change when she goes away to college and is irrevocably and unintentionally changed after the crash. In what ways is she different and the same in her hometown and at school, and before and after the crash? Who is the "real" Avery?

3. One of the themes in *Girl Underwater* is family. How does Avery's concept of family change over the course of the novel? How does Colin's?

4. Do the characters' decisions seem real and believable? Can you relate to their predicaments in the wilderness? What would you have done in their situation?

5. Avery's father and her brother Edward play significant roles in the book, but her mother and other brothers less so. Do you think this was an intentional choice on the part of the

author? How did this narrowed view of Avery's family affect your perception of her? Of the family as a whole?

6. How did the alternating present-past framework affect your reading experience? Did knowing that Avery survived her ordeal compromise the suspense or enhance it?

7. Why does Avery lie about what happened in the wilderness? Do you agree or disagree with her choice? What do you think would have been different if she'd been honest from the outset?

8. Avery's story is as much about her psychological recovery as it is her physical recovery. Who do you think played the most important role in Avery's battle with PTSD? Why? In what ways was Avery forced to overcome her ordeal on her own?

9. Avery is an elite college swimmer raised by a tough-nosed father, but her survival and recovery are fraught with setbacks. Did you perceive Avery as a strong or weak protagonist? Did your view of her change over the course of the novel?

10. What do you think about Lee? Why do you think Avery was drawn to him? If her plane hadn't crashed, do you think she and Lee would have made it as a couple?

11. What do you think about Colin's relationship with his family, particularly his mother? Do you think her illness helped him to cope with the possibility of death out in the wilderness or did it make him fight harder to survive?

12. What role does guilt play in this novel?

13. How would you characterize Avery's relationship with swimming? What role do you think swimming plays thematically in the book?

14. Were you satisfied with the book's ending? Why or why not?